Enemy at the Gate

Book 9 in the Anarchy Series

By

Griff Hosker

Enemy at the Gate

Published by Sword Books Ltd 2016

Copyright © Griff Hosker

Cover by Design for Writers
Thanks to Simon Walpole for the Artwork.

Contents

Prologue

Stockton Castle - January 1138

I do not think my spirits were ever as low as they were that Christmas. There was no happiness to be found anywhere and I found myself despairing that the sun would ever shine on the world I ruled. We were a tiny enclave of the supporters of Empress Matilda and her son. Around us was a sea of enemies.

Wulfric, my Sergeant at Arms, had almost died after fighting the enemies of the Empress. He had recovered but it had been a close thing. We were surrounded by those who wished us harm. The nearest allies were in Normandy! In England, I had but half a dozen knights on whom I could rely. There were more who would fight alongside me but they were in Normandy, with my son, William, at my Angevin manor of La Flèche. Leofric of Stockton and now my new squire, Gilles, had left for there too. I felt alone. I had also lost my first warhorse, Star. Scout had been retired but I had ridden Star whenever I could. Latterly, I had used Badger, but he was in Normandy and now Aiden, who cared for my animals, told me that Star had died of some illness. It was as though I was fated to plumb the depths of despair. My brave horse should have died in war and he had not; he had wasted away. That alone had depressed me more than I could say.

Rolf, who had been, like me, a Knight of the Empress, had also died in Normandy. He had died the death he wanted; a warrior's death defeating our enemies but I still missed him. He and the rest of the Swabians had all fallen. Now there were just three of us left. Sir Edward in Thornaby and Sir Guy in France at his manor of La Cheppe.

It was the memory of my dead wife who brought me back to some kind of sanity. After Christmas, I had been in the church close to my castle and reflected on all that had gone wrong. I had tried to do as King Henry had asked of me and defended Empress Matilda's right to the throne but I had failed. My dark church seemed to suit my mood and I prayed there. Perhaps it was a trick of the candlelight, I know not but the effigy which William the Mason had carved of my dead wife, Adela, seemed to smile. I knew it could not; it was stone but I swear that it did smile. In that instant, I remembered how she had always had the ability to make me see that the beaker was half full. It was that smile that made me realise that we still managed to cling on in my island of the Empress. I had allies: Thurstan, Archbishop of York, was a friend, a supporter. There were knights who secretly supported me, like Sir Hugh Manningham of Hexham. And I still had my son as well as allies in Normandy. More than that I had Henry, the son of the Empress. I owed it to him to make him king.

I stood, angry with myself and thankful to my dead wife. I went to the effigy and kissed the stone lips. "I am sorry that I allowed doubts to creep into my heart. You were ever my rock and I was never good enough for you. I will try to be the man you deserved."

As I turned, I heard Father Henry say, "Amen, my lord. Amen."

Part 1

Scottish Invasion

Chapter 1

One major problem with being surrounded by our
enemies was the proliferation of bandits and brigands. They
took our predicament as a sign of weakness and their
numbers increased. They thought we were weakened and
gathered like carrion to pick at the carcass while we still
lived. My men still had the reputation of being the fiercest
warriors in the land but like a pack of dogs trying to take
down a bear, they nibbled and bit at the edges of our land.
We now controlled the river only as far as Barnard Castle to
the west and Thornaby to the east. All else was lost. To the
north, I had no knight at Norton but there was a stout
garrison of those who had fled from the lands around
Hartness. They would hold the town wall and the manor for
a brief time at least. Sir Richard of Yarm had been a dubious
ally until his son Tristan had almost been slain by the De
Brus clan. Now he guarded the southern approaches to my
land. The east was my main problem. There Robert de Brus
still ruled and he was an ally of King David of Scotland and
Stephen the Usurper of England.

Aiden acted as my gamekeeper as well as the master of
my animals. Since the troubles had begun, he had ridden
further afield with his two hawkers, Edward and Edgar. The
two brothers had been with me for some time and Aiden had
trained them well. The days when I could enjoy the pleasures
of hawking were long gone. Knightly pleasures were a thing
of the past. We were fighting for survival and our backs were
to the wall. The three of them ranged far and wide and were

my eyes and ears. They scouted. They looked for signs of strangers. They were my guard dogs.

The nights were still long and few men were abroad when they returned one dusk, cold and shivering. Aiden sent his two acolytes to the fire in the kitchen while he sought me, Sir John, my castellan, and Wulfric. We were together in my Great Hall. "Lord, I have found tracks of bandits north of here, towards Thorpe."

"Were there many?"

He gave a grim smile, "If there had been but a few of them then they would be dead already. There were too many for the three of us. They have a camp in the forest north of Thorpe. Thorpe has been destroyed." He shrugged, "There were no people there, none alive anyway. The ground was hard with the frost and it was difficult to ascertain numbers. I am guessing twenty, perhaps more." He shook his head. "When last we visited, a month since, it was prosperous and the people were happy. Now it is a graveyard."

"You have done well. Go, warm yourself and tomorrow you shall lead us to this nest of vipers."

After he had gone, Wulfric made to rise. "I will warn the men."

"Stay, Wulfric. You will not be riding tomorrow."

"Why not, lord?"

"The thirty stitches in your leg for one."

"It is nothing."

"That is not what Father Henry says. I will not risk my rock for bandits. Sir John has been yearning to leave the castle and he will accompany me. You will remain here and enjoy a day or two of being a castellan. You can groom your fine horse, Roger. I believe that, come the spring, you shall have need of him. I will leave you here with Erre. I take but Dick and his archers. Cedric and Oswald shall be my men at arms. Go tell them."

He nodded and left.

Sir John had been my squire, along with Sir Leofric who was now my castellan at my Angevin manor. He knew me well. He now felt confident enough to talk to me where once he would have been afraid. "Lord, you hunt these bandits because you are restless."

"I do. I have written letters to the Earl of Gloucester. We need him to end the unrest in Normandy for only then can the Empress and her son come to England to reclaim her birthright. I know not why he delays."

"There are rumours he urged Theobald brother of Stephen to become King."

I nodded, "I have heard those rumours. They may have been a ploy to drive a wedge between the brothers. The Earl knows how to do such things. In any case, I owe the Earl enough to wait for judgement on that." Sir John's words echoed my fears. The Earl had not been as strong a supporter of his sister as I had expected. "The greatest threats are the Scots and the northern rebels. Since Barnard de Balliol and De Brus have joined Stephen of Blois, I fear treachery for they are Scots at heart. Stephen may have been taken in but not I. King David and his son Prince Henry are cunning. They may have planted those two cuckoos in Stephen's nest."

"Does that not suit us, my lord?"

"No, for although I wish Stephen defeated, it is not at the expense of the loss of the north of England. I fight not only for the Empress but the people of this valley. Those two play games to gain power and land."

Sir John shook his head. He was low born. I had elevated him but such games were beyond him. He struggled to grasp the concepts of chess. With a sword and a shield, there was no finer knight but my former squire would never lead armies. "I would not be you, my lord. You have a task such as would have been set Hercules."

I laughed, "At least Hercules knew who his enemies were. I can count my knights on one hand and the rest..."

"Better a few men that you know, lord, than an army of men like De Brus." I nodded for he was right. I did not have many men but I could rely on them all.

I rode my newly acquired horse, Rolf, when we rode abroad the next morning. I had brought him from Normandy and named him Rolf after the last of the Swabian bodyguards of the Empress. My new horse was not a warhorse but he had destrier blood in him. Scout was now too old to ride and with Star gone, Rolf would be my first choice. Badger and Hunter were my warhorses. I would have need of them when we faced knights.

I took Dick and ten of his archers. I could have taken more but I was loath to risk my castle. Although our treacherous neighbours had been quiet of late, I would not put it past them to have created this problem in order to lure me from my castle. Besides, I felt I had enough men. With two men at arms, Sir John and his squire, Ralph of Yarm, we would be the equal of any bandits.

My three scouts did not range far ahead. They knew where we were going. We headed up the Durham Road. Once this had been a busy thoroughfare as men travelled to and from the Palatinate but the Bishop of Durham had sided with Stephen of Blois and he was another enemy. The only thing in his favour was that he did not wage war upon me. He owed me much for I had saved him and his castle before now. He waited and watched to see who would rule this land. When the dust settled then he would decide. The land rose towards Thorpe and then a mighty forest stretched on both sides of the road for many leagues. It was fine hunting there. As soon as we reached the eaves of the forest, we stopped.

"Lord, their camp is in the heart of the forest some two miles away. Look on the ground, you can see tracks here. The frost makes it hard to see how long ago but this is the path they use."

I nodded. "Dick, it is time for you and your archers. Would you go on foot or horse?"

"Two miles is nothing. We will walk."

"Edward, Edgar, guard the horses." I saw the disappointment on their faces. "Keep a close watch. You may have to defend the horses."

"Aye, lord."

Aiden also dismounted. He was a fine archer too. They strung their bows and set off in a long line. The five of us rode. We would be the bait. I had no doubt that the bandits would have sentries. If my archers chose to then they would be invisible. A horse is a noisy creature. They would hear us coming. The trail we followed was clear and my archers did not wait for us. They vanished into the trees. Although our horses made noise, we did not. We had each brought a spear. I preferred using a sword but fighting a man on foot necessitated a weapon with a longer reach. We had brought long spears.

I rode at the head of our small column with Sir John on my right side. Cedric and Oswald rode together behind and the least experienced, Ralph, rode at the rear. We might only be facing bandits but would take no chances. My shield was held tightly to my body. Rolf suddenly snorted. I looked around and saw the dead man with an arrow sticking in his chest as he fell from his perch. My archers were silent killers. The body alerted us to the dangers ahead. I knew that we were getting close and I hissed, "Cedric, Oswald, flank us."

The two men at arms rode to my left and Sir John's right. Dick and his archers might be the shield but we would be the hammer that smashed the bandits. Suddenly I heard cries ahead. I spurred Rolf who responded immediately. He was a powerful beast and I had to pull back on the reins lest he outrun the other three. They caught up with me as we galloped towards the sounds of combat. An arrow came straight at me. It was a blur but I knew what it was. I flicked up my shield and the arrow pinged off the surface and into the trees. Then I saw the bandits. They were crouched as they tried to take advantage of the low bushes and send arrows towards the enemy they could see; me and my four men on horses. My archers were hidden but their arrows were taking their toll. Dick and his men had surrounded the camp and all the bandits' attention was on us.

There were more bandits than I had expected. Some I could see as soon as we reached the clearing. A handful wore helmets and leather hauberks. Some had been soldiers. Their weapons and their demeanour told me that. I could not restrain Rolf any longer. He had the smell of battle in his nostrils and he leapt forward. A brigand with a poleaxe swung it at me. Had I had a sword, he might have caught me but I jerked Rolf to the left as I thrust at him with my spear. His two handed weapon meant that he had no defence against the blow and my spearhead went into his throat. I twisted and pulled as Rolf galloped into the heart of the camp. Two bandits stood thirty paces from me and pulled back on their bows. Suddenly they pitched forward as Dick's archers' arrows struck their backs. They fell and their backs looked like a hedgehog.

Sir John had only one man who was bigger and stronger than he and that was Wulfric. He rode directly at the leader of the bandits. He had a short mail byrnie, a shield and a spear. Sir John rode straight at him. Cedric galloped to his right and his spear took the bandit who was guarding the side of the leader. Sir John's spear smashed into the shield of the leader. It was such a powerful blow that the spear shattered in two but the man was thrown to the ground. He lay stunned. Sir John whirled around and drew his sword in one practised motion. As the leader rose to his feet, he brought his sword around and took his head. It rolled into the middle of the camp and its dead eyes stared at the grey skies.

The last few bandits threw down their weapons and fell to their knees. "Mercy! We beg mercy!"

I reined in Rolf. He had not had enough and would have charged again. My men emerged from the forest. I saw that we had not lost a man. I had not expected to. Then a movement to my left caught my eye. Five women and two children emerged from the dell in which they had sheltered.

The grey-haired gammer dropped to her knees. "My lord. You have saved us."

I dismounted and handed my reins to Oswald. "Rise. Who are you?"

"I am Anna wife of Arne of Thorpe. These are my daughters and granddaughters."

"These are the bandits who killed your men?"

She glared at the eight who had surrendered. "Aye, lord, and worse." I saw the younger women pull the two young girls closer. She did not need to elaborate.

One of the men said, "We only did what Alan of Trimdon told us, lord. Give us mercy!"

I turned to Anna, "It is your decision, Anna wife of Arne of Thorpe, what is the fate of these men!"

"Give me your knife, lord, and I will mete out justice myself."

I saw the men recoil and knew what she intended. "No, mother, for you would have to live with that. Whatever punishment you decide, we shall deliver."

"Death!"

One of the women stepped forward, "No, mother. That one should live," She pointed to a young man no older than Gilles, my squire, "he was kind and tried to stop them. He should not die."

Anna wife of Arne of Thorpe looked coldly at the youth. "He was part of them! He should die!"

I saw that the young man did not beg but stood, awaiting his fate. "What is your name?"

"I am William of Wulfestun, lord."

I peered at him. "You are related to Old Tom?"

"He was my grandfather, lord. When my family were slaughtered by the Scots, I was taken as a thrall." He pulled back the lock of hair that hung over his forehead. There was a sign of a slave burned into it. It was not a fresh wound. "I escaped a year since and would have starved but these bandits took me in."

The bandit who had spoken earlier said, "See lord, we are not all bad!"

I ignored him. "Cedric, Oswald. The boy lives, hang the rest!"

They wailed and they cried but my men ignored their pleas. They were taken to tall trees and hanged. Their seven bodies jerked and thrashed for a few moments and then lay still, swinging from the branches.

"Anna wife of Arne, would you go back to Thorpe? If you do not wish to return to the farm, there are places for you at my castle."

"My husband and his father built the farm by the valley. I would go back but we have no man. We need someone to do man's work."

I nodded and looked at the youth I had saved. "William of Wulfestun, I have a mind to let you live. But I charge you with working for this woman and her family for seven years to make amends for your misdeeds. What say you?"

"Aye, lord. I am no bandit."

And you, Anna of Thorpe, what say you?"

Her face was hard but two of her daughters came close and one said, "Please, mother! You are angry and the boy did naught. He took no part in the attack on the farm. He held the horses."

She relented, "I will agree but only because the Earl of Cleveland says this. It is known he is a wise and a fair man."

"We will accompany you. Collect any weapons, armour and treasure they may have taken and fetch their horses. Your family shall have horses from this at the very least. We will keep watch over your settlement from now on."

Even as we escorted them back to their village, I began to wonder if I could deliver on my promise. It would have been bad enough in times of peace but I now had both the Scots and the usurper King of England to fight. How could I promise to fight for the weak when I had so many enemies? Even as I thought it, I knew the answer. My father would have defended them. That was his way. My namesake would have defended them. I would too. I could not run away from my obligations or my heritage. I left Henry Warbow and Ralph of Thirsk with them. "My men will stay here for a few days and provide game for you and help make your home habitable."

Anna of Thorpe curtsied, "Thank you, my lord, and I am sorry that I did not seem more grateful."

"You held your family together and you did what you had to. Do not reproach yourself."

I was mounting my horse when William of Wulfestun approached me. "I swear I will not let you down, lord. I know that my body could be swinging in the trees and I would be meat for the birds, but you have to believe me that I did not choose that life."

I pointed to Dick and the other archers, "All of those were bandits and outlaws once. The difference is that they did not prey on women and children. I believed you and I believed the young woman. You have the chance for a new life. Consider today the day you are reborn." He looked at them with new eyes. To him, they were the men of the Earl of Cleveland. Now he knew their past, he could see the way to redemption.

I was quiet as I rode home. I believed I had done a good thing and I believed that William would keep his word. Only time would tell. Life had a way of changing a man and his nature. I had been betrayed and let down before. Most of those who had done so were now dead. I had a vengeful side to my nature.

The days of winter were so short that by the time we reached home, it was dark. The only saving grace of this time of year was that our enemies rarely moved in such times. My land was harsh and unforgiving whilst in the grip of icy winter. That did not stop us from keeping a close watch on our borders and our homes but it was unlikely that we would be attacked.

When we rode through my gates, I was greeted by John, my steward. "My lord, did you find the bandits?"

"We did and they have been despatched. The land to the north is scoured."

" Alice has prepared food, my lord."

"Good. Tell me, John, when do you expect the '*Adela*' back?"

"At this time of year, lord, it is a twelve-day voyage there and back. Captain William is a good captain and a careful one. He will return as soon as he can."

"I know, John, but I hate this lack of news. It is sad to think that we cannot find out what is happening in our own country save by what we hear from Normandy."

"We cannot make the winds and the seas obey us, lord."

We entered my hall and Alice, who was ready and waiting with her cooks, began to serve up. It was her way of telling me to eat! She was very much the mother of the hall. She never shouted, at least I had never heard her do so, but Wulfric and all my men at arms obeyed her words as though commands from me.

"This smells good, Alice. Have Wulfric and Dick join us. You two as well." I pointed to my steward and my castellan.

Sir John and John were frequent guests at my table but they never took the honour for granted. They nodded their acceptance and sat. We ate the warm rye and barley bread while we waited. Alice had warmed some ale with a poker and that warmed my chilled bones. I waited until all of my guests arrived before I spoke.

"Eat and I will tell you my thoughts. This day has sharpened my mind." They nodded and began to eat. Alice's frown left her face and she hurried her servants away to fetch more food. We never went short. "The problem we encountered this day was a foretaste of the future. How stand we for war, John?"

"Thanks to the monies and jewels you brought from York, we are financially sound. Our coffers are full and we do not need to burden the people with heavy taxes this year." He waved his hand at Wulfric and Dick. "Thanks to the skills of you and your men, we have both ransoms and arms from battle too. The goods we trade also bring in money. The problem is buying what we do not produce and cannot capture. We no longer have local markets such as York and Durham. Other traders do not visit the port and we have but the one ship."

"And what are we short of?"

"Wheat, lord."

I shook my head, "We can get that and wine from my estate in Anjou. We are at war. We can eat oat and barley bread. What of the iron we need for weapons and armour? What of horses?"

"We have iron aplenty, lord, but if we have trouble with the De Brus clan then there may be a problem for the mines are close to their lands."

"Do we have trouble?"

John nodded, "Men have raided the mines and taken some of what the miners have gathered and they fear for their lives. None have been killed yet but that is because the miners flee at the first sign of raiders."

I looked at Wulfric, "Then we make war on the De Brus again so that they cannot interfere." He nodded, "And horses, John. I am aware now of the need. Star has gone and others, like Scout, are no longer able to endure a long campaign. We need horses for the future."

He looked out of his depth, "I know money, lord, not horses. We have stallions and we have mares. They mate...."

"You are right, John. I will speak with Aiden." I looked at my three warriors. "We have food and we have weapons. When I see Aiden, we shall have horses but what of men?"

They looked at each other and it was Wulfric who spoke. "The men we have are good men. More than that, they are the best men that we could have but..."

"There are not enough of them."

"Aye, my lord."

"Archers?" I looked to Dick, my captain of archers.

"I am more hopeful than a couple of years ago. We now have many young men who will be as good an archer as you could wish for but not until next year or the year after. From then on we will have a steady supply of replacements."

"And that is good news. Sir John, if I take away my archers and men, have you a garrison?"

"I will be blunt, my lord, I have only the Varangians and the men of the town. They are keen but lack skill."

Wulfric shook his head, "Erre and his brothers are getting old."

Dick said, "Aye, they are like your father and his men when they returned from Miklagård." He shrugged apologetically, " No offence, lord."

"I know. I take no offence. My father and his men should have enjoyed their last days telling tales and enjoying grandchildren. They should not have had to die defending their land against Scottish raiders and bandits. Erre and his should enjoy a more peaceful old age. Steward, I want the money made available to Sir John here. Hire ten men at arms and ten archers. They will be your garrison."

"That is easier said than done, lord. We no longer have the markets to hire such men we once did and what about their loyalty?"

The wind suddenly whipped the shutters open on the eastern end of the hall and Wulfric jumped up to shut them. "There is always Denmark and the Low Countries. Our ship would have a shorter journey and they are not our enemies."

Wulfric snorted, "Not yet."

"Come, Wulfric, we have fought against these men have we not? I am sure Sven the Rus could help us to choose some good men at arms."

He nodded, "It is worth a try, lord."

John the Steward asked, "My lord, I mean no impertinence but can we win?"

"Win?"

"My lord, I am no warrior, I am a bookkeeper. However, being a bookkeeper I know numbers. I have been reckoning up the men at your disposal. If we stripped all of your castles of your knights, archers, squires and men at arms then you could field an army of no more than a hundred and sixty men."

I smiled, "A hundred and sixty-five, John, I can count too. And your point is...?"

"When the Scots come, they will bring more men than that. They will bring hundreds more than that. King Stephen can bring more than that from the Palatinate and York alone. The Scots hate us and every village north of the wall and south of it too would send men who were eager to ravage this land. We are the thorn in their side. I am just a bookkeeper but I can see that. How could we defeat them?"

I sipped my wine. "In all honesty, I do not know. But then, answer me this, how did King Harold manage to march from one end of the country to the other, defeat rebels and Vikings and then march all the way south and come within a whisker of defeating King William and his Normans?"

Poor John looked confused, "I know not, lord. It sounds impossible."

"And so it seems, yet the fact of the matter is that they managed this. You ask me how will we do so and I say, honestly, I do not know. Perhaps we will be as King Leonidas and his three hundred Spartans. We might face an army of ten thousand men and defeat it but die in doing so. If that is what we must do to save the valley then that is what we shall do. What I do know is that I will not cease to fight for my Empress, my land and my people until they hack my head from my body and tear my sword from my dead fingers."

My three warriors banged the table. Wulfric roared, "And the Earl speaks for every man at arms and archer. We are warriors and it is what we do. Moneyman, you give us the means to fight and you shall be safe here in Stockton's walls."

Chapter 2

The mood of my men after the meal was ebullient. They felt we could take on the world. I was not so sure but I did not break the mood. Our first task was slightly smaller in size and in my mind achievable. We had to eliminate the threat of the De Brus clan from the area south of the Tees. They had been a thorn in my side and that of my father since we had first arrived in England almost twenty years earlier. I had driven them from Normanby and they had fled to their other castle at Guisborough. Allies of both King Stephen and King David, they could switch sides with ease. They were the masters of following the line of least resistance. Whatever happened to them, they would survive and emerge on the winning side.

I rode out, the next day, with Dick and Sir John. We took but four archers with us. I intended to visit with Sir Tristan and Sir Harold before calling at Thorpe. Sir Tristan had been badly wounded in our last campaign. He had been close to death and was still recovering. His would be a social visit but if I was going to attack De Brus then I would need other knights and Sir Harold was always keen to improve the skills of his men and to gain treasure. He had recently married and was the poorest of my knights. When I had seen them, I would visit with Sir Edward.

Hartburn was so close to us that we could be there and back in under an hour, Elton was even closer to Hartburn. We went to speak with Sir Harold first. His wife, Lady Eloise, was with child and Harold was most attentive towards her. It was his first. I had been the same when Adela had been expecting William. By the time Hilda was due, I was less worried.

"My lord, this is unexpected."

"It is partly social, Harold. I have not seen you for some months and wished to see how you fared. I also came to let you know that we caught and executed bandits yesterday in the woods north of Thorpe. We scoured those woods of them but there are also forests to the west of you. You should be on your guard."

"Thank you, my lord, I will do so."

I nodded, "And I also came to invite you to raid De Brus at Guisborough." He frowned. I smiled, "It is an invite, Harold, and not a command. You know me well enough to know that."

"I would like to, my lord, but if there are bandits then I would like to protect my home. And my wife needs me." I saw Eloise squeeze his hand in gratitude. Hartburn was no castle. It had but a manor house. Well made to protect against the elements, it would not last a determined attack.

"I understand but know this, Harold, war will come to our valley this year. You will have to choose sides. Remember that my castle is always open to your family for protection. We have thick walls."

He hesitated, "When war comes, we will take you up on your offer but I will forego the riches I might have attained on this attack. My wife is more important."

"As she should be."

I was slightly disappointed but I was not the kind of lord who dragged his knights away from family obligations. I was going to punish a knight and his people. I was not going to war against King David. I had enough men to do this.

After I had visited Tristan, I felt a little happier for he was well on the way to recovery. He would be ready for war when spring and the campaign season started even though he was not ready to raid. Our last visit was to head north to Thorpe. I was relieved to find that Thorpe had been secured. My men at arms had worked hard. The doors and ditch had been repaired. The women looked happy and young William appeared to have been accepted by all the women. Anna of Thorpe said, "I was wrong about him, lord. He is hardworking and he is kind. I misjudged him."

"Often we do that, mother, we should give some people a second chance."

Once again it was dark as we headed home. "Can we do this with just our men, lord?" I heard the worry in Sir John's voice. This was my fault. I had left him behind my walls for so long that he had forgotten what it was like to ride to war. I was confident we would win but I understood his reservations.

"You forget Sir Edward. He may well wish to fight." Sir Edward was the oldest of my knights and the most experienced warrior outside of Wulfric. I hoped that he would join me but if he did not then I was prepared. "The way to look on this, Sir John, is that the fewer men we take, the richer we shall be when we triumph."

"De Brus has a castle."

"He has wooden walls. He has a motte and he has a bailey. We have a castle. That is the difference. And we have the advantage that we have good, well fed horses. We have mobility. We take only mounted men with us. We force him to make war on us by taking from his people."

Dick asked, "What is your aim, lord?"

"To make De Brus flee to one of his two masters. I care not which one: Stephen the Usurper or King David. When they have departed, we can safely mine the iron we need to make weapons and we will be stronger. We need a few months to extract as much as we can before summer. It will also give us protection from enemies from at least one side of the valley. The enemy will soon be at the gate. We have to buy time."

"Buy time, my lord?"

"Aye, John, until the Empress invades England." I sipped my wine. The letter I had entrusted to Gilles for Robert Earl of Gloucester had been blunt and unequivocal; I had called upon him to honour the oath he swore to his father. It had been less than polite but the Earl and I had butted heads before now. I had thought the loss of the land in the west to the Welsh would have spurred him on; Stephen had managed to lose all the land he had conquered. However, he seemed happy to grab manors in Normandy. He and the Empress' husband, Geoffrey of Anjou, were winning against the rebels and Stephen's supporters. However, I wondered at their ultimate aim. Were they both trying to carve out larger tracts of land for themselves?

"I will visit with Sir Edward tomorrow."

Dick sensed my mood and said, quietly, "Earl, we have yet to be beaten. God is with us, I am certain, for we are in the right. Your soldiers' spirits are high. Our weapons are the best and we have the finest leader. We will win."

"I like your optimism and I believe that you may be right but here, at the end of this cold dark month, I see no glow of a victorious spring."

Sir John said, "You should not be alone, lord. You need someone to replace Lady Adela." I know he meant well but I did not appreciate the comment.

I shot him an angry look and then relented immediately. John was young and did not understand. "Replacing a love is not as easy as replacing a horse, John. Forgive me, friends, I am in ill humour this night. It has been a long day and I will retire."

As I prepared for bed, I mentally berated myself. I was being less than honest. There was love in my heart and it was for a woman I could never attain. The Empress and I had lain together, we had a son and that son would become King of England one day but my life would be empty and lonely. All that I did was for England and naught was for me. I might as well have been a Templar, a warrior monk. As I lay down to sleep, I could almost hear my dead father and my mentor Wulfstan say, *'and that is how it should be, Aelfraed, for you are a knight of the realm'*. For some reason, that thought helped me to sleep. I did not determine my course; higher forces did.

Sir Edward was keen to visit his wrath upon the De Brus clan. "Over the winter they have been raiding the outlying farms and stealing cattle. At first, it was far to the east and did not concern us over much but they have raided the farm at Marton and the one at Acklam. That is but four miles hence. They grow bold and my people begin to hunger. I think your plan is the right one."

"Then we will leave in seven days. We take mounted men only. We will travel to Stokesley first and then head east. I would approach not from the north but from the west. They will have learned from our last attack."

"When we chased them after the raid at Acklam, we rode as far as the bridge at Ayeton. They have put small towers up. They watch the approaches from the valley."

"The hills and the rocks give them the illusion of protection. Do they have a garrison at Ayeton?"

"No, lord. There is a small hall there but it is not fortified. They have the bridge which they could defend but the river is shallow enough to ford on horses!"

"Then we take Ayeton first."

I did not take all of my men at arms. I left half at home but I did take my entire troop of archers as well as Aiden, Edgar and Edward. My three scouts were worth a conroi of knights. I left clear instructions for my castellan. "Sir John, keep a close watch on the north. I will be away for three days, perhaps four. Keep me informed if there is news from anyone." Although Sir Harold and Sir Tristan would not be sending men with me, they would both watch the borders to the west. We were vigilant these days. Even our farmers walked the fields with short swords while their boys kept slingshots close to hand. An enemy would pay dearly for every inch of our land that they tried to take.

It was just ten miles, as the crow flies, to Ayeton but our route down the York Road added five miles to our journey. It would, however, deceive any spies and scouts who might be lurking in the woods to the south of Thornaby. They might think I was going to the Manor of Yarm. I had not visited Richard of Yarm and asked for his help. He had sided with Stephen until his son had been injured. As far as I was concerned, his loyalty was still a little dubious. Both his son and son in law had assured me that he was of our heart but I had my doubts. Passing so close to his land, however, meant that the first part of our journey was through that of an ally.

They were tracks over which we passed but the hard frosts of winter still lay upon them. Jack Frost had an icy grip upon the land. We were well wrapped against the cold and our horses were well fed. I had had John, my steward, prepare great stores of hay and the poorer quality grains and cereals to feed my horses. They were each as important as the men I led.

With my three scouts far ahead of us, I was able to ride easily. We would have a warning of danger. I was growing accustomed to Rolf, my new horse, but I still missed my old mounts. Scout was still the finest horse I had ever ridden. He had a nose for danger and a heart as big as that of Wulfric. Star had been a warhorse who would face down any enemy. I wondered what type of horse Rolf would turn out to be. He was bigger than Scout and not as big as Star but I had yet to put him in extreme danger. That would be his first test. I knew that, in the years to come, we would both be severely tested.

The fields could not be worked; the ground was too hard but the people of Ayeton had cattle, sheep and a few goats. They were penned close to the village itself and we descended upon the village as the animals were being watered. My banner and device were recognised. Our arrival was sudden and unexpected. They had no time to flee to their hall. The villagers dropped to their knees. I was blunt, "Who is your lord and your master?"

The farmers looked to their headman. I was aware of the dilemma in which I had placed him. It was why I had not asked him for his loyalty. "Our lord was the Baron of Normanby, lord, and he is dead."

"Who collects the taxes?"

"Henry de Brus will come in the spring."

"He will not this year. I am your lord and master now." I pointed to Sir Edward. "Sir Edward and Sir Richard of Yarm shall protect you. If tax collectors come from the east, pay them but send word and we will recover them for you."

"We pay no taxes to you, lord?"

I smiled, "We will recover your taxes and take half." He looked disappointed. "Half is better than none and this way your animals will be protected."

A voice from the back said, "Ralph, let us take the offer. This way the bandits and brigands will not have free rein. You will rid us of those will you not, lord?"

Sir Edward answered for me. "Aye, I will rid the land of those for you when you swear allegiance to the Earl of Cleveland!"

The men all made the sign of the cross and chorused, "We swear allegiance."

"Have you one among you who knows the land twixt here and Guisborough?"

A young man, a little older than William, my son, stepped forward. "I am Alan of Grange. I was the Baron of Normanby's man, lord, and I helped old Harold, his gamekeeper. I know the land as well as any."

We had brought four spare horses. "Edward, give a horse to Alan. Lead us safely to Guisborough and you shall be rewarded."

"Thank you, my lord." He mounted the horse well. This man had ridden before. I saw that he had a bow which he had picked up. No one said goodbye to him. I needed to find out more about this man later. He took us across a low path that passed beneath the strange rock the locals called the Topping. It was little more than an animal track but the frost had made it passable. When the land thawed we would have struggled to stay upright. The path meant that we approached the castle and settlement from the direction of the woods. It had been a good decision to use him. We arrived unseen.

We halted and Alan turned to me. "They have built a watchtower a mile in that direction, lord." He pointed to the north. Had we stayed on the road then we would have been seen.

I turned, "Ralph of Wales, take four men and capture the tower."

"Should we burn it, Lord?"

"Not until you see flames from Guisborough." They rode off. I had been to Guisborough before but not for some years. I waved Alan of Grange over. "Have they improved the defences of the castle?"

"Improved, lord?"

"Have they added stone?"

"No, lord. It is still wood." We were now close enough for me to use my archers and men at arms rather than my scouts. "Alan, go with Aiden. Aiden, stop any message leaving Guisborough to head south."

"Aye, lord."

The four of them trotted off. I was confident in their skills. My three men could stand next to a warrior in the woods and be invisible. I had no doubt that a gamekeeper who had survived the slaughter of Normanby would also have such skills.

Sir Edward nudged his horse next to mine. "What is your plan, lord?"

"The gate faces north. The priory is to the west. We use the priory to hide our approach." I pointed to the sky, "It is past noon already. Both the monks and the garrison will be at ease. There will have been no signal from the tower. They will not expect an attack. It is winter. We ride through the gate as hard and fast as we can."

"Aye, lord."

"Dick, I want your archers to clear the gate into the bailey."

"Aye, lord."

Guisborough had a wooden wall and a ditch. There was a gatehouse that led to the outer bailey and a second below the hall and mound. All that we had to do was to take the gate to the outer bailey. I gambled on a garrison at the gate of four men only. We tightened girths and loosened weapons and then I led my men forward. In the absence of a squire, Stephen the Grim carried my banner and rode behind Wulfric and myself.

We emerged from the woods and headed across the narrow, shallow stream. Some monks who were gathering from the hedgerows saw us but they would not have time to sound the alarm. They were too busy fleeing. My banner was known. As we wheeled around the front to the stone priory, I saw the castle. It was less than a hundred and fifty paces from us. Even as I turned and readied my spear, Dick and his archers dismounted and were knocking arrows. The guards and sentries were chatting and looking to the north. It was the cries of alarm from villagers which drew their attention to us. Had I been more ruthless I might have had my archers slay them. I was no De Brus; I would kill only warriors.

The five sentries saw us and they wasted time laying down their weapons as they tried to draw up the bridge.

Fifteen arrows plummeted into their bodies. One lived long enough to try to raise the bridge but it was too heavy and Dick himself ended his heroic efforts with a well-aimed shaft. We thundered over the wooden bridge and under the gate. The main gate was up the slope and already men were pulling up the bridge there too. We would not reach it in time. Dick and his archers were too far away, however, we had attained our first aim.

"Sir Edward."

"Yes, lord."

"Have six of your men secure the leading burghers and hold them as a hostage."

"Aye, Earl." He laughed, "That was easy enough."

As he rode off, I shouted, "Dismount." I handed Rolf's reins to Stephen the Grim. He would stay by the gate with my banner and the horses. The rest of the men at arms tied their mounts to the wooden ramparts. Dick and his archers did the same. "Come, Wulfric, let us see if they are in the mood to surrender."

"My lord, you spoil all our fun."

"Remember, Wulfric, that Father Henry said to take things easy for a while. Your stitches have almost healed. Do not undo the father's good work."

"I know my body, lord. I will take it easy but if you are inactive for too long your body does not fully recover. I do not need a priest to tell me that."

I saw men hurrying to the walls of the inner bailey. The banner was that of De Brus but it was not Robert who led these men. From what we had heard in Ayeton, I guessed that it was Sir Henry. I did not know him. I was no fool and I held my shield before me. Sure enough one of the crossbowmen risked a bolt. It thudded into the shield. Before a second could come my way, four arrows struck the walls. One of them hit the crossbowman whose weapon fell into the ditch followed, a moment later, by the dead man. We had so many archers that shields' came up and those with crossbows decided that discretion was the better part of valour.

Dick shouted, "Right lads, loft your arrows."

They began to send their arrows vertically. Crossbows had to aim horizontally. I heard a cry from the ramparts. The defenders would need shields. We stopped thirty paces from the gate. I shouted, "Surrender your castle and I will ask for ransom. Fight and you shall die."

A shield with a red diagonal cross on a yellow background appeared. "I will not surrender to a rebel and a traitor."

Wulfric growled next to me. "I believe I am both, Wulfric. He is right to address me thus." I lowered my ventail so that I could speak a little clearer to the walls. "Then that should tell you I am a dangerous man to cross. I repeat my offer. Surrender your castle and I shall demand a ransom. You will live."

"My Uncle left me in command of this castle while he is with the King. I will defend it."

"Then you are brave but foolish. Had you stone walls then you might hold us off. Ask your men. They know me."

There was silence and then raised voices. Finally, the shield disappeared and I heard, "Very well. We will come out. Promise me that your archers will not release arrows at us."

"You have my word!"

Next to me, Wulfric lowered his axe. He sounded disappointed as he said, "They used to fight us."

I heard raised voices within the walls. I smiled, some must have objected to the surrender. I had just turned to shout for Dick when the gates opened and ten horsemen galloped out. Far from surrendering, they were attacking. The men nearest me reacted the quickest. Wulfric stepped before me and swung his axe at the horse which hurtled towards us. My other men at arms made a hasty shield wall. Dick and his archers were unsighted. They could not release their missiles for fear of hitting us. The rider whose horse was hacked by Wulfric flew over his head and landed at the feet of Ralph of Thirsk who stabbed him in the neck.

The ones who had not had the chance to take a horse now flooded out. I turned to shout. "Stop them!" Stephen the Grim had a horse in each hand and could do nothing about

the men in mail galloping towards him. The knight rammed
his spear at Stephen who spun and fell to the ground. Then
they were through. Sir Edward's men charged at their side
for they were still mounted and they slashed and stabbed at
those towards the rear. My men at arms were angry and they
fell upon the men on foot. Sir Henry and two men escaped
the carnage beyond the gate. None survived within.

"Wulfric, take my men and search the hall. Fetch
anything of value and then burn it!"

"Aye, lord, with pleasure!" he shook his head in disbelief.
"They had surrendered!"

"They will pay."

I ran down to Stephen the Grim. The horses had not
wandered far and the standard was still planted by the gate.
He lay on the ground and I saw blood. His eyes opened, "I
am sorry, lord."

"It is not your fault. Where are you hurt?"

He held his hand to his shoulder. The tip of the spear had
broken some mail links and entered his left shoulder. It was a
flesh wound only. "Henry Warbow, find me a priest or a
monk. I want this man looked at."

"Aye, lord."

My men began to drive the thralls and servants from the
hall. They carried the valuables from within and were
watched by my men at arms. Behind them, I saw flames
licking the roof of the hall. "And burn the ramparts. Tear
them down in the ditches. I want nothing to remain of this
nest of dishonourable knights!"

The servants and slaves stopped close by me at the gate. I
was aware that I had an angry look and they would fear for
their lives. I pointed to the best dressed of them. "You, what
is your name and what is your job?"

"I am Philip of Clitheroe and I am the Steward of the
Baron of Guisborough."

He stood erect but I could see the fear on his face. "And
who surrendered and then fled?"

"Sir Henry de Brus, my lord."

"You and the rest of the servants and slaves are now my
property." He nodded. "Do not try to escape and serve me

well and you may be returned to your master." I swept a hand around them all. "The same goes for all of you."

Philip of Clitheroe said, "You are known to be a man of your word, lord."

"Which is more than can be said for your former master."

"He was young, lord..."

"If I meet him again he will not age!"

Wulfric and Sir Edward joined me. "We have the burghers. They fear that they will be killed."

"Good, for I am angry enough." I saw that Stephen was being tended to. "When the monk has finished with Stephen burn the rest of this castle. I want the walls burned and the ditches filled."

As I passed, the monk said, calmly, "The Prior hopes that you will leave the Priory alone, lord. He had nothing to do with this."

"Save that he is the Prior appointed by Robert De Brus. I will speak to him when I have time."

I went to the villagers who were awaiting my judgement. The representative of their lord and master had fled. He had not stayed to protect them and now they were at the mercy of the Warlord of the North.

I did not waste time; that was not my way. "Your lord has deserted you. He saved his own skin. I am the Earl of Cleveland and until the rightful heir to the throne of England is crowned then I intend to rule this land. If you pay your taxes to me then I will give you protection."

The leader of the village rose, a little fearfully, "We will live, lord? You will not enslave us?"

"That is what I said. I will go further. If you feel that you cannot stay here and pay taxes to a warlord then leave. I will not hinder you but, " I raised my voice and pointed my finger, "if you are disloyal to me or treacherous in your actions then I will hang you."

"What of the Prior, lord?"

"What of him?"

"We give him a tithe."

"You give him a tenth of all that you produce?"

"Aye, lord."

I shrugged, "That is up to you but as far as I am concerned, you need not. I will speak with the prior before I leave." I looked at the sky. The evening was approaching. "We will stay here this night. You will feed us." I pointed to the two dead horses. "We will eat the horses." I would not begin my rule by taking food from their mouths.

The headman looked relieved, "Of course, lord. And where will you sleep?" He looked pointedly at the burning hall.

"I will see the Prior."

I heard hooves and turned to see Ralph of Wales leading his men and Aiden, his. "No one passed us, lord."

"The tower is destroyed."

"Aiden, return to Ayeton. Stay there this night. Tell them De Brus is fled and they will pay their taxes to me."

"Aye, lord."

"Wulfric arrange for sentries. Sir Edward and I will visit the Prior. Gilles, his squire, will bring you the news."

"Aye, lord."

We mounted our horses and rode around to the priory. We dismounted at the gate where novice monks awaited us. "The Prior is inside. He asks that you leave your weapons outside."

Sir Edward laughed, "I cannot see anyone making us do that so out of the way, boy."

We strode towards the hall. Robert De Brus had built well. It was a stone hall and a stone priory church. The huts in which the monks slept were made of wood but they looked to be comfortable. The prior was seated on a leather-covered chair on a raised dais. He looked to be a king receiving foreign dignitaries. His pomposity was about to be pricked. He was a large overweight man in contrast to the thin and emaciated villagers we had seen.

He frowned, "You are the Earl of Cleveland, the renegade I believe?"

"That depends upon who is speaking. Empress Matilda and her son Henry Fitz Empress, believe me to be the only power in England. If you speak with the usurper, Stephen, then he will call me a renegade."

"What have you done with Sir Henry?"

"Did your monks not tell you? He has fled. Guisborough is now mine."

For the first time, he looked worried. He had not been told. His tone changed. "You are a knight of the realm and I hope that you will behave as such."

"I am the new lord of the manor. The Priory is on land belonging to the manor. I am now your lord. And as I am Warlord, I do not answer to any other lord in England."

I saw him thinking of a way out of this. He could not. He gave a thin smile, "So long as you protect this land from enemies then we are happy."

"I promise you that the people of Guisborough will be safer in my charge than they ever were under the rule of De Brus. My men will be fed but we need somewhere to sleep. This hall will do."

"That is out of the question. This is a holy place and I will not have it filled with men of war."

It was my turn to smile. "I am sorry, did I not make myself clear? I was not asking; I was commanding. We will be sleeping here this night." I turned to leave and, before I did, I paused, "One more thing; I have told the people that they do not owe you a tithe any longer. They can pay if they wish. I advised them not to."

He stood up and coloured red with anger, "But where do we get our money? Where will we obtain our food?"

"If this was church land then you would be entitled to take from your tenants but this is my land now. Have your monks grow their own food. Other monasteries and priories do. We will return when we have eaten. We will arrange the hall ourselves."

Sir Edward chuckled as we left, "I thought he would erupt like a volcano back there."

"This De Brus is a clever man. He endows a church and then has his people pay for it. That way he ingratiates himself with God and the Church and yet it costs him nothing."

"Well, it is ours now."

"I do not think we have seen the last of Sir Robert. But we have rid ourselves of one problem; at least for a while."

Chapter 3

Following our return from our successful capture of Guisborough, Sir Edward's men had actively scoured the woods for any bandits or remnants of the De Brus soldiers. My men had kept the north clear. I was still distracted by the lack of news. The Archbishop of York had sent nothing to me for many months. I trusted Thurstan but who knew if he could send a letter to me? His nephew, Philip of Selby, served me still, but the Archbishop was the most important man I knew who still lived in England and sympathised with me. He had not sent a message to me for many months. I was blind.

The *'Adela'* returned to Stockton three weeks after we drove Henry De Brus from Guisborough. The return of my ship filled me with joy. John, my steward, as well as Sir John and Father Henry, waited at my dock as my battered ship came in. Gilles, my squire, was waving madly from the bows as it edged up the icy river. Winter had not loosened its grip yet. Captain William brought the ship to a gentle halt and his crew threw lines to secure my vessel to the bank. Even though I was desperate for news of the Empress and my son, I was patient. The fact that the ship was lying low in the water suggested that she was heavily laden but I was concerned with the state of the sails and the ropes. She looked to have been in the wars.

Captain William made sure that the ship was securely fastened before he ran out the gangplank and stepped ashore. "Good voyage, Captain?"

He shook his head, "Winter storms plagued us all the way north. We had to put in at Frisia. It cost us silver to sit out the storm there. Then, after the first storms abated and we sailed, we were struck by an even greater storm. I lost a ship's boy overboard."

"I am sorry. Can I do anything to make your voyages safer?"

He looked at me with surprise, "You are worried about us?"

"You are my ship and you serve me. Of course, I worry. Perhaps we could make ropes here in Stockton and you could carry spares."

"Aye, and sails too. If that could be managed we would be better off. As it is, we will need a month, at least, to repair and clear the weed."

"Take all the time you need but I have two more voyages for you. I would prefer you to be ready to sail safely rather than risking a damaged ship."

"We will be shipshape, lord."

I sensed John, my steward, behind me. "I think my steward wishes to know your manifest."

He grinned, "And Gilles is bursting with news for you." He turned and shouted to his Bosun, "Harold Three Fingers, have the chest with the letters and the coin brought up."

"Aye, Skipper."

"Henri, start unloading the cargo!"

Gilles struggled over with the chest. Sir John said, "Here, give me one handle."

The two of them walked behind me. I said, over my shoulder, "Did you enjoy returning to your home, Gilles?"

"This is now my home, Earl. I enjoyed meeting the Empress and the Earl but this is where I belong. I could not wait to get back. You will be a grandfather by summer, lord!"

Sir John burst out laughing, "I must teach you to be more discreet."

"I did not know that my son was married."

Gilles was an innocent, "He is not, lord. It is one of the girls who works in the manor kitchens. She is pretty. She laughs a lot."

Sir John said, quietly, "He is young, lord. Do not be critical of him. Why even King Henry sired many bastards in his time."

"But he was not my son!"

They both sensed my anger and were quiet. My father would have been appalled at such behaviour. A man had to be honourable in his dealings with women. And then my own hypocrisy struck me. The sins of the father were visited upon the son.

I changed the subject, "And how are Leofric and his bride?"

"He is to be a father too. Perhaps he is one already. I lose track of time. The voyage was hard, lord."

We placed the chest on my table. Alice hovered nearby. Her face was filled with joy now that Gilles had returned. She shook her head, "You need fattening up, Gilles! You have not been eating!" She began to straighten his hair, much as a mother might do.

I saw Gilles looking embarrassed at the attention. "The ship has a cargo for us. Unless I miss my guess there will be wine. Have a jug brought to me and the rest placed somewhere cool."

"Aye, my lord, and I will fetch young Gilles some food too. He looks a little thin to me. This foreign food is not as good as our English food you know, my lord. You always look half-starved when you return from Normandy!"

She bustled away and I felt in better humour already. Alice's priorities were all her brood in the castle and well fed faces.

"Before I read the letters, tell me what your view is of the war in Normandy. Is it won yet?"

The young squire frowned and then smiled, "The Earl and the Count control all but a small part of Normandy. I think there were talks of surrender but I am not certain. It was easy to move around the country and there was no danger to us."

I nodded, relieved. That was good. I could open the letters now without the dread of bad news. Alice brought a jug of wine and another of water along with three beakers. "Better bring another for my steward, Alice." I sat at my table and poured the three of us a beaker of wine each. I poured in a little water. It was not yet noon.

"Yes, lord."

I took out the letters. There were four of them. One each from the Empress, the Earl, my son and Leofric. I put the one from the Empress to one side. I would read that one when I was alone. The one I read first was the one from the

Earl of Gloucester. I read in silence. When I had finished, I downed the beaker of wine in one swallow. It was good news.

Sir John looked at me expectantly. "The Earl of Gloucester has heard my pleas. He has declared that he will invade England soon and he has sent word to his knights in the south. We are not alone."

"He will come soon, lord?"

The joy I felt evaporated. I re-read the missive. The letter was a promise and nothing more. I looked at Gilles. He was young but he was clever. "Did you see any sign of invasion?"

"No, lord. I saw much activity in Normandy where the Count and the Earl were busy besieging the supporters of Stephen who still held out."

"Then the answer is no, John. We hang on still but I take hope from the fact that there will be help from the Earl's allies in the south."

John, my steward, arrived. He was ebullient. "Your son and Leofric have sent many valuable goods; food, wine, linens."

"Linens?"

"Lord, linens and pots please the women. If the women of the town are happy then so are their husbands. We need the women as much as the men." Alice's arrival with food seemed to emphasise his point. "Is it good news, lord?"

"It seems the Earl has raised a rebellion in the south. We are not alone."

He frowned, "However, here, in the north, we are. If the Scots come again, we will be alone to fight them. Stephen is not likely to come north and defeat them again. The last refugees that arrived spoke of the land around Carlisle, Durham and Newcastle falling to the Scots. They are seeping south and encroaching gradually. They will be here by summer."

He was no warrior but he knew numbers and he was clever. "You are right, John. We cannot wait for a month to send for your garrison, Sir John. You had better press on training your men of the town. I fear they will be needed sooner rather than later."

"Aye, lord, and what of Leofric and your son? Their letters are unopened." He pointedly did not mention the missive from Matilda. I wondered just how much my men knew.

"You are quite right." I read Leofric's first. It dealt initially with the war and then, briefly, his own circumstances. "He confirms what Gilles has told us. The war in Normandy goes well. He has not had to campaign this year. The demesne prospers. He mentions my son and begs me to be forgiving." I shook my head. Leofric and John had been as big brothers to my son after my wife died. "He and his wife prosper as does my manor which yields much."

"Aye, lord, I can see that from the goods we have brought within our walls today."

I laid that to one side and, with a heavy heart, opened that of William. It was brief.

December, the year of our lord, 1137,
La Flèche
Father, I must beg your forgiveness. I have fathered a child out of wedlock. Eliane is the love of my life and I would have married her but Leofric and the Empress urged me to wait until I had spoken with you. When you come to Anjou you will love her as I do. Until then I will curb my desires. I pray you to sanction our marriage.

Your son
William

I laid down the letter. I could see now that this was not a wilful act but an impulsive urge. I blamed myself. He had spent a great deal of time with King Henry and the young knights and squires. He had picked up their habits. I should have kept him closer to home and my side. It was a distraction and I put it, briefly, from my mind. He was in Anjou and I could do nothing about it.

Sir John said, "Well, lord?"

"It is as Leofric said and I will reserve judgement on my wayward son."

Gilles said, innocently, "Lord, the letter from the Empress remains unread!"

Sir John shook his head and I smiled, "I am tired, Gilles. I shall read that later. Now come. Tell us of your voyage and your travels."

He needed no further urging and his tale confirmed my belief that I had the best of crews for my ship. He told of how every man had had to fight the sea and the weather to bring my ship home safely. He spoke of the haven that was the Frisian port they had discovered.

"Were there many men in Frisia who were hiring out their swords?"

"There were, lord. We spent time in the taverns and inns there while we waited out the storms. It seems that the Count of Flanders is waiting to see how things develop in Normandy. There were swords looking for masters. Many of the men we spoke with had been hopeful of employment in that war but the Count is safe from attack and watches to see what develops."

"Clever. He can wait while Normandy tears itself apart and when peace comes there, he can pick up juicy morsels at little cost to himself."

Gilles looked amazed, "Lord, that is strange for those exact same words came from one of the men at arms with whom we spoke. He had served the King of France too and said that the French King had not sided with either side in the civil war as he thought it more prudent to let the Normans kill themselves first. He did say that Blois was being threatened from the east. Count Theobald is sheltering behind his walls."

"Then, Sir John, I think you should go to Frisia and hire these men. Take Gilles with you. It will be a good experience and he seems to have knowledge of the men we might need."

"What of my duties here, as castellan, lord?"

"I will not be abroad. Now that I know what the Earl intends, I can plan. Tomorrow I will send Philip of Selby on an errand." I stood. "And now, I am tired and I shall retire. Thank you, Gilles. You have not let me down. You shall be rewarded."

"I have been rewarded already, lord; I serve you. In Normandy, your name is oft spoken. They say that the war there would be over if we had your standard and your sword."

"They are kind words but I listen not to flattery."

"It is no flattery, lord. It is common talk. None would gainsay you."

I took the letter from the Empress to my chamber. There would be little in it which would be incriminating. Maud was a clever woman and would not leave herself open to anything which would jeopardise her position. I would have to read between the lines. I knew her well; my father would have said too well. Although she would have trusted Gilles, she could not allow the letter to contain anything which would help our enemies if it fell into their hands. Geoffrey of Anjou had to hold Anjou and then Normandy if we were to win back England too. He could not be allowed to know of the feelings we had for each other

I opened the letter. Perhaps it was my imagination but it smelled of her hand.

La Flèche, January
My Lord of Cleveland,
I hope the letter reaches you and finds you well. Although the war goes well here in Normandy there are many enemies who surround us both. I urge you to take great care in your dealings with all who come to offer aid. There may be many who purport to come from me. Know that I only use those who are dear to us both. Be wary of any others.

41

Your squire, Gilles, is a delight and he has regaled us with tales of your courage. My son Henry is once more filled with admiration for his favourite knight of the realm. He echoes his mother's thoughts. I pray you to be more careful. Gilles has told us how you are sometimes reckless. You are a puissant warrior but it would harm our cause if you were to fall in battle.

I have to tell you that your son is to be a father. Do not judge him harshly. After all, my brother was conceived out of wedlock and he, like you, has been my rock. When hands touch and lips meet who knows what may follow? I advised him not to marry until he has spoken with you. It may be the impulsive act of the young but, who knows, it may be a love that will endure through the years. Such things happen. Such things are what make us human.

Your son is someone of whom you can be proud. He has taken young Henry under his wing and it is good to see the two of them together. It is a sign of the bond and the links we share. There are but three Knights of the Empress who yet live. You are all three precious to me.

I hope that we shall meet again but that will not be for some time unless you return to La Flèche.

Your friend,
Maud

I read and re-read it four times. To me, it was a love letter for I recognised the nuances and hidden meanings but one thing was clear; the warning of enemies. There was a plot afoot. Neither the Earl nor my son had mentioned it and so it was a deep secret. I would be wary.

The repairs on the ship went far quicker than I could have hoped. Partly this was John's doing. He set up a rope walk where we could manufacture our own ropes. It was on a flat piece of land close to the Ox Bridge. With the extra coin we had from the two new manors, we could afford to pay some of the women to make ropes. As we had many more women than men in my town, this proved advantageous. Sixteen days after he returned, Captain William, Gilles and Sir John sailed across the German Sea to hire men in Frisia. They hoped to return within ten days.

I rode, with my men at arms, to Barnard Castle. I worried about Hugh of Gainford. We had captured the great castle overlooking the Tees from Barnard of Balliol but Sir Hugh did not have a great number of men in his garrison. I would be away but one night. Even so, I worried about my home; I had sent Sir John to Frisia. The words of the Empress worried me. She had suggested treachery.

The young knight who had survived a Scottish attack when all his family had been killed was now one of my most trusted confederates. He and his wife, the daughter of Richard of Yarm, were now my bastion in the west and controlled the upper Tees but I now worried about the Scots. Barnard de Balliol had fled to London to join Stephen of Blois. King David could, by taking Barnard Castle, control the whole of the north of England. There would be isolated pockets such as Hexham but, by and large, it would be under Scottish rule. We had to hold Barnard Castle.

Fatherhood had brought maturity to the young knight. The callow youth was gone; in his place was a seasoned warrior. "Welcome, Lord. How goes the world? Here we are isolated."

"I am not much better in Stockton but we survive. How is your wife?"

"She is with child again and this one is proving troublesome. The priests and her women have confined her to her bed."

I nodded, "I am glad that we do not have to bear children. Nine months is eight and a half months too many!"

"You are right there, my lord! Come, let us sit in my solar. You have business to discuss. We can be private."

"I have information to impart." Our two sergeants at arms, Wulfric and Harold of Huntcliffe, sat in with us. They were as much part of the defence of the north as any. "The Earl of Gloucester and the Empress have begun the stirrings of rebellion in the south. I have sent Philip of Selby to his uncle to glean more information but there is a danger that Stephen's eye may be drawn to the south."

Harold of Huntcliffe said, "Surely that is a good thing, lord."

Sir Hugh said, "I think not, Harold. It means that King David could take advantage of the movement south and attack. That is why you are here, lord, is it not? You fear that we will be the focus of the attack."

"David has three choices: attack here, Stockton or Chester. Chester is well garrisoned as is my castle. However, the Earl of Chester appears to lean towards Stephen of Blois. I believe he has received monies from him. Yours would be the place I would attack. It takes a day to reach here from my castle. That means if you were attacked, you would need to hold out for two days. Could you do that?"

He walked to the window which looked to the west. That would be the direction the enemy would attack. "We have the bridge and that is a major obstacle. The gate there is strong and well made. An enemy could not take it quickly. Then they would have to travel to the east, around the outer wall, to attack the main gate. That would take them a day, at least. My main gate is well made but it is a dry moat. I do not have the luxury of a river running around it."

I smiled, "I know, I am lucky. The Tees is a friend."

"Have you anything which can pour boiling pig fat or water at your gate?"

"Not yet, lord, but I could build something."

"You have thick stone walls. Fire is a danger but if you could heat the water or the pig fat there then that would help."

"I could do that, lord."

"The most important thing you must do is keep a close watch north and west of the river. At the first sign of an enemy then send to me. By the first sign, I mean hoof prints and scouts. If you wait until you see King David's banners then it may be too late."

"I will."

I hesitated before I made my next suggestion, "If you wish your wife to stay with me at my castle, I will guarantee her protection."

"I thank you for the offer and I would take you up on it but I fear the journey there might be worse than the dangers she might suffer here."

I left him the next morning feeling happier than when I had arrived. I still feared for the safety of the castle but I now knew that its salvation would lie with me. We had walked the bridge and the perimeter. I had given him suggestions to make an attack difficult for our enemies. The only place it could be attacked would be from the east.

Two days after my return from the west, Philip of Selby arrived back from York. I was closeted with him, Wulfric, and Dick. He had news of great import. "Kent has risen in revolt under the banner of the Earl of Gloucester."

"The Earl has landed?"

"No, lord, but Baldwin de Redvers and other friends of the Earl have been taking castles. Stephen of Blois has had to return from Normandy."

Wulfric said, "This is great news, my lord."

Philip shook his head, "My uncle fears for the North. He begs you to be ready to join his standard and to fight the Scots should they come." He paused, "He believes they will come. The north is ripe for plucking."

"And I concur with your uncle. I fear you will have to return to him. I will join him but I protect the Tees Valley first and foremost. I will not leave Sir Hugh alone at Barnard Castle. If the Scots come from the north then I will try to stop them and the Archbishop can help me, and welcome. If they come from the west then I will endeavour to join him but I will not leave my castles undefended." Philip nodded, "I am being both blunt and honest, my friend. I wish no misunderstanding. Your uncle has my word but there are conditions attached."

"And I believe that he will understand. There is more. We have news from the north. Norham has fallen to the Scots and an army is besieging Wark. Just Hexham and Wark remain in our hands. The rest is now Scotland."

"Then that hardens my resolve. We will hold, and when time and resources allow, we will relieve their siege."

Alf, my blacksmith, had used the iron we had mined to produce great quantities of weapons. I went to see how Gilles' armour was coming along. That was the gift I would give him when he returned from Frisia. Alf had four workshops. He looked like Vulcan himself as he pounded the iron and steel amidst the smoke and flames of his smithy. He stopped when I approached and joined me outside. He wiped the sweat from his head and downed a whole half gallon of ale.

"God but I needed that. You have come about the mail, lord?"

"I have. Is it ready?"

"It has been ready these two days since. As your squire has not returned, I have had my grandson oiling it link by link. It takes time but it is worth it and it is good practice for someone who would be a smith. It teaches them patience."

"Good. War is coming."

"King Stephen?"

"No, the usual enemy, the Scots."

He spat and shook his head, "They are like lice. They have no honour. Animals! All of them!"

Until I had come to England, I had thought that the people of the island were one. I had since learned that there were more differences on this tiny island than in the whole of the Empire! The Welsh hated the English. The Scots hated the English and they all hated the Irish. I nodded, "This will be the last bastion. Barnard, Yarm, Elton, Hartburn, all may fall but this castle cannot! When the enemy is at the gates then I want every man, woman and child to defend it. The consequences of failure do not bear thinking about."

"We know, lord, and every man does too. They will not let you down."

"It is I who fear letting you down, old friend."

He laughed, "You could not, even if you tried. I will fetch the mail and you can give it to him when he returns."

It was four days later that the *'Adela'* came into port. It was the first time in some years since Sir John had left Stockton. A number of us waited for its arrival. I saw new men waiting on the deck. That was a hopeful sign. Captain William was careful and the ship was tied fore and aft before the gangplank was run out. Sir John, Sven the Rus and Gilles were the first off.

"Well?"

"We hired fifteen men. I hope that is satisfactory?"

Poor John could not get over being my squire and he was ever hesitant. "That is fine." I looked at Sven. "You are happy?"

He grinned, "I am but the twenty we rejected are not."

"Twenty more wished to serve here in Stockton?"

He nodded, "Aye, lord. They know they can make their fortune here. It is why I rejected them. I wanted men who were true warriors. These fifteen are just the sort of men we will want. You have my oath on that."

"That is good enough for me, Sven. Come, let us get them in the warrior hall." I could barely contain my joy as we headed for my castle. Fifteen men at arms, added to Erre and his Varangians, were more than enough to hold my castle. If we added the men and boys of the town who were all archers and slingers of note then I could go to Hugh's aid knowing that my castle was safe and secure.

Easter was early. It was the end of March when it arrived. We had had blue skies and warmth in the day and freezing temperatures at night. We had had sea frets and fogs. The month was out of sorts with itself. Father Henry was keen to make the oldest Christian festival a good one. We invited my neighbouring knights over so that we could feast. Alice made Simnel Cakes and decorated the hall. It was a good celebration.

I sat with my knights and their families in my hall. We had been to church and now we celebrated Christ's death. I took the opportunity to tell my knights and their ladies our situation. I spoke true for that was the only way I knew. When I spoke of the danger of Barnard, Sir Richard and Lady Anne held hands tightly. Their son, Tristan, had almost died and now their daughter and newest grandchild were in danger.

I said, "I believe we will come through this but I am no fool. It will be hard. If they attack Sir Hugh then I will take my archers and men at arms and go to his aid. I will need all of my knights and half of each knight's men at arms and archers. If the Scots attack Barnard then there will be enough left to defend our homes. I will not leave Sir Hugh alone!"

I saw the gratitude on Sir Richard and Lady Anne's faces and was gratified by the nods from the others.

"My intention is to ride as soon as I hear of danger. You must follow as soon as you can. Sir Tristan and Sir Harold, you are the closest. I would expect you to ride with me. Sir Richard and Sir Edward; get there when you can."

Sir Richard asked, "And what if it is here that they attack?"

I smiled, "I hope that it is. I would rather bear the brunt of the Scottish attack than your son in law. If it is here then you assemble at Thornaby and use my ferry to come to our aid."

The feast ended well. For the first time in a long time, I felt that we were all, even Sir Richard, of one accord.

Chapter 4

A full five days after Easter, my sentries announced the arrival of armed men. They did not ride with shields on their arms and their hands were on their saddles. Nonetheless, I was wary for I knew none of them. Then Wulfric said, as they drew closer, "I recognise that device, lord. It is Sir William Redere. He is a Scottish lord of Norman descent. You captured him two years since on the border. His family paid the ransom."

"I do not remember him. Can we trust him?"

"He is Scot but, for a Scot, he seemed to have some honour. Best be wary, lord."

"I will." I shouted down, "Admit them!" There were but ten and we could easily defeat them. "Maintain a watch on all of the gates in case this is a ruse."

"Aye, lord." Erre had his new Frisians on guard and they were all keen to impress.

I descended to my inner bailey. I saw the knight taking in the defences. Was he a spy? My castle held few secrets but it was as strong as any I had visited.

The knight, who appeared to be my age, had dismounted and taken off his helmet. He bowed, "My lord, I come from King David and I have news for your ears only."

"Your men can stay here. Come with me." I strode off, not waiting for him to follow me. He spoke to his men and scurried after. In my hall, I waited for him to enter and shut the doors. "Well?"

I examined him as he spoke. He had fine armour and a good sword hung from his side. This was a warrior. I remembered him now. He had fought well but he lacked the experience I had. The ransom I had extracted had been high for his family was rich.

"My lord, I bring a message from my King. It is not written down for he did not wish it to fall into the wrong hands." I nodded. "The King of Scotland has decided to support his niece Matilda, Empress of the Holy Roman Empire and Countess of Anjou."

I do not know what reaction he expected but my face of stone was not the one. "And..."

He was put off his stride; I could see that. "And he will help to conquer her lands from the north. Now that rebellion is in the south then we can reconquer the land which is the rightful inheritance of his niece Empress Matilda."

His face looked as though he expected effusive praise for such altruism. "And the King has no desires on England?"

"None save the return of his rightful inheritance; the land north of the Tees."

"My land."

"The King assures you that you will retain the title and lands of the Earl of Cleveland. More than that he will give you the lands of Guisborough and Northallerton."

"Very generous of him. And yet the land between the Tweed and the Tees is English and has been since the time of the Romans. You would have me fight for a Scottish King and then give him the very land that belongs to us. I do not see the appeal!"

"But the Empress will rule England."

"A smaller England and a greedy neighbour to the north."

"The Empress has said she agrees."

As soon as he said that, I knew that he had been lied to. I did not doubt his honesty. They had chosen an honest man to deliver a dishonest message. Even had Matilda not warned me, I would have been suspicious of such an offer but with the letter in my mind, I knew that it was a lie. The Scottish King would let my men bleed for him against Stephen of Blois and then he would take my lands.

"I will think about the King's offer, which is a most generous one. You will have my answer before midsummer day."

He then made his first mistake. It reflected his honesty. "But my King needs to know before Whitsun. He has plans."

I nodded, "Very well then I will tell him seven days before Whitsun. Whom should I send with my answer?"

"Send your priest. That way God will be happy too."

"Very well. Will you stay?"

"No, I fear I have a long journey home."

After he had left me, I sent for my captains and Sir John. I told them what had transpired. They knew me well enough to wait for my words. "The Scots are about to invade. If they do not attack now then it will be by Whitsun at the latest but I fear it will be now. The messenger was sent to allay my fears and lull me into indolence. Dick, have Aiden and his falconers follow the Scottish knight. I would know where he goes."

"Aye, lord."

"Wulfric, send a rider to Sir Hugh and tell him to be on his guard. The Scots are abroad."

"Aye, lord."

"John, send to my knights. "I would see them on the morrow."

John, my steward, nodded. "I will do so."

Left alone with Gilles, Sir John and Philip, I said, "The question we must divine is where this Scottish attack will come?"

Sir John said, "Perhaps this is a true overture of peace and aid."

Philip shook his head, "It confirms my uncle's worries about the Scots. I agree, Earl, they will attack."

"Sir John, I intend to leave once Aiden tells me where they are. I am guessing that Barnard Castle will be their target. You need to ensure that the castle is secure. We will speak with Alf and the burghers in the morning when my knights have been informed. Assume that any stranger is a spy or an enemy. These are parlous times. Captain Philip, go to your uncle and tell him the news. He needs to know."

I was alone in my chamber and I reread the letter from Matilda. She had warned me of the danger. Had King David approached her? I suspected he had. He could feel righteous that he was helping his niece but I knew that he had an ulterior motive. There was no one I could consult. I was Warlord. I was the only representative of the Empress and the Earl for hundreds of miles. I had no one with whom I could share this burden. I steeled myself. The worst decision I could make would be to make no decision. As soon as I discovered where the Scots had gathered, I would formulate my plan.

Edgar arrived back at noon. I had just finished my meeting with my knights where I put them on a war footing. Edgar rode in. "Lord, they took the old Roman Road north and west. They are heading for Carlisle."

I smacked my palm. "Then they are coming through Barnard Castle." I looked at Edgar. "Where are your brother and Aiden?"

"Aiden said he wanted to make sure that the knight did go to Carlisle."

I smiled. Aiden had been bought as a slave but since his manumission, he had been the most loyal of my men.

"I want the men for my conroi gathering by tomorrow. If you fear for your families then bring them within my walls. I guarantee that they will be well guarded. Bring your warhorses for we will need to break the back of this Scottish attack.

"Aye, lord."

They left immediately. I sought out Father Henry. "I go to war, Father. The Scots are coming."

"And you need shriving?"

"No, Father, I need a priest to tend to our wounded and our injured."

"Father Abelard is a good healer. He will come with you. I will bless the men before they leave. When will that be?"

"Tomorrow afternoon at the latest."

"We have time then."

John, my steward, had sent me to war enough times to know what he needed to do. He had servants and slaves filling the wagons. They would carry spare weapons, tents and bedding as well as food. He had ten servants ready to accompany us and serve our every need. There would be food and enough beer for five days. We had learned from our earlier campaigns. Gilles had his new armour but also our horses to deal with. I would be taking Badger as well as Rolf. He had but one horse, a palfrey. He had been a squire long enough to know that this was his best chance to get a warhorse at little cost to himself. His life would be the coin he gambled in the heat of the battle.

Even though my messengers had not returned, we left as soon as the army was gathered. I wanted to meet the enemy as far from Stockton as I could. We met Edward as we passed Piercebridge. "Lord, Aiden says they are moving east. The Scots are coming over the high passes."

"He watches them?"

"Aye, lord. He says if you do not see him before you see the Scots then they are heading for Barnard."

Aiden would only be seen if he chose to be seen. We would not reach Barnard before dark and so I headed for Gainford. Sir Hugh's old castle was still manned and we could defend it if I was wrong. If the Scots decided to pass Barnard Castle then they would come down the river and attack Stockton.

As I walked around the camp, I spoke with as many of my men as I could. My father had taught me to do so. He had told me that you must know the hearts of the men you led. It had proved a successful strategy in the past. Those with whom I had never fought always asked me about the legends which surrounded me. I told them the truth. They were still impressed which I did not understand.

We broke camp and headed west. I sent two of Dick's archers south of the river in case there were Scottish scouts there. If there were then that meant they were heading for Stockton. As we travelled along the old Roman Road, I remembered when we had taken the castle from Barnard de Balliol. I had seen how it could be taken and I had to learn from that. Barnard de Balliol had fled before he could be taken. Like De Brus, he was a wily adversary. In those days, he had allied with the Scots; now he had fled to Stephen of Blois. Men like that were dangerous for you never knew their true allegiance.

It was just eight miles to the castle and we reached it by noon. Hugh opened his gates to welcome us. My two archer scouts crossed the bridge from the west and reported no signs of the Scots south of the river. While my men set up camp close by the town, I held a council of war.

"We will have every archer within the walls of the castle. This is too good a vantage point to waste. We will keep all the horsemen, including yours, Sir Hugh, outside the castle walls. We will hold the horses in the woods to the east of the castle. When Aiden reports their presence then we will take down our camp and wait in the woods."

Sir Hugh nodded, remembering our earlier conversation. "You intend to wait until they attack our east gate."

I nodded, "Once he is committed then our knights and men at arms can fall upon them and wreak havoc. Their men at arms will be on foot trying to take the walls."

Sir Edward, like me, had fought the Scots his whole life, "I still worry that he will take the route south of the river. The road is not as good as this one but the whole of England would lie before him. He could advance as far as York and that, my lord, is an even greater prize than either Barnard Castle or Stockton for it houses the archbishop."

"And you are right. It is why we camp here. As you said, Sir Edward, the road is better north of the river. We can be at Gainford in an hour. From there we can head south and cut him off close to the junction of the two Roman Roads, hard by Northallerton. In many ways, I hope he does just that for our valley will be safe and we can trap them between the archbishop and his men and ours."

Sir Edward bowed to me, "I should have known that all was well thought out, lord."

The enemy did not make an appearance for two more days. Aiden rode in late one night looking weary. "The Scots have come, my lord. This night they camp just four miles away at the old Roman fort by the farm of Bowes. I estimate that they have the banners of twenty knights. I saw few archers but there was a company of Flemish crossbows. Half of their men at arms were mounted. Their army is in excess of four hundred." He paused. "The King is not with them. They have that fat slug Gospatric with them and the Earl of Moray's banner was amongst them."

Bowes farm and the old Roman fort of Lavatrae was the point at which the road forked. One road came to the castle but the other headed towards the Great Road in the east.

"Do you know if they intend to attack here?"

He smiled, "The reason they have taken so long to get here is that they stopped at Brough Castle where they built ladders and a ram. They have the parts of the ram in wagons. Unless they intend to lumber across the north of this land so slowly that a one-legged man could catch them then they are coming to Barnard Castle, lord."

"Thank you, Aiden. Your news is all the better for your judgements."

"Do the ram and the ladders change our plans, lord?"

"No, Sir Hugh. You will have, within your castle, over one hundred archers. The twenty-two men at arms can defend the bridge gate but it is the archers who will slaughter them as they cross the bridge and then travel around your castle. Captain Dick will thin their numbers. They may have mail and shields but the ones who carry the ladders and fetch the wagons will not. They will have to find somewhere safe from the arrows to construct the ram. That is the only change. My seventy horsemen will destroy their war machine and the men with the ladders. Your men at arms will not be able to hold the bridge gate for long. Do not risk them. When the gate is lost, recall them to the curtain wall. That is the advantage of a second gate. Your bridge gate is the point that is the narrowest. They will only pass it slowly."

"But Aiden said there were over four hundred in the army."

I smiled, "Sir Richard, with seventy such men I would happily fight the Tartar horsemen of the east. Trust in your son and trust in your men. We have right on our side."

That evening in our camp, for I shared the hardships with my men, Gilles sharpened my sword and oiled my mail. My shield had been repaired after the bolt had struck it and I was as ready as I would be. "Will you ride Badger tomorrow, lord?"

"I will. And we will need to look out for a young warhorse for you, too, Gilles."

"I am barely a squire, lord. I may wear mail but we both know that I have not yet the skills to fight in a conroi. I am there to fetch your spear and your spare horse."

Unlike most squires, Gilles was overly modest. I liked that trait in him. "Do not underestimate yourself, Gilles, besides, I did not say you were ready for a warhorse but you need a young horse that you can school so that you can grow together. Sir William, Sir Leofric and Sir John all had unschooled warhorses which are still not at their peak but horse and rider are growing as one. We shall put Badger with a good mare and you shall have the issue. Aiden knows horses and he will help you to grow close. Wulfric there will teach you how to school the beast."

Wulfric had acquired his magnificent grey, Roger, in Normandy when he had slain the knight who rode him. He had only ridden palfreys before then. Most men at arms would never be allowed a warhorse. Men who served me did not follow the same rules. Perhaps that was why I had little trouble in attracting new men.

We were going into battle and that night Father Abelard heard confession and then absolved the conroi of its sins. Men fought better knowing that their souls had been cleansed. He had with him a cross that Archbishop Thurstan had given to me many years earlier. Father Abelard would make sure that the cross would be as visible as my banner. Although priests were supposed to be safe in battle, I had seen too many die to take that for granted. My banner would be carried by Gilles. I had too few men at arms to have the luxury of a standard guarded by a valuable warrior. Gilles could defend the standard; I hoped he would not have to.

We broke camp before dawn and moved all into the shelter of the woods. We walked our horses there rather than riding them. I had Aiden, Edward and Edgar with me. I sent them down to the river with orders to slay the Scottish scouts whom I knew would be crossing the river soon. They were fine hunters; this day they would hunt men.

We then waited. Most battles are hours of waiting followed by a brief but vicious fight and then it would be over. Some men lost the battle while they were waiting, for they defeated themselves in their minds. Their enemies' numbers grew. Their belief in their leaders diminished. All of my men had fought enough times to ignore those doubts.

By noon, we had received a message from the castle that the bridge gate had fallen and the Scots were crossing. To us, it was a distant noise but from then on the noise grew as more Scots and rebels crossed the bridge and tried to move around to the east gate. The curtain wall, which was above the bridge, had been built on a slope that was impossible to climb one handed. Four men could guard the whole wall. Instead, the army endured the arrows, slingshots and stones of the south wall of the castle as they hurried to the flatter ground to the east.

Gilles pointed and said, excitedly, "There, lord! I see banners."

"You have sharp eyes, Gilles." The vanguard was approaching the east gate. The castle was just three quarters of a mile from us. I had had my men pace it for I needed to know the exact distance for our charge. I turned, "Prepare for war. The enemy approaches. Gilles, fetch our mounts."

When he returned he said, "Do we not charge them now, lord?"

"No, for first they will ask for the surrender of the castle while their men prepare the ram. I want the ram almost completed before we destroy it."

Sure enough, we heard the trumpets as the Earl of Moray or whoever led them approached the walls.

"Mount!"

There would be no further orders until we left the safety of the woods. It would take some minutes to organise into our three battles. Sir Richard would lead the right. Sir Edward, the left. I would have Sir Tristan and Sir Harold with me and we would form the centre. There would be forty heavily armoured men in the centre column and but fifteen on each of the flanks. It was my job to go for the heart of their lines. The other two were to protect my flanks and enable me to do so.

I waited until I saw activity and heard the shouts and cheers as the Scots prepared to attack. Half a mile from us they had set up their camp and I saw men unloading the parts of the ram from their wagons. I shouted, "Forward!"

I led my men from the wood. It did not take long to form our lines. I rode at the head of my column and I was flanked by Wulfric and Sir Harold. Sir Tristan was to Sir Harold's left. Gilles and the squires were tucked in behind the four of us and then the rest of my men at arms, warriors all, formed the sides of the wedge. We were using my father's favourite formation. The four of us would be the point of the arrow and we would charge the heart of the enemy.

Wulfric said, "Ready, lord!"

We trotted forward. We were not seen by those constructing the ram until we were four hundred paces from them. By then we were cantering. When we struck the enemy, we would not be going much faster. Behind us, the men who guarded our camp were running to finish off any men we wounded. We would slay the men at the ram and they would destroy it. Without a ram, the castle could not be taken.

As soon as we were seen, pandemonium ensued. The men who had been building the ram had no armour and they fled towards the river. Our horses opened their legs and we covered the last couple of hundred paces quickly. Ahead of us, the Scots had seen our approach. They had their best men facing the walls and few mounted men. The mounted men were their twenty knights and they hurriedly turned to face us. I eased Badger's head to the left so that we approached the knights head-on. We had our long spears. Unlike wooden lances, these had a long metal head. Alf had tempered them and they would penetrate mail.

The Scots had no lances for they had not envisaged fighting horsemen. The four of us were so close that our stirrups were touching. The enemy line was loose. The four of us struck the two centre knights. I pulled back my spear and punched it at the chest of the knight with the yellow cross on the blue surcoat. Harold's spear struck his shield. My punch and my sharpened spearhead broke the mail and tore through the gambeson to enter the knight's chest. Harold's spear knocked the rider into the path of the fellow next to him and Wulfric lost his spear when it shattered in the throat of his opponent.

I pulled back my arm and lowered my hand for there were no horsemen before me. My men at arms were engaged with the outnumbered knights behind me. Sir Richard and Sir Edward had brought their men to add their swords to that unequal contest. Before us, lay the mass of the Scottish army and they were all on foot. Dick and his archers rained arrows down on men who now had two foes to face. If they turned their backs on the archers to face us, they had no shields to protect themselves.

Twenty or so Scottish men at arms had formed a shield wall. Three of us still had spears. I shouted, "Bear left!" It allowed us to ride obliquely across their line and thrust our spears at the waiting shield wall. Wulfric had drawn his axe and he could swing that mighty weapon one handed. I thrust with my spear at the man at arms who had just stabbed at me. My spear was longer than his and it entered his cheek whereupon the head shattered. I felt the blow from his spear but my mail prevented penetration. I heard a loud shout as Wulfric's axe took half the head from the leader of the men at arms.

"Bear right!" Drawing my sword, I swung Badger's head to the right. We were now inside the shield wall and the slaughter began. The squires could use their spears and we had our swords and axes to hack and slash at the heads of the men at arms. Few had mail coifs and our long swords found flesh. They were brave and struck at us with their swords. One managed to strike Badger which was a mistake for he lunged, teeth bared at the Scot. I thrust under the man's outstretched arm into his side. The Scots were either dead, wounded or had thrown down their weapons and prostrated themselves on the ground. I reined in Badger. The wound to my mount was not serious but it would need stitches. He stamped the ground angrily. It did not do to upset a destrier.

I saw that Sir Edward and Sir Richard had captured most of the knights or slain them. Two had managed to escape and now gathered with the rest of their army. It was much smaller in number. They had formed a huge circle with shields on every side. I smelled burning and turned to see that my men had set the parts of the ram alight. Close to the wall were the remains of the ladders. Barnard Castle would not be taken.

Wulfric and Sir Edward reined in next to me. Wulfric pointed to the two knights who had escaped, "That is Sir William Redere there with the Earl of Moray."

Sir Edward said, "They still outnumber us, lord."

"But they cannot defeat us. We have an impasse. We do not have the men to defeat them and they are looking for a way out. Come, Gilles, Sir Edward, we will go and speak with them. Sir Richard, take command."

I sheathed my sword and took off my helmet and rode slowly towards the enemy with my right-hand palm uppermost. It was the sign of peace. When I was twenty paces from their wall of spears I stopped. Just then I saw a crossbow come up. I barely had time to bring up my shield before a bolt struck my shield. I lowered my shield as I heard the cries as my archers killed the last four crossbowmen.

"I might have expected such dishonour from Scots." I pointed my hand at Sir William, "And you, sir, had best stay clear of my sword for you lied to me." He had not been as innocent as I had assumed. He had deceived me.

He shrugged, "A ruse of war, that is all."

The Earl of Moray was a greybeard He had negotiated before, "Make your offer!"

"Leave your horses and go back to Scotland. Send ransoms for your knights and pay a hundred gold pieces to Sir Hugh of Gainford for the unwarranted attack on his castle and his lands."

"We outnumber you!"

I was close enough to see the walls and for them to hear me. "Dick! A demonstration!"

An arrow flew and struck the squire next to the Earl in the hand. The shocked squire looked in disbelief at the shaft in his palm. "Enough! You call this honourable?"

"He lives, does he not? Had the position been reversed then I am not so sure."

"Very well. I agree to your terms, reluctantly. I do so to save my men's lives." He turned his horse's head.

"No horse is to leave the field. You can walk back to your home. You have one month to send the ransoms, that is all!"

The four remaining horsemen dismounted and the Scottish army trudged west. They had to endure the jeers and shouts from the walls of Barnard Castle and it was not a quick departure. The narrow bridge gate slowed them down. The humiliation would last all the way west.

It would have been impossible not to lose men in our attack against such odds and we had lost men at arms who were impossible to replace. Others had wounds. Our horses had been hurt. We had to stitch Badger and a number of other animals. However, we had achieved our aims. The Scots had been thwarted. I was, however, worried that King David was not with them. This meant that this was not the main Scottish army. This was a test to see our reaction. Had they captured the castle then it would have allowed them to take the whole of the north. The war was not over and the enemy warriors were still sniffing around our borders, our walls and even our very gates.

We took the prisoners into the castle. There they would be closely guarded. Sir Edward organised the sharing out of the spoils of war and they were better than we might have expected. It showed that they had been confident they would win. We had seven warhorses, one for each conroi. There were suits of armour as well as many weapons. The baggage train was abandoned and we found gold and coins. Gospatric had escaped us once more. He was always too canny to be caught. He had been the first to flee with his bodyguard. He would live to fight another day.

We feasted that night. It was always the way of warriors. We had come close to death and yet, by banding together, we had survived. None of my men had died but we knew those who had and we spoke of their deeds. We recounted past battles where they had gained honour and we toasted their souls to heaven. None of us doubted that we would meet again in the Otherworld, heaven.

The next morning I sent Sir Richard, Sir Tristan and Sir Harold home with their booty. I wanted their homes protected. We could not risk spending long periods away. Sir Edward and I would wait until the ransoms and damages had been paid. Sir Hugh was delighted. His castle had held and he had seen ways to improve his castle.

"I believe, Earl, that we could last five, six, even seven days without aid. I intend to build a double ditch before my gate. If a ram is the best that they have then they will never defeat these walls."

"Then make sure you have a cellar with plenty of food. Your well and the river give you water but a determined enemy can lay siege for months."

"I will, lord, but, thanks to your wisdom I am much richer now. I can hire more men and employ William the Mason to make my castle stronger."

By the time that the ransom and damages had arrived, I was satisfied that Barnard Castle would be a rock upon which the Scots would break. The next time they would come a different way. As we rode back, I discussed it with Wulfric, Dick, Aiden and Sir Edward. Aiden knew the land better than any.

"I was worried, lord, when they reached Bowes for, from there, they could either cross the river or head south. I gambled."

"We all gambled, Aiden, and it paid off. But you are right. What do we do if they come south of the river? They could head for Gainford, Piercebridge or Yarm. None of those castles is as strong as Barnard. King David can muster a much larger army than the one we saw last week. We must be vigilant. I asked Sir Hugh to keep his foresters far to the west and the north. We need early warning of danger and our enemies."

Sir Edward laughed, "Lord, we have even more enemies to the south of us. The Baron of Skipton is no friend to us. One of the prisoners was saying that the Earl of Chester has now allied himself with Stephen. Our list of friends shrinks and that of our enemies grows."

"The Earl and the Empress are coming. We have to hold on until they do. We have yet to be defeated and our losses are acceptable." I saw the scowl on Sir Edward's face. He had lost men. "Sir Edward, when you were a man at arms would you have accepted such small losses as part of the victory?"

He nodded, "You are right. We fought in some battles and only Wulfric and I survived but when men fight for you there is an unspoken bond; a responsibility."

Wulfric said, sadly, "It is good that you say that but we know lords who were not like the Earl. They would have discarded men and not lost a moment's sleep. We have changed, old friend, and it is for the better. Sadly, it will not help us to sleep at night. We will both suffer the nightmares of lost comrades."

Chapter 5

Not long into May, I had another visitor from Scotland. This time it was not the Scottish knight I had threatened to kill, it was the Bishop of Glasgow. There was an assumption that, as a man of God, he would be safe. To be honest, I would have lost no sleep had I had him killed but it suited my purpose to speak with him. I found that I could learn much from what men did not say and what they assumed I knew. I made sure that Father Henry was present when I interviewed him.

"King David is less than happy that you rejected his offer of help for the claims of his niece."

"And I am disappointed that King David's men attacked without provocation."

"The King knew nothing about that, Earl."

I looked in his face for dishonesty but I saw none. "You believe that?"

"I was told by the King himself and I have no reason to doubt him."

"I might have given him the benefit of the doubt had his last emissary, Sir William Redere, not been with the attacking army. Perhaps I might see you in the next attack, your grace."

He was not put out by the insult. "I am a man of peace, my lord. I will not be present."

"So, what does the King wish now?"

"He makes the same offer he did before. He will support the claim of the Empress if you will help him conquer the north of England."

"And I say again that I will only do this if I command the army. That way I can dismiss the Scottish troops when I no longer need them and send them back to Scotland."

"Some might argue that this is Scotland, my lord."

I shook my head, "When the Roman Emperor came many years ago, he put a wall between the barbarians of the north and civilisation in the south. That wall stands yet and is the only marker between the two countries. Carlisle, the New Castle, both of those castles were treacherously taken by an opportunist king when King Henry was murdered!"

The Bishop frowned, "I thought King Henry died from eating too much?"

"Do not believe the stories of his enemies. He was murdered. I was there and I killed the murderer."

"Then I am wasting my time."

"You are indeed, and tell King David to send no more emissaries. I tire of them. The next one he sends will have his head decorating my walls."

"That is not the act of a civilised man."

I laughed, "I will take that from many men but not a Scot. Leave, Bishop. I tire of you!"

"You would not offer us hospitality?"

"You slept last night in Durham. Leave now and you can sleep there again!"

After he had gone, Father Henry said, "He was not treated as a Bishop, my lord."

"Did he come here as a bishop or an emissary of a treacherous man? I am sorry, Father, if I have offended your sensibilities. That man is not a priest; he is a political animal. Do not confuse the two. You are a good man. Not all priests are as noble as you." I saw him reflect on those words as he left.

We held our sessions and collected our taxes. I had no one to answer to now and that made both tasks hard. We needed taxes to pay for the men at arms who would defend my valley but I did not want my people to suffer. I taxed them the lowest amount I could. The Sessions were even harder for I had no one to whom I could refer those cases which I found difficult. It was where I missed Adela the most. She had a kind heart and a sharp mind. I found the taxes and the trials drained me more than a battle. I no longer kept to the usual dates for taxes and sessions. I was Warlord and made my own rules.

I went to Ayeton and Guisborough myself to collect taxes. I made them as fair as I could. When I was there, I told the burghers of both places that I would happily offer employment to any who wished to fight for me. Surprisingly, I had many who wished to take me up on the offer. It was known that I paid well. Seven young men came back with me. Wulfric and Dick would assess their skills and decide how best we might use them.

I sent my ship back to my manor in Anjou with letters for the Empress, the Earl, my castellan and my son. I had waited to write them as I wanted a considered reply to them all. I asked Captain William to see if he could hire any men when he was in Anjou. Gilles had told me that my name still commanded respect. Sir John thought I should use that to my advantage. It was not my way but I conceded.

By the end of May, we had added thirty men to our garrison. The Scots had not attacked again and the allies of the Earl of Gloucester were succeeding in their Kentish rebellion. It was June when we heard of movements in the west. Sir Hugh's scouts had grown bold and using the fine weather had travelled as far as Carlisle to spy upon the Scots. There they saw the royal banner and an army gathering. Sir Hugh knew that it did not bode well and he sent a messenger to me.

I sent for Sir Edward and we sat with Wulfric and Dick to discuss the problem. John, my steward, was also present. I began. "We do not need to hasten to Barnard Castle this time for Sir Hugh has made it stronger but we still need to prepare for a campaign."

"The problem, my lord, is that it is summer. Farmers are in their fields and all else are working from sunrise to sunset."

Sir Edward shook his head, "We will not take the fyrd. We will leave them at home! We pay men at arms and archers to fight."

"But lord, if you take the men then we have to man the walls of our castles with those who live in the borough. They cannot do both and we need them as sentries. With the Earl's men away, we are vulnerable."

I saw the dilemma. "You are saying that the twelve men of my garrison are not enough." John nodded. "I daresay that

Sir Edward, Sir Tristan and Sir Harold will be even worse off for many of their men at arms had farms too."

Sir Edward looked glum. "The bookkeeper is right, lord. I had forgotten."

I smiled, "Do not berate yourself. I have a plan. If I take the knights from your three castles, your squires and half of your men at arms and archers, I will have enough men to slow an enemy up and ascertain the danger."

John looked flustered, "But lord, what about Stockton?"

"I am coming to Stockton. I will take Sir John but leave eight men at arms and Philip of Selby's archers. That is enough to defend the White Tower!" He looked relieved, "What say you, Wulfric? Will that work?"

"Aye, lord, although if it is the whole Scottish army, we may be outmatched."

"Gilles, go to my chamber and fetch me the parchment with the map upon it."

He quickly returned with the calfskin vellum. John, my steward, had a fine hand. He had copied the map from an ancient one we had seen in York. He had not copied all of the detail for we had not had time but it had sufficient for my purposes. At the time, I had been welcome in York for it had been when King Henry still lived. Gilles spread it out.

I jabbed my finger at the map. "We are mounted and we will be faster than any enemy. We concentrate at Bowes. We know that the King of Scotland is in Carlisle. If we are threatened then he must come through Bowes. It is his only route east. We can cover both roads and delay an army long enough to fetch our people within our walls. It will buy time to sow the fields and tend animals. Life has to go on."

Dick nodded, "I agree with you, lord. The land is perfect for my archers. There are forests aplenty. We can ambush and delay an army. If the Scots send their men into the forests then the beasts will feast well on their corpses. We have spent the winter laying in a great store of arrows. We have good fletchers in Stockton."

"Then we leave but we will not take warhorses. I would travel light. Philip of Selby may well need every man to man the walls; even horse holders and carters."

My counsel of war ended and I think that all were satisfied with the plan. They would have to be for I had no second in case it went wrong.

When we left for Bowes, we could only take one long spear each. We were travelling light. When that spear shattered, we would have to rely on our swords. We would use Barnard Castle for food. It was but a few miles away from Bowes. The battle I led was mainly my men. However, my three knights had chosen their best three men at arms and best three archers to accompany us. We would have no peer in combat. The five banners, for Sir Hugh of Gainford, would join us, might confuse an enemy and suggest a larger force of men. Scouts tended to count banners and make assumptions about numbers.

Sir Hugh, when he joined us, brought more news about the Scottish force, "It is led by the King's nephew, William Fitz Duncan."

"Do we know anything about him?"

"Nothing, lord."

We reached Bowes by the end of the first week of June. The old Roman fort was just a ruin but I saw that it would make a good site for a castle. If we had the men, I would build one but this was not the time for building. We needed Matilda or young Henry on the throne first. I kept that information in my head. I had to remember that there would be a future when this anarchy was but a distant memory. If I did not have that hope then I would go mad.

Dick and his archers hunted the land around the deserted fort. It allowed them to spy out the terrain and watch for the enemy whilst filling my men's bellies. We had been there for some days when a handful returned earlier than expected. Will Red Legs led them. "My lord, there are men at arms fleeing this way."

"Fleeing?"

"Aye, lord, Dick and the others are watching. They are coming from the west up the old trackway from the southwest. They are five miles from us."

I turned to Edward, "The southwest? That makes no sense." I closed my eyes and saw the map in my head.

"Unless William Fitz Duncan has headed south towards Chester."

"Then he would meet Sir Edgar Mandeville."

Sir Edgar was the new Baron of Skipton. An unpleasant and treacherous man, he had been appointed by Stephen the Usurper. The men who were fleeing towards us might be his men. "That is fifty miles south of here. Why would they head north? This may be a trap. Come, we will head south to the track from the south and west."

We rode in a column of fours. We found Dick and his archers dismounted by the edge of the thinning trees. Ahead of us, the moors and rocks rose to the highest point on the long ridge which ran down England's spine. I saw, in the distance, standards and mounted men as they hastened towards us. Dick pointed half a mile ahead. There were ten men, four of them mounted and the rest on foot. They were hurrying towards us.

"These were the men we saw, lord. Since I sent Will Red Legs we saw more of them." He pointed further up the slope. I saw another ten mounted men. They kept their line to charge those with standards and banners behind them. Even as we watched, I saw one of them fall.

"You have good eyes. Do you see the banners?"

He peered, "The ones chasing are Scots."

"Then they are our enemies. Whoever they chase we will aid. We ride. Dick, mount your archers and sweep to the west. We will charge them head-on."

We galloped south. The ten we had first seen cowered as we galloped by. They looked stunned to see our horses and banners. If we were to save the others then we had no time for pleasantries. However, as we rode by, I recognised that two of them wore the livery of Sir Edgar Mandeville. I was helping a supporter of Stephen the Usurper!

The dips and folds in the land aided us. We disappeared from the view of the Scots as they concentrated upon the men they were chasing. We knew where they were. The track was little better than the moors around it and we rode in one long line. We burst over the crest and the nine men who were fleeing towards us on horses already close to death stopped and hung their heads as though they expected death. The thirty Scots who were pursuing must have been confident of catching their foes for they rode in a single column of twos. We saw each other when we were but fifty paces apart. Instead of charging us, which was the only option I would have taken, they halted.

Sir Edward and I rode at the two leading men, a knight and a man at arms. I punched my spear at the knight and, although he brought up his shield, he could not prevent my spear from striking and penetrating his shoulder. He chopped through my spear with his sword and I drew my own. He rode a palfrey and Rolf was bigger and more fierce. I swung my sword at his shield and his weakened left arm could not stop the blow. It hacked down across his neck and he fell from his horse.

His standard-bearer lowered the standard and screaming, "Scotland!" charged at me with the standard held like a lance. I jerked Rolf's head to the left and hacked at the standard. Holding my own banner in his left hand, Gilles brought his sword sideways to take the head of the brave young standard-bearer. The rest were all quickly slain. Dick and his archers appeared from the south.

"We found four Scots who were on foot. They are dead. My archers are fetching their possessions."

I dismounted and picked up the standard. I recognised it. It belonged to Redere. I returned to the knight I had slain. Lifting his helmet I saw that he looked to be of an age with William my son. The seal he bore marked him as a knight. "He must be a son or brother of William Redere. Our lives, it seems, keep touching."

"Aye, lord."

"Wulfric, collect the horses and the booty."

"And the bodies, lord?"

The moorland was dry for it was summer. I did not want a fire that might destroy this land. "Put them together and cover them with rocks." Wulfric scowled, "Wulfric, they fought well enough."

"Aye, lord. You are too kind. I would have left them for carrion."

As we rode back to the men we had rescued, I reflected that perhaps he was right, but a man cannot change his nature. I was not naturally cruel. I had fought men who were.

The nineteen men who had survived had joined together and stood not aggressively but apprehensively. They had dismounted for their horses could carry them no further. I took off my helmet as I approached and handed it to Gilles before dismounting. The leader of the group had a wound to his head; a blow had cut him from his eye to his chin and his ventail hung in two parts. He looked to be an older man at arms.

"Who are you?"

"I am John of Craven and I lead all that is left of the men of Skipton."

"The Baron of Skipton is dead?"

"No, my lord. " He almost spat the words out and I could hear the hurt in his words. "Sir Edgar fled the field with his brothers. They left us."

"The field? You had better start at the beginning. Gilles, give them water for they look like they need it."

"Thank you, lord, we have ridden for a day and a night without stopping. There were a hundred of us when we began."

"Then you have lost friends. Go on."

"Sir Edgar had word that the Scots were harrying Furness and my home of Craven. He sent my lord, Ralph de Umbraville, to investigate. We found a mighty army. We fought our way back to Clitheroe where the Baron had gathered his army. He had raised the levy and we had a good position but after the Scots charged he fled south. My lord could not leave the men of the west to die and we fought on to allow them the chance to escape the slaughter. We were surrounded. When it became clear that we could not win, my lord decided to gather the survivors and fight our way out. The enemy soldiers were the weakest to the north and we broke through. My lord was heading for York and Archbishop Thurstan." He shook his head and I could see that the old warrior was upset.

Wulfric and his men returned with laden horses. "We will return to Bowes shortly. Carry on, John of Craven."

"My lord could have escaped for we were well mounted but he would not leave those who were on foot. The Scots pursued us relentlessly. They picked off the weak and my lord kept turning to fight. He was a mighty warrior. He was young but he was puissant. We thought we had escaped. There were fifty of us this morning when we came towards the high ground. We were heading east when this latest conroi found us. Sir John charged them but he fell as did his squire and his young brother. The Scots hacked their bodies. I was left in command. I had heard that the Tees was safe from the Scots and I headed thence. They kept coming. Had you not arrived then I fear I would have joined my lord. Thank you, Earl. We owe you our lives. At least now the perfidy of Mandeville will be known."

I now regretted the burial of the Scots. I should have treated them the way they had treated Sir Ralph de Umbraville. "Tell me, sergeant, who commands the Scots?"

"William Fitz Duncan. He had a claim to Skipton through his father in law, William de Meschines."

"The army you fought, how big was it?"

"I would guess, from the banners, at least a thousand men. We had but five hundred. The Galwegians had no armour but they fought well. My lord wanted to charge them but Sir Edgar declined. That cost us the chance to defeat them. We slew many but I would guess that five hundred or more survive."

"Come, you shall rest and then we will decide what happens to you."

His eyes narrowed, "Happens to us, lord? Have we done wrong?"

I smiled, "No. Your scars bear testimony to your honour. I merely mean that you have, it would seem, three choices: return to fight for your land, join the Archbishop in York or join my men. If it is the first of these then I can help you no longer but if you choose the latter then I can help you."

He smiled, "I am sorry, my lord. I am suspicious of great lords now. Sir Edgar was base. I should have known that the warlord of the north, the man who chose honour over riches, would be honourable. For myself, I would serve you, lord. There is naught for me in Copeland or Craven now and so long as you fight Scots then I am your man."

"But there may come a time when I fight Stephen, the one you call King."

He shrugged, "Kings? Queens? Emperors? It is all the same. Soldiers like me just want a leader they can trust."

Wulfric nodded, "Then you have made the right choice, John of Craven."

We headed, not for Bowes but for Barnard Castle. The news we had heard meant that there was no immediate danger of an attack from the west. Even a thousand men could not take Barnard. The men we had rescued joined us, to a man and welcome they were. It was propitious, for Sir Hugh's wife gave birth to a son, John, on the day we returned. It seemed a good omen.

However, a messenger from my castle towards the end of the month scotched that idea. "My lord, there is a message from Sir Hugh Manningham. King David himself has brought an army. Sir Eustace Fitz John has declared for King David and handed over Alnwick Castle. Parts of Yorkshire around Malton have declared for King David. Sir Hugh says to prepare for war. He fears that we are the target of the enemy. "

"And any news from York?"

"Archbishop Thurstan has raised the levy in Yorkshire. There is a sealed letter for you at Stockton."

I turned to my knights. "We return to our castles. Sir Hugh, I fear that I must leave you alone and without our aid. Prepare for a siege."

"Aye, lord. The enemy is truly at our gates now."

Part 2
The Battle of the Standards

Chapter 6

My ship was already in port when we returned. Sir Tristan had been despatched to visit with his father and tell him our news. I summoned Captain William, "I need to keep you in port but be ready to sail at a moment's notice."

"Aye, my lord. We have heard the gossip. The Scottish King himself comes. I can take families to safety if you wish."

"I do not think that any will wish to leave but I thank you for your offer. My walls are high and they are thick. The only way across the river is by ferry and we can tether that on the southern bank. No, Captain William, I need you to take a message to Anjou."

"Then I will await your orders."

John, my steward, had already begun making plans. We had amassed a great deal of salted and preserved meat. We needed no more but the first of the vegetables were now ready and he was storing the best of those. "We have a little wheat but plenty of rye, barley and oats. We will not need to ration it for a while."

"I hope it does not come to that. Keep me informed. We have new men to place on your books. They cost but, in the long run, they will save us."

"I know that now, lord."

Finally, I summoned Philip of Selby. I told him, in detail, what we had learned and the parlous state of the north. "You must ride to your uncle. I believe he may wish a conference with me. I will meet with him anywhere but I believe that he will wish it to be a discreet meeting. The Carthusian Monastery at Mount Grace would seem a logical choice."

"Aye, my lord. I will ride there immediately."

"Take your men with you. These are dangerous times and I would not have you ambushed."

I was not yet done. I went into my town. Gossip had spread and there were worried looking burghers gathering and talking. "Lord, is it true? Does the Scottish King come?"

"He can come but we will resist him." I pointed to the walls of my castle. "Do you think he can breach those walls? You have seen my warriors; are there any better men in the land? It is the Scots who come. They are like fleas on a dog. They irritate and they bite but they do not hurt the beast. We will endure and emerge successfully." They seemed mollified and I headed for Alf. I found him speaking with Father Henry, "This is fortuitous. I can speak with you both at the same time."

"We have heard the news, lord."

I shook my head, "You have heard the gossip. I will now tell you the news!"

Father Henry nodded and Alf said, "I am sorry, my lord."

"A Scottish army has attacked castles in the west and captured them. King David is bringing an army south. That is the news. However, we know not the size of the army nor when it will come. We deal with what we know. My steward has supplies laid in. I suggest that the people of Stockton share their supplies and you two ration them. Remember that we will have those from the outlying farms joining us. The folk of Hartburn and Elton have no castle. They will be housed in my bailey for the duration of the incursions. The people must know that I have made plans and that we know what we must do."

"Aye, my lord." Alf looked relieved.

"Father Henry, the Archbishop has summoned the levy. There will be succour from the south."

"They will help us? Even though we fight against King Stephen."

"You should know that King David says that he comes here to aid Empress Matilda but I know it for a lie. He seeks to enlarge his kingdom while anarchy reigns." They both nodded. "I have also gained seventeen more men at arms as well as the new members of the garrison. We might not be able to meet the King of Scotland in the field but we can greet him from behind our walls."

"I will speak with the people, lord, and give them comfort."

"Thank you, Father."

That done, I walked my walls. Would the King come this way? He had to. If he did not then he left a dagger at his back. He would come. I would need to send a messenger to Norton. They had been raided many times before and they would require my protection. Luckily, they were as close by as Hartburn Manor and could wait until the enemy were seen on the Durham Road. I looked north. Would the Bishop of Durham fight? There was so much that I did not know. I had made plans but this was not like fighting a battle where you knew the lie of the land.

I glanced down and saw Aiden and his two hawkers. They were just returning from the hunt. A deer was slung over the rear of Aiden's mount. "Aiden, a word."

He quickly joined me. "Yes, lord?"

"The Scots are coming. I need your eyes and ears again. He is coming down from the Tyne. I need to know numbers but, most importantly, I need to know when he arrives so that we can gather the people within my walls."

"Should I leave now?"

I nodded, "I think we have some time but take Edward and Edgar with you. Take care for I would not be without your services."

He smiled, "Fear not, lord, if I cannot hide from an army of Scots then it is time for me to take up telling tales in the ale wife's kitchen. We will leave in the morning."

As he turned to leave, I asked, "Where could an army cross our river?"

"In winter there is nowhere until Piercebridge and the bridge there but in summer, if there has been no rain, then there are places by Neasham, Hurworth and Croft which a bold general could use."

"Thank you, Aiden. As ever, your knowledge is invaluable."

I was disappointed. I had hoped that we could deny the King the crossing of the river. I had contemplated sending men to hold the bridge at Piercebridge but if there were fords then there was little point. The next days were spent in frenetic activity as storehouses and granaries were filled and more weapons made.

Philip of Selby returned before Aiden. He had left sooner and had less distance to travel. "Lord, Archbishop Thurstan will meet with you at the priory as you suggest. He was leaving at the same time as I did. He will be there by now."

I looked at the sky. There were still some hours before dark. These were still long days. "Then I will leave now."

I sought Sir John. "I go to visit with the Archbishop. I shall return on the morrow. You command until then." He nodded, "Wulfric, I want ten men to escort me. You stay here with Sir John."

"Aye, lord."

Gilles and I led the men as we left the ferry and galloped south. It was only fourteen miles to the priory and we rode hard. The horses were strong and speed was of the essence. We reached there in less than two hours. The Archbishop had brought a company of men at arms with him. Gilles and I were admitted immediately. We were taken to the Prior's chambers. The Archbishop and the Prior were there along with the High Sheriff of York, William Espece. I had met him before but I did not know him well. He was Stephen's appointment.

The Archbishop looked every day of his seventy years. He held out his ring for me to kiss, "It is good to see you, Aelfraed."

"And you, your Grace."

"You know the Sheriff?" I nodded. "These are dangerous times but we are joined against a common enemy. I have persuaded the Sheriff that you are a noble who puts loyalty to the land above all else."

It was diplomatically put. "I am, your Grace. How stands our defence against the Scots?"

"We have men coming from Nottingham, William Peverel, Geoffrey Halsalin, and from Derbyshire led by Robert de Ferrers. The King has sent De Brus and Balliol from London with mercenaries." I frowned and the Archbishop held up his hand. "They are on the side of

England in this. I know that you doubt their loyalty." He paused. "I have sent them by ship to meet with King David to discuss terms."

I began to lose my temper, "They have allegiances in Scotland; you cannot trust them! What were you thinking? They are traitors!"

He waited for me to subside, "I hope, my son, that you trust me." I paused and nodded. "We still prepare for war. Will you join us?"

"That may be a moot point, your Grace. If David comes south then he will have to cross the Tees. I believe that he will come to take Stockton. I may not be able to join you for I may be the only thing which keeps King David from Yorkshire."

"My sources tell me that he has more than twenty-five thousand men with him, Aelfraed, can your castle hold out against those odds?"

It was a grim smile I gave him, "Whatever the outcome you would not have to face twenty-five thousand men, your Grace. for my castle is strong. We will make them bleed for every inch of my land. I know what you are asking and the answer is no, I will not abandon Stockton to the Scots. They are beasts and my people deserve more."

Sir William spoke for the first time, "My lord, you are wilful! Think of the country! We need your men here with us! It is known that the Scots fear you. Abandon Stockton. We can rebuild a town but if we are defeated then we lose the country."

"What is the country if it is not the people? Would you have me abandon my people? I would not be a knight if I did so. I will bleed for you, your Grace, we will die for you. But I will not leave my castle. When we are gone, they will have to cross the river upstream of Yarm. They will have to come down this road. If you dispose your men between here and Northallerton, you can halt him. My people will be as the three hundred Spartans, Themistocles, and buy you the time!" I smiled as did the Archbishop.

"I am flattered by the illusion but do not die just yet, Earl. Our emissaries may yet succeed."

I laughed, "And the sun may rise in the west! Balliol and De Brus will not bring you success. They bring only treachery!" I rose. "I will return to my home and prepare for the worst. If that worst becomes fact then I pray that you will tell the Empress, the Earl of Gloucester and my son that I did my duty."

"Do not throw your life away, my son. The loss of the land north of the Tees would not be the end of things."

I stared at him, "It would be for my people, your Grace. Farewell."

I rode north, in the dark. I could have stayed but I was angry. The lives of my people rested upon the shoulders of two hypocritical traitors. Once more I was on my own. Sir Hugh's words came back to me. We would have twenty-five thousand Scots descending upon us and I had less than two hundred and fifty warriors to defend my valley.

I headed through Yarm even though it was after dark. "Who goes there?"

"Stockton!"

I was admitted. "My lord! What is the danger?"

"It is the Scots. An army of twenty-five thousand is heading south. We will hold them at Stockton. I came here, Sir Richard, to offer your wife and the family to sail to safety on the *'Adela'*. She waits in Stockton."

Lady Anne put her arm through her husband's. He smiled, "There was a time, my lord, when I doubted my duty but no longer. What can I do?"

"The Scots will attack me but they may try to force a crossing here. Deny them and slow them down. That is all. The Archbishop has an army south of us but there will be no more than ten thousand of them. If we live then we will join him."

"I will do so, lord. But I do not fear for Stockton. With you on the battlements, the Scots will waste their fury on its fine walls."

It was beyond late when I entered my gates. "Alice, fetch me some red wine! I have need of it. Sir John, Gilles, Wulfric, Dick, join me I have need of like-minded fellows."

They came warily. Gilles knew my mind, he had been with me. The others said nothing of my mission and they drank with me. I needed no words of support. I just needed the companionship of men with whom I had faced danger. We were about to be destroyed and I wanted some memories to take with me. When I had had enough drink to make me smile and to loosen my tongue, Dick asked, "Lord, what troubles you?"

"We face twenty-five thousand men and the Archbishop has sent Balliol and De Brus to negotiate the peace. That is like letting the fox in the henhouse!"

Wulfric filled his beaker, "Lord, it makes no difference. They are treacherous and the Scots will still come here. We know that. We hold the walls and they die. It is as simple as that."

Sir John smiled, "He is right, lord. You were wise in the times of plenty and you put your gold into the walls of this castle. We will laugh away a siege. The King could have a hundred thousand men. He has to cross a moat and scale our walls. Even if he does that, he has to face us beard to beard on our walls and we now have more men. I would back any of your men against ten Scots."

They all nodded, even Gilles.

"Are you all mad? Is it the full moon?"

Dick said, "No lord, we are not mad. We are your men... to the death! We fight with you and stand shoulder to shoulder. We face whatever comes our way. I fear no man when I am led by," He stood and raised his beaker, "the Warlord of the North!"

The others joined him and suddenly I felt at peace. If I was to die then what better company than that of these men!

On return from my meeting, I visited my knights and made their families the same offer I had made to Sir Richard. None took me up on it. They understood my offer but wished to stay. Sir Tristan and Sir Harold, however, had their families prepare to leave their homes and join me as did the people of Norton. Their manors could not be defended. We would lose the men who defended them and gain nothing. Better to protect the people. We could rebuild manor houses.

My leaders were now aware of the seriousness of the situation and they all worked harder than ever to prepare for the enemy. We were a people under threat and we worked together.

I wrote letters to the Empress, the Earl and my son. They would be both my will and my legacy if the worst came to the worst. I told them what I intended and what I foresaw as the outcome. I would send them on my ship at the last possible moment. William the Mason worked every hour he could to add defences to my already impressive castle. Each extra stone would slow down the enemy.

Aiden and his two scouts arrived back two days after I had finished my visits. They looked dirty and dishevelled but they were all full of news. "Lord, they are at Durham and encamped outside."

"Numbers?"

"More than twenty thousand but only fifteen or sixteen thousand are warriors. To be honest, my lord, I have never seen as many banners and standards."

"Did they try to reduce Durham?"

"No lord, for they were visited by two lords, De Brus and Balliol. They spent some time talking and the two knights left for the river. I think they came by ship. I do not think the Scots will attack Durham. They have captured all the other castles of Durham. Wark and Hexham are the only two places which remain in the hands of our knights."

"How do you know?"

"We captured two of their scouts and, before they died, they told us all."

"So they are a couple of days away?"

"Yes, lord."

I shouted, "Dick!"

He had placed himself within earshot as soon as my scouts had returned. "Send riders to Norton, Hartburn and Elton. They should come here now. Send riders to Yarm and to Thornaby. Tell them that the Scots are two days away."

I actually felt better now that we had something to do. The castle became a hive of activity as shelters were erected in the inner and outer baileys. Alf and Father Henry organised the town and I fell asleep that night, exhausted.

I was summoned to the walls the next day by my sentries. When I reached the gate, I saw De Brus, Balliol and their guards. "Yes!"

"We have to come to tell you to flee. King David marches here to destroy you."

"I thought you were sent to discuss terms?"

De Brus said, "We failed. He will come no matter what we offered."

I wondered what that was. "It changes nothing for me. I enjoy killing Scotsmen as you both know."

"Earl, this is no time for petty squabbles. We have been enemies before but now we fight on the same side."

"No, we do not, for you two fight for yourselves and I fight for this land and the rightful ruler of England. Ethelred!" I pointed to the ferry. "Take the ferry and tell the Archbishop that the men of the valley still fight beneath my banner and we will die before we surrender!"

De Brus shook his head, "You are my enemy but I admire your courage. I will see that you are buried with honour."

Ethelred looked up at me, "Take them across the river and then anchor by Sir Edward's castle until this is over."

Ethelred turned to his son. "Take this over. I fight with the Earl for my home! I am an Englishman and I know where my loyalty lies."

When the ferry had left and Ethelred entered my castle, the doors slammed shut. With those of Hartburn, Elton and Norton within it felt, somehow final. At least we knew where we stood; alone. I walked down to the jetty with my letters and handed them to Captain William, "Take these to Anjou. If we are not here when you return or if the castle has fallen then serve my son."

"My lord, you will prevail. This is not the end!"

It felt like the slamming of a door as the tiny ship sailed east. My last lifeline was now gone. We were alone.

The last of the villagers from Norton trickled through the north gate as Dick and my archers stood watch in a protective half-circle. When they were within, the gates would be slammed shut for the last time and we would hunker down to await whatever King David had to throw at us. The last time they had come to besiege us, I had been in Normandy and they had almost captured the castle. That had been a weakness of the design and we now had a stone tower by the ferry and a curtain wall that joined the town wall. The tower was strongly garrisoned. We had prepared the ground around my town and my castle. We knew what to expect. We were ready this time.

The first Scottish outriders and scouts arrived at noon the next day. They were cautious and stayed well beyond arrow range. My archers were respected and feared. Some watched the town walls while others went east and west along the river. My castle was calm for we had prepared as well as we could. We had enough archers and men at arms to man the castle walls, the towers, and, with the men of my town, the town walls. Every man had a helmet; even those from the town. Every hand held a weapon, most of my men had two. Even the boys had their slingshots and a leather cap. Below the ramparts, the women were ready, under Father Henry's supervision, with bandages, catgut and ointments. We were a valley at war. No one would hide from the enemy.

We signalled Sir Edward's tower on the opposite bank of the Tees. It told them that the Scots had come. Until they crossed the river, the burghers of Thornaby could continue their daily lives. Our signal merely warned them of their presence. A rider had ridden to warn Sir Richard. The King of Scotland took two days to reach us such were the numbers of men he led. By then the town and the castle were ringed with campfires. There were neither cattle nor sheep for them to eat. They had been taken south of the river or brought within our walls. I had no doubt they would hunt our deer but the army which lay without would take much feeding.

Each morning I was on my walls as dawn broke. I was cautious. If I was King David that would be the time when I would attack. Perhaps he was confident for he did not attack at dawn. I stood with Wulfric as he looked at the winking fires of the Scots. "How many?"

"I would guess more than twenty thousand. I confess it is many years since I have seen such a host."

"Are you worried?"

He laughed, "Lord, they are limited in where they can attack. I am guessing it will be the town walls but when they fall the enemy will have to scale these mighty battlements. My only fear is that I will need a spare axe to hew the heads as they appear. A blunt axe is no weapon at all."

He was right. The huge army he had brought would be better used on a battlefield. He would waste his men attacking such strong walls. I had no doubt that he would bring a ram. That might work on the walls of the town but the ditches to the castle were double ditches. We had copied Roman design. He would need to build a bridge first. Any attack would be expensive. My fear was for the town. Although we had a strong wall and it was manned, equally, by my men and those of the town, it could be breached. The hard work of years could be undone by the vandals that were the Scots.

That August morning I heard trumpets, and a rider bearing the banner of the Scottish King rode to the gate. He bore no helmet and he held no weapon. My men respected the sign for a truce. "His majesty, King David of Scotland, would speak with the Earl of Cleveland."

"He may approach with no more than five riders."

My knights joined me at the north gate. We looked down on the west gate of the town which abutted up to the castle wall. I waved to Alf who was armed and armoured as well as any man at arms. In his hand, he held a war hammer. Woe betide any Scot who came within range of his powerful right arm. Sir Harold pointed, "That looks to be Prince Henry with him."

Sir John said, "Aye, lord, and your friend Redere."

I recognised both of them. Prince Henry had grown somewhat and he had a reputation as a good leader. The Archbishop had told me that Stephen had allowed De Brus to offer him the title of Earl of Northumbria in exchange for peace. I would not have done that but I could see that as the present incumbent was Gospatric, a rebel, it made little difference.

They halted before the gates. I had already annoyed them by making them look up to my walls. Kings never liked that. King David spoke but I could see that his son was already angry at the disrespect shown by us. "Earl, you rejected my offer of friendship and now you close your gates to me. As my envoy told you, I fight for my niece. You are her foremost supporter. We are on the same side."

"You fight for Scotland. I fight for England and I respect patriotism so do not dress it up as an offer of friendship. The Empress does not wish to give up one piece of land. You have already taken advantage of the usurper and grabbed Carlisle. When time allows, I will take that back."

Prince Henry jabbed an angry finger at me, "That land was ever Scottish!"

I laughed and saw the young man redden, "Do not believe your singers of songs. The Romans built a wall to divide the civilised world from the barbarians of the north. Carlisle is English!" I pointed to Redere, "And a word of warning for you, dissembler. Come within the reach of my arm and you shall lose your head. That is fair warning."

King David raised his hand, "Enough of these threats, Earl, do you join us or fight us?" He gestured behind him. "I have twenty-six thousand men and you are no obstacle to us. If we attack then we give no quarter. We will slay the men and enslave the women and children."

I shook my head, "Hypocrite! You talk of ending threats and then threaten us in the same breath. Do not waste any more breath. If you can take us then do so but do not insult us with the sound of your voice."

"That is the King to whom you speak! He deserves respect!"

"And, pup, I am the Warlord of the North. There is neither King nor Emperor who commands my respect. When the real Prince Henry, the son of the Empress, is anointed, then I will bow my knee to a king, until then they are merely men and they should avoid the edge of my sword."

The King said, "Then it is done. You have consigned your people to an ignominious end."

As he turned, a chant began. I think Alf began it but all took it up. They banged their spears on the wooden walls and on their shields. All joined in, men, women, children; burghers and warriors. "Warlord! Warlord! Warlord! Warlord!"

It continued until the King rejoined his men and then all began to cheer. The words of the King had not frightened my people, they had inspired them. The King had done me a favour.

Chapter 7

"That was well done, lord."

"If you were the Scots, Wulfric, where would you attack first?"

"The town wall and their north gate. It is stone and the walls next to it have stone foundations but it is a lower obstacle than our walls."

"I agree. Sir John, take command here with Sir Tristan and Sir Harold. Wulfric, fetch Erre and his Varangians as well as the Frisians. This is their sort of work."

Philip of Selby and the Archbishop's archers manned the north gate of the town. We had identified it as a target. There were also some of Sir Harold and Sir Tristan's men at arms there but I would take my elite warriors. Wulfric and the Varangians. King David would want a demonstration of his power and he would use his best men at arms to assault the gate. I, too, would make a statement and they would be thrown back.

Philip nodded as we ascended the gatehouse. "I see I am in elevated company this day. The mighty Wulfric joins me."

Wulfric laughed, "Aye, for the few who survive your arrows shall be hewn as trees." The banter was a good thing it showed that my men were unworried.

I saw the Scots forming up. The mormaers were assembling their chosen men. The ones who would attack us were the men of Lothian. They had helmets and a few had leather hauberks. Their shields were as large as ours. Unlike my men at arms, only the front rank wore full hauberks. I saw no knights amongst them. They were making a shield wall to advance over the killing ground which lay to the north of the town. It was grazing land. The cover was almost a mile away, north of the Ox Bridge. Behind the shield wall came men carrying ladders. They waited and I wondered what for. Then I saw it. They had a ram.

Next to me, Wulfric chuckled. "They are in for a shock." The ram rumbled down the track from the north towards the gate. We had taken out many of the cobbles which normally made the road surface smooth. We had replaced them with mud. The ground on both sides had been soaked by river water and was now spongy and soft. There was a layer of clay not far below the surface which stopped water from draining off. It was the reason we used it for grazing. Once again the land would come to our aid. The Scots marched towards us, oblivious to the hazards. The shield wall had split in two and flanked the ram.

The soaked area was two hundred paces from my walls and Philip and his archers had marked the spot with white stones. As the shield wall stepped onto the boggy area, they found themselves in difficulty. They looked to their feet and the archers struck. Their arrows found flesh where they should have found shields. Twenty men fell before order was restored. Shields were raised, dead men replaced and then, when it was pushed forward, the ram found the first of the broken sections. The front dipped alarmingly exposing the leg of one of the men within. Philip's arrow found the leg. They righted the ram and carried on. It was the third break in the road which destroyed the ram. The constant falls had weakened the axle and the wheels. The front axle and wheel broke. It was eight paces from the walls. The men from within tried to escape but were cut down.

I heard a mormaer shout orders and the shield walls joined once more and continued their advance. The cloying mud sapped their energy and it took forever to reach the walls. My archers wasted not an arrow. Their targets were the flesh they glimpsed. They did not miss.

The ditch had no water but it was filled with stakes and it was deep. It would take many bodies to fill it. The original one had been just two paces across. We had discovered that our enemies could bring wooden boards to cover that distance. Now it was as wide as a Roman ditch, almost four paces. The sides were steep and made with the slippery clay of the valley bottom. Soaked by the same river water which had made their progress slow, it was as deadly as ice.

The mormaer halted them at the edge of the ditch. He raised his sword and archers ran towards the rear of the shield wall. They had the same problem as the shield wall had encountered. In addition, they were now close enough to be subjected to the stones and arrows hurled and loosed by the villagers. Most of the archers did not even get to release an arrow. The ones they did release thudded into the wooden walls. Realising that the walls could not be cleared, the Scots, no doubt emboldened by their numbers, began to descend into the ditch. They could not keep their footing and the first ones slid down the slippery slope to be impaled upon the stakes at the bottom. Philip and his archers now joined the villagers in slaying the Scots who could not both keep their footing and their balance while holding a shield. By the time the ditch had been filled with bodies, the mormaer had had enough and they withdrew.

The villagers cheered as though we had won the war. We had not even won the battle. Erre spat, "We have not even dented their numbers!"

"I know, Erre, but it will give the people heart. They are not used to this as you are. They now know that numbers alone will not win this battle."

"But lord, the ditch is almost filled. When next they come they can walk across their own dead!"

Wulfric said, "And you have walked on corpses before now, Erre, they shift and they move." He pointed to the stones we had removed from the track and placed on the rampart by the gate. "Any who survive arrows will have their heads crushed."

Erre nodded and stroked his axe, "True, my friend, and the lucky ones to survive will meet me and my lady friend here!" Most of the Varangians liked to name their weapons. Erre's was Medusa's Blade! His time in Miklagård had not been wasted and he knew classical allusions.

I saw the Scottish leaders, half a mile away, as they gathered to discuss what to do. I saw Prince Henry gesticulating, angrily, in our direction. I looked at the sun. It would soon begin to dip into the west.

I turned to Wulfric, "A night attack?"

"Aye, and here. They know the ground and they have filled the ditch. They will use it."

"Then have the men eat in shifts. Philip, have fire brought for we will need fire arrows this night. I will go and speak with Alf and the townsfolk. Come, Gilles, I may have errands for you. Leave the banner here on the walls. Let the Scots know where I shall be."

I climbed down the stairs. At the bottom, I was cheered by people who thought the retreat of the Scots meant victory. Alf descended from his section of the wall too. "Do not blame them, lord. To them, it seems like we have won."

"But you know we have not." He nodded. "They will come and probably this night. Have your men on the walls eat and rest; I would suggest one in two. The ones who attack us will have been resting. They will be fresh and they will be angry."

"Aye, my lord, but the people are angry too. They know what privations the Scots inflict upon their enemies. There will be no surrender. The King's words just stiffened their resolve."

As I went back to my castle, I knew that he was right. "Aiden!"

My forester ran towards me. "Yes, lord."

"Slip out this evening and take a boat upstream. See if you and your two hawkers can upset the sentries of the Scots. Make them fear the woods."

"Aye, lord. I do not like sitting on my backside doing nothing."

"If you can hear aught of their plans then so much the better but take no risks."

"I hear your words, lord."

My three knights and Dick descended to meet me. "We have beaten off one attack but Wulfric and I fear a nighttime assault. Rest one man in two. I believe their main attack will be on the north gate of the town. I would expect them to probe for weaknesses all around our defences. They have the men to do so."

"Do not put yourself in danger, lord. We have our best men guarding the gate from the town. Leave yourself enough time to escape."

"I will escape only when the townspeople are safe. But I do not fear this night attack. It is what King David does next which has me worried."

Alice ran up to me. She had a wooden platter. There were thick slices of ham, cheese and some bread which was still warm. A servant girl held a jug of beer. "Here lord, eat now before you return to the walls. If you fail then we are lost. You must keep up your strength." She looked at a grinning Gilles, "And you too!"

I smiled, Alice had no family of her own and God had not blessed her with children, and so she regarded me and Sir John and Gilles as her family.

"We had better do as she says, Gilles." I was hungrier than I had thought and the warm rye and oat bread was smothered in butter. Washed down with freshly brewed black beer, I was ready to face whatever the Scots threw at us. The sun was slowly dipping in the west when I reached the walls again. I had sent Gilles for my cloak. It would be colder later, but, more importantly, it would hide me from view. When the Scots came, they would be greeted by dark apparitions which rose like wraiths from the walls. It would add to their fear and apprehension. I saw that only four of my men stood on the walls. The rest sat, hidden from view. I wished the Scots to think we had all retired.

It was pitch black when we heard the first cry. It was away to the west close by the willows which dipped to the river. Philip of Selby whipped his head around, "What was that, lord?"

"That is Aiden and his men upsetting the Scots. It will distract them as well as alarm them. It is hard to sleep when you think you might have your throat cut."

The sporadic cries lasted for some time. I could not see them but I knew what they would be doing. They knew the woods as well as any, and they would lead any pursuers a merry dance. They would approach the fires and loose arrows into the air. When hunters came for them, they would have their throats cut.

"Lord, I see something." Gilles had young eyes and they were sharp. I peered into the dark and could see nothing.

Philip of Selby said, "I saw movement too. They come."

Wulfric hissed, "Stand to! Pass it on!" The whisper slid down the wall and, unseen by the enemy, men rose to stand at the walls. All were well wrapped up in cloaks.

I picked up the throwing javelin. We had placed thirty of them by the walls along with the stones from the track. They would be our first defence. Thereafter it would be swords and axes. It is hard to climb a ladder and hold both a sword and a shield.

Turning to Philip of Selby, I said, "Prepare fire arrows. Use your own judgement when to release."

"Aye, lord."

We had pig fat to use but that would not be yet. Boiling water and pig fat were for the final assault. That would be many days off yet. I could now see the darker shadows of the Scots as they moved cautiously across the ground. No matter how silent they were they could not avoid the squelching of their feet in the mud. We heard them as they crossed the muddy ground.

Philip said quietly, "Release!"

The fire arrows had been hidden from view by the bodies of the twenty archers. As they turned, the walls were illuminated as well as the sky. As the fiery arrows descended, we saw the Scots frozen in the light. The men and boys of the town saw the targets and they needed no urging to slay the Scots. Arrows and stones were loosed and thrown as fast as they could be reloaded. The loosely advancing line became a shield wall but the littered bodies told the tale. They had been hurt. Darkness descended again as the arrows were extinguished. Two had struck the Scots and they were the last to go out as they burned out on the two dead men.

There was no need for secrecy now and we heard a shout and a roar as the Scots advanced from every direction. They even attacked the castle walls. I had no worries about those. The ditches had water within and traps and stakes would take a heavy toll. The attack would bleed to a halt there but in front of this gate, there was danger. We had had no opportunity to clear the corpses from the ditch and the Scots had a bridge of bodies. My eyes were now accustomed to the dark and I watched the mormaer as he led his warriors across the ditch. As I had expected, they found the footing was less than stable. As the mormaer's arms flailed to keep his balance, I threw my javelin. It struck him in the chest, penetrating the mail he wore. He was thrown back to add to the dead in the ditch.

The night had aided the Scots and more of them were able to reach the ditch unharmed. I heard the smack of wood on wood as the ladders were thrown up. The gatehouse was higher than the walls. My archers were able to pick off the Scots from the side. My Frisians and men of Copeland hacked and hewed the Scots as they tried to clamber over the walls. The numbers were so great that, inevitably, some Scots found a foothold. I saw Alf sweep three of them from the wall with one strike of his hammer. "Wulfric, take Erre and his men. Clear the wall to the west. Gilles, come with me and we will clear the wall to the east. Leave the banner here. This is sword work." I drew my dagger which was more like a short sword. A shield might encumber me.

We left the gatehouse by the small sally port. There were dead townsfolk close by the door and we stepped over their bodies. A head appeared over the wall. I swung my sword and it smashed into the helmet and the skull. The Scot fell, his dead hands still grasping the ladder, his body pulled the ladder and his companion to the ditch of dead below. I knew that Gilles would guard my back and I went towards the last Scots who had made my walls, confidently. One must have sensed me for he turned around. He swung his sword. I blocked it with my own and then rammed my dagger under his arm. I tore it sideways as I withdrew it. The limb was almost severed from his body and he tumbled into the town. I stabbed forward at the mormaer who was raising his axe to strike Alf. My sword went through his mail and grated along his spine. His arm froze in mid-air as he died. His body fell from my sword as it dropped to the town below.

"Thank you, lord."

"Thank you, Alf. You have defended like Horatio at the bridge!" I looked down the wall and saw that the ladders had been cleared. Philip and his archers were now loosing at the Scots who fled. The night attack had been beaten off.

We kept watch all night but they did not return. Aiden and his foresters slipped back into the castle before dawn and we watched the sun rise together. It was like a charnel house around my walls. Many hundreds had died. We had lost none from my castle walls but there would be empty hearths in Stockton. As I ate breakfast with Alf and Wulfric, I saw that the Scots were breaking camp.

"Lord, they are leaving!"

"Alf, it may be a ruse. Let us wait. Wulfric, take command."

I hurried back to my castle. "Dick, signal for the ferry. Take ten men and ride to Yarm. The Scots are breaking camp. If this is not a ruse then they will try to cross the river upstream and try to trap us. Warn Sir Richard. If it is not Yarm, let me know where."

By noon, half of the enemy had left. A line of knights and men at arms protected the departing warriors. They would not risk us sallying forth. Aiden had not heard anything during the night which might give a reason for the departure. My own guess was that King David had decided I was costing him too many men. He had bigger enemies to defeat. By late afternoon, the Scots had gone. My townsfolk were keen to strip the bodies and burn them. We all knew the dangers of rotting bodies which would attract all sorts of unwanted animals.

"No, Alf, let us do our job first. Philip, Wulfric, take my men and make sure that they have gone."

"Aye, lord."

"Alf, find Father Henry. We have our own dead to bury."

My men arrived back before dark and it was they who began the grisly task of emptying the ditches, stripping the bodies and making a pyre for them. We used the wood from the ram and the ladders as a base for the pyre and, as darkness fell, burned the Scottish dead.

Wulfric and the others had assured me that the Scots had headed west and no sign of them had been seen. Hartburn and Elton halls were burned as they passed but that was to be expected. It was vindictiveness. There was nothing to be gained from that senseless act.

Wulfric chuckled, "We found Aiden's handy work. He had placed the heads of the dead on top of their spears and they surrounded the Scottish camp. They must have been filling their breeks. He is a good man to have on your side."

I allowed the villagers to return to their homes the next day although Sir Tristan and Sir Harold's families stayed in my castle. Dick returned with news that the Scots had tried to cross the river at Hurworth but the water had been too high.

"Then they will cross either at Croft or, more likely, over the bridge at Piercebridge. We have time. We ride to Northallerton to join the Archbishop."

It was less than a few hours riding to reach Northallerton and we left a skeleton force to guard our castles. I doubted that the Archbishop would have been able to muster anywhere near the numbers available to the Scottish King. We had hurt him but not mortally. With Stephen busy in the south, it would need my men to help the ancient Archbishop defeat the enemy. It took time to cross the river and I set each party off as soon as they landed. Speed was of the essence. We were all well mounted and the road was a good one.

As we approached Arncliffe, we met the first of the Archbishop's men. These were loyal to Stephen the Usurper but they had been warned of our arrival. "The Archbishop has received your news and he is gathering men two miles north of Northallerton."

We headed there. I knew the place well. There were small ridges which would give a slight advantage to us. It would also allow us to fall back to Northallerton should we be defeated. If we fought closer to the town then we would have nowhere to run.

I knew where the Archbishop was by the armed guards around the large tent. "Wulfric, organise our camp." I smiled, "We will introduce ourselves to our new allies. I suspect we will have a wary welcome. Gentlemen, follow me."

I led my four knights towards the tent. Two warriors wearing the livery of Walter Espec put their spears across the entrance. I said quietly, "I would move them before you are cut down."

"I have orders to prevent anyone from entering."

Sir Edward said, "This is the Earl of Cleveland. He has just fought the Scots and slain a great number of them. I think he is just warming up. Besides, I have a dagger here and it is close enough to your manhood, or what passes for your manhood, to guarantee us entry." The sentry looked down and saw the savage-looking blade Sir Edward held. The spears were removed.

When we stepped in, I saw that the men who were gathered there were all the leaders. I turned to Sir Edward, "Stand guard with the others in case we have difficulty."

"Aye, my lord, I will get to know these two guards a little better."

I stepped into the tent. I heard Barnard de Balliol shout, "What is he doing here? He is an enemy!"

I laughed, "Coming from you, Balliol, I take that as a compliment but I am here to fight the Scots. Tomorrow will be time enough to take your head; if you stand this time. Normally you flee when I appear."

"Your Grace, I protest!"

I saw the hint of a smile play about Thurstan's lips, "Behave yourself, Aelfraed."

"I will try, your Grace."

"We appreciate your efforts at Stockton. Can you give us an accurate report of what we can expect?"

"The numbers reported were relatively accurate although we have thinned them somewhat and my scouts reported some desertions. Even so, I would expect twenty thousand Scots within the next day."

De Brus said, "The most we can muster is ten thousand! We should retire to York, your Grace!"

I snorted, "And do what? Watch the Scots ravage and pillage the land and enslave the people? We are Englishmen! We fight. That is the only reason I am here. If you wish to fall back then do so. You and Balliol are ever self-serving! As for the rest, I know not." I glared at them.

Hands went to swords and the Archbishop's voice cut like a knife. "Do not draw a weapon! I would not have the Earl of Cleveland slay you before the battle! I have seen him fight. He is a warrior. Aelfraed, control your tongue! I should have introduced you all first." He gestured as he introduced each of the knights, "William of Aumale, Walter de Gant, Roger de Mowbray, Gilbert de Lacy, William de Percy, Richard de Courcy, William Fossard and Robert de Stuteville. You know De Brus, Balliol and Espec. Gentlemen, I think you all need to cool off. Leave me alone with the Earl. I will summon you when I am ready."

They glared at me as they went out. I smiled, especially at Balliol who made sure he had Walter Espec between us.

He shook his head as he poured us both a beaker of wine. "What am I to do with you, Aelfraed? You grow worse."

"Your Grace, we have just fought off twenty-five thousand Scots with a handful of knights and the people of Stockton. I come here and find knights ready to run. What would you have me do?"

"I would have you advise me. You are a warrior and I am a cleric. None of the men here has fought in a battle of this size. If we are to survive then we need a clear head to guide us."

"I am sorry, and you are right. Firstly, we do not have enough knights and mounted men at arms to make this a mounted battle. We use the land and our best weapon, our archers. Array the army between the two areas of boggy ground you see to the north of us. It is just wide enough for our men and will stop us from being outflanked. The boggy land will be a barrier. They will be wary of that. Have the men at arms and knights in the front rank and the archers behind. Place the fyrd behind them. Keep the horses behind the ridge."

"That is it? We let them come on to us?"

"Our strength does not lie in the levy. It lies in knights and men at arms. We face them beard to beard and use our archers to thin their numbers. Put your nephew in command of the archers."

"Not your man?"

I smiled, "Philip of Selby will be more acceptable to the other barons and besides, Dick will be with him. When we have broken their back, we mount our horses and pursue them back to Scotland."

"You think we can win?"

"I believe we can but you, your Grace, must put steel in their hearts. They will not listen to me. Tomorrow morning you must inspire them. As much as they hate me is the measure by which they love you."

He nodded, "Very well; I have brought the cross from York and Pyx with relics within as well as the consecrated banners of the minsters of York, Beverley and Ripon."

"Then place them in a cart in the centre of the line so that all men may see it. Have you and your priests there so that men will defend the standards and your good self. Even Balliol will baulk at fleeing in those circumstances."

"Aelfraed!" He shook his head. "Go fetch them. It is time."

I went to the flap, "Come, the Archbishop has made his dispositions."

I think they all knew it was my plan but despite their opinion of my politics all respected me as a leader. I had been King Henry's champion and fought alongside him many times. They approved the plan.

I sent my own scouts to discover the enemy before we retired and discovered that they were close enough for us to smell their campfires. The next day would be the day that battle would be joined.

Chapter 8

I urged the Archbishop to have the men ready well before dawn. The Scots would use the dark to advance close to us. The knights and the rest of the army gathered around the cart, lit by burning brands, as the ancient Archbishop addressed us. His words were formal but they were delivered with all the gravitas of the most respected cleric in England.

"Most illustrious nobles of England, Normans by birth, consider who you are, and against whom, and where it is you are waging war; for then no one shall with impunity resist your prowess. Bold France, taught by experience, has quailed beneath your valour, fierce England, led captive, has submitted to you; rich Apulia, on having you for her masters, has flourished once again; Jerusalem so famed, and illustrious Antioch, have bowed themselves before you; and now Scotland, which of right is subject to you, attempts to show resistance, displaying a temerity not warranted by her arms, more fitted indeed for rioting than for battle. These are people, in fact, who have no knowledge of military matters, no skill in fighting, no moderation in ruling. There is no room then left for fear, but rather for shame, that those whom we have always sought on their own soil and overcome have come flocking into our country.

This has been brought about by Divine Providence; in order that those who have in this country violated the temples of God, stained the altars with blood, slain his priests, spared neither children nor pregnant women, may on the same spot receive the condign punishment of their crimes; and this most just resolve of the Divine will, God will this day put in execution by means of your hands. Arouse your spirits then, ye civilized warriors, and, firmly relying on the valour of your country, nay, rather on the presence of God, arise against these most unrighteous foes.

And let not their rashness move you, because so many insignia of your valour cause no alarm to them. They know not how to arm themselves for battle; whereas you, during the time of peace, prepare yourselves for war, in order that in battle you may not experience the doubtful contingencies of warfare. Cover your heads then with the helmet, your breasts with the coat of mail, your legs with the greaves, and your bodies with the shield, that so the foeman may not find where to strike at you, on seeing you thus surrounded on every side with iron.

It is not so much the numbers of the many as the valour of the few that gains the battle. For a multitude unused to discipline is a hindrance to itself, when successful, in completing the victory, when routed, in taking to flight. Besides, your forefathers, when but few in number, have many a time conquered multitudes; what then is the natural consequence of the glories of your ancestry, your constant exercises, your military discipline, but that though fewer in number, you should overcome multitudes?"

For me, it was too cold a speech but it seemed to work on the nobles who all stood and began to cheer loudly! Many dropped to their knees and began to pray. I did not need the inspiration of the old Archbishop to fight well. I was fighting the old enemy and for my people. That was enough. We went to our positions. I chose the centre of the line and stood flanked by knights on one side and my men at arms, led by Wulfric on the other. The rest of the barons stood with their own men amongst like-minded fellows. It was not a bad way to deploy. Behind us were the archers. Philip of Selby, Dick and the archers from the valley formed the centre of the line. I knew that their accuracy and their rate of release would guarantee that the enemy before us would be weakened. The mist limited our view to three hundred paces. I did not mind for that was as far as the best archers could release. Realistically, they would not begin sending their arrows at the enemy until they were two hundred paces away.

Many of the men had heard the Archbishop's words and felt inspired. They banged their shields and shouted at the, as yet, unseen enemy. All that could be discerned were their advancing banners above the early morning mist. I turned to Sir Edward. "I think that King David tried to catch us unawares."

On the other side of me, Wulfric laughed, "Wait until he sees your banner in the front rank! You make sure you wave it, Master Gilles!"

"I will! I promise you."

We each held a long spear. If the enemy tried to use their horse against us then we could defend ourselves. For my own part, I did not think that the Scottish King would do so. He did not have enough heavy horses. I guessed he would use his own spearmen to punch a hole in our ranks. When they had weakened us, he would send in his knights. They were too valuable to throw away. We would be outnumbered. If he had committed all of his men and not left some to guard his line of retreat then it would be two to one. It was why I had suggested to the Archbishop that we place our flanks between the boggy ground.

I saw spears approaching. It was as I had expected. Then through the mist, I saw the first rank of the Scots. They were Galwegians. They had shaven heads and many were tattooed on their half-naked bodies. They carried a small shield, a long spear and throwing spears. By their sides, they carried a long knife. They relied on speed and terror. They lined up, two deep. Behind them, I saw the banner of Prince Henry, his knights and the men at arms. As they moved forward, I saw that the men of Lothian were behind the knights.

Sir Edward said, "He will let loose his wild men at us first and then attack with his knights and men at arms. He will hope that we are weaker after his barbarians are done with us."

Sir Harold said, "With the archers behind us, he will stand little chance. They wear no armour at all. Not even a helmet!"

I cautioned those around me, "But they are fast and they are fierce! I want a solid line of men; at least here in the centre. They will try to get to the Archbishop and the standards! We stop them!"

As we waited for the attack, I saw that the Scottish King was also dismounted. He stood with his picked knights and best warriors. They would be the final attack. He intended to attack with his men. That proved he was no coward, at least.

A horn sounded and the Galwegians launched themselves at us. That, in itself, was a mistake for Prince Henry and his mailed men could not keep up with the wild men.

I heard the command from behind me, "Release!" as Philip of Selby ordered the arrow storm. The sky was black with arrows and they plunged into bare flesh. Amazingly many of the wild men ran with four or five arrows sticking from them. Even so, many more fell but the wave of warriors did not diminish. "Brace yourselves. Lock shields!"

They hurled themselves physically at us but our shields, helmets and mail held firm whilst they impaled themselves upon our spears. The two men who threw themselves at me were both pinned with one spear. I dropped it and pulling out my dagger slashed it across the throat of the first one. His falling, dying body brought the other forward and I stabbed him through his screaming mouth! I put my dagger in my left hand and drew the sword. The blue pommel stone, which had come from Harold Godwinson's sword, always filled me with a power I did not understand. It made me feel invincible. The centre was holding but I could see the two wings pushing back our own flanks. The men there had recoiled.

I yelled, "Archers, clear the flanks!" We could hold but if the flanks fell then we would be surrounded. I saw Prince Henry and his men as they advanced. Before me, I saw a mormaer as he urged his men forward. He had arrows sticking from him but he seemed to care not. He hurled his javelin and it would have struck Wulfric had I not held my shield up to block the blow.

"Stockton, forward!"

I stepped forward with Sir Edward and Wulfric in perfect time. That came from years of practice. I brought my sword up to tear it into the stomach of a Galwegian. I ripped it to the side and his entrails fell before him. I punched my shield at the mormaer next to him who dropped his javelins and went to draw his sword. I did not give him the chance. I brought my sword diagonally across his neck and chopped his head. He had been screaming when I struck and his mouth appeared to be grinning. It tumbled from his neck. I reached down and picked it up. There was no hair and so I rammed my sword into the open mouth and held it aloft. At that moment, Sir Tristan slew the second mormaer. I swung my arm behind me and hurled the skull high into the sky. His men all looked up to see their dead leader. It proved too much and the survivors broke and ran.

Their rout broke up the second line which was led by Prince Henry and consisted of English and Norman knights. "Forward! For Archbishop Thurstan! We have them!"

My archers turned their attention to Prince Henry and his men. Already disrupted by the fleeing Galwegians, more fell to the deadly arrows. When we struck them, we did so as one solid line of mail, metal and muscle. I brought my sword down onto the shield of a knight who was defending the Prince. Wulfric's axe took out a second defender. I punched my opponent with my shield and he was forced back. I brought my sword up and hit him in the middle. I winded him and as he bent I stabbed down into his spine. Wulfric's axe hacked into the Prince's shield and it split. He turned and ran towards the waiting horses. Wulfric and I had enemies through which to wade.

Those on our flank had now joined us in the charge and our archers were causing mayhem amongst the third rank, the men of Lothian. Unbelievably, the Scots were falling back before our charge. I heard English voices amongst the men we fought. I recognised some and I made my way towards them. As I did so, I saw the Earl of Northumbria, Gospatric. He shouted for his horse. The obese lump of lard was going to escape. I hacked and I slashed at the men before me. They all fell but I saw the Earl mount his horse.

"Dick! Gospatric!"

My furious charge had broken the second line of Scots who began to flee. It took the men of Lothian and the islanders with them. I saw King David mount his horse. I yelled, "Gospatric, you traitorous dog! Stand and fight!"

As he turned to face me, Dick's arrow plunged into his face and knocked him to the ground. The man I had fought for more years than I cared to think was now dead. I turned, for no enemies remained before me. "Gilles, you and the squires fetch the horses. This will now be a chase."

The rest of the English line was now flooding forward but the men they pursued were without armour. To my amazement, I saw knights stripping off their hauberks so that they could run faster. We had not left our horses with the others. Instead, they were close to the cart with the standards and Gilles and the other squires soon returned with our fifty horses. I mounted and rode to Archbishop Thurstan.

"Your battle is won, my lord, but we must pursue the enemy and slay them or capture them. We can win back the north this day."

He smiled, "And you were the right Captain, Earl. Go with God! You have served your country well this day!"

I rode back to my men. "Dick, take command here. Make sure we have our share of the armour for we did the most work today!"

"Aye, lord."

Just then we heard a shout from the ridge. One of the Archbishop's priests shouted, "Earl! The Scots are amongst the horse holders!"

My plans to catch King David and end this war were thwarted in that instant. I wheeled my horse around and galloped back to the horse holders. As we crested the low ridge, I saw the Scottish and Norman knights slaying the unarmed horse holders. I became angry. This was not well done! "After them!"

The thundering of our hooves alerted the enemy. I saw Prince Henry and his banner. He had taken his opportunity to garner some glory. Rolf needed little encouragement and he soon began to outstrip the others. I heard Gilles shout, " My lord! Slow down! You will be alone!"

I cared not. I soon began to catch those at the rear of the line as they fled north. Their horses were tired from their charge. I let my shield hang loosely from my side and I galloped towards the rearmost knight. I brought my sword down on his back. I used all the force I had and I heard his spine as it broke. He tumbled from his mount. I kept my eye on the Prince's banner. If I could not have his father then I would have him. Some of those before me turned and recognised my livery and my device. Few wished to face King Henry's champion and some pulled to the side. I ignored them. I heard cries from behind me as my men caught up with the ones I had passed. They had escaped my wrath but not that of my men.

I saw that we were heading northeast, towards Stanwyck and the bridge over the Tees. I knew this land. Soon their horses would tire for the ground would rise and I reined Rolf in a little. Any gains the enemy made would soon be lost as their horses tired. They were riding warhorses and they were powerful beasts but they tired quicker than a horse such as Rolf. Even though I had slowed a little, I was still catching them. I saw William Redere. He was four knights away from me. I shifted Rolf to approach the next knight from the right. As Rolf came abreast of the knight, the Scot swung his sword sideways. He made the mistake of not looking where his blow struck and it hit my shield. I stood in the stirrups and lunged forward to strike him under the arm. He fell from his horse.

I could see both the standard-bearer and the Prince. They were with a third knight of the household. The Prince turned and saw me. He shouted something and Sir William Redere drew his sword and turned to face me. He had been given his orders. He was to take on the nemesis of the Scots, me.

I did not slow down but I gripped my shield. I would need it now. Sir William Redere was a knight I had fought before. He would know my tricks. I would need to be wary. I had, however, to despatch him quickly else the Prince, as well as the King, would escape me. As he galloped towards me, I had to gamble. Would he go for my right side, and my sword, or my left? I jerked Rolf's head at the last possible moment and swung my sword at chest height. Had I swung at head height, he might have ducked. He raised his shield and flailed harmlessly with his sword. My sword smashed into his shield and I saw him reel. I pulled Rolf's head to the right. I had the advantage. I pulled my arm back and swung my sword again. This time I hit the base of his spine. I hurt him but his horse was moving to the right and I did not manage to get the full effect. I followed his turn around and took a chance. I stood in my stirrups and stabbed at his back. I felt the tip slip through the mail and crack a couple of links. I pushed harder and felt it slide through his gambeson. I saw his back arch and pushed as hard as I could. His arms came up as my sword grated along his backbone and he fell from the horse twitching and dying. I reined in Rolf and looked down at his face as he died before my eyes.

"That is the payment for treachery and deceit; a painful death and ignominy!"

Gilles, Sir Harold and Sir Tristan joined me. The rest were still finishing off our enemies. "Come, we have a prince to catch."

The Prince and the last of his men had a head start now. Sir William had bought them time. We settled into the easy rhythm of hunters who were following prey. I took a chance and rejoined the road rather than following the hoof prints. We knew the area and the Scots did not. We made better time along the road. As we passed the ancient fortress of Stanwyck, I wondered if the people who had lived here all those centuries ago had had the same problems we did. It was probably ever thus. As we crested the rise above the Tees and the bridge, I saw that my gamble had paid off. I could see the Prince, his standard-bearer and three others as they crossed the bridge. We were less than a quarter of a mile behind them.

Gilles said, excitedly, "We have them, lord!"

"When they are dead or surrendered, Gilles, then we have them. Be careful for a cornered animal is always dangerous."

The Scots disappeared from view as they rode through the huts and homes of those who lived close by. The old wooden castle which had belonged to one of my knights, William of Piercebridge, was long gone. It had been destroyed years earlier in another Scottish raid. I had put off appointing a new lord of the manor and now that came back to haunt me. Had I had a castle and a lord then things might be different. They might have stopped the Scottish retreat.

The road headed north and west and passed through some trees. The day was still hot and it was gone noon. The trees would give us some shade. Even a brief respite would help. I contemplated stopping to give the horses some water but knew that I could not afford to lose touch with our enemies. Their horses would give out before ours did. Rolf's nose gave us warning of the ambush. He twitched and I reined back a little thinking he had spotted a hole in the road. Instead, three Scots burst from the trees to our left. The standard-bearer was using the Prince's standard as a lance. It punched into my shield and almost unhorsed me. I swung Rolf around and, drawing my sword, went for the standard-bearer.

I heard the clash of steel on steel behind me as I brought my sword over. The Scot brought the standard up to block the blow. The staff was shattered in two. As the standard-bearer tried to reach for his sword, I punched him hard with my shield and he tumbled backwards over the cantle of his saddle. He screamed as he fell. When I turned Rolf around, I saw that he was impaled upon the severed branch of a lightning-struck tree. His body twitched and then was still. I turned and saw that the other two attackers had been slain.

The Prince and the other rider were long gone. "Water the horses. Gilles, fetch the standard. I fear it is all that we will have of this Prince. It seems he has fortune on his side."

"Will we not follow, my lord?"

I shook my head. "His men have bought him time. He will be long gone now. I should have brought archers, Gilles, but their horses were stampeded by the Prince. There will be another day. Besides, this day has been a great victory." I pointed to the three Scottish bodies. "These are knights. The Scottish nobles and the English north of the border have filled the land with their blood. We have the chance now to end this war and regain all that Stephen the Usurper gave away."

We loaded the hauberks and arms on the backs of the three horses and headed back to the battle. We found Sir William's body and added his hauberk too. Close by, we found Sir Edward and the rest of my men with the Scottish knights and men at arms who had survived. There was a pile of booty with them. When the enemy saw the banner of their Prince, their shoulders slumped.

Sir Edward asked, "Did you catch the Prince?"

"No, he is as slippery as an eel but he only escaped with one man. Tomorrow I take my men and we head for Carlisle. If the Archbishop gives me the men we can catch him there and, perhaps, his father too."

It was late afternoon when we reached the site of the battle. There were great piles of Scottish dead and the prisoners had been gathered to stand forlornly together. I saw that Dick had adhered to my orders and he and Philip of Selby guarded our share of the spoils of war. I dismounted. "Gilles, feed and water Rolf, he has done well."

I walked over to the Archbishop who was with the other leaders. Despite the battle, I could see that I was still an intruder. They resented me. The Archbishop, in contrast, beamed. He threw his thin and blue-veined arms around me, "My son, a great victory! England and King Stephen owe you much."

"Thank you, your Grace, but it is not over yet. Let us take the army and follow the Prince to Carlisle. Mayhap his father has gone there too. We can recapture that castle and the north will be safe from the Scots once more."

Walter Espec shook his head, "We have just spoken of our plans. We have won a great victory and secured Yorkshire. That was our avowed intent. King Stephen will be told of the victory and he can make the peace. That is not for us to take upon ourselves."

I rounded on him and the others, "You are all spineless jellyfish! I might have expected this of cowards like De Brus and Balliol but I expected more of the High Sheriff of Yorkshire!"

Their hands went to their swords and Walter Espec said, "I resent that! Take back the words."

I laughed, "Or what? You will face me sword to sword? Good. Let us end it here and now. I will fight each of you one to one. Who will be first? You De Brus? Balliol? Ferrers?" They all stepped back. None would dare face me in single combat. I shook my head, "It is as I expected. You are cowards and dissemblers all. There is not an ounce of honour amongst you."

I turned to the Archbishop, "You have courage, your Grace, but I cannot stay here longer. I will go to Carlisle with my men. Our brief truce is over. If any of Stephen the Usurper's cronies and chancers come near my land," I turned to face them, "they will receive the same treatment as the Scots. I do not discriminate. Rebellion is in the south and I am the spark in the north. I stand for Matilda and Henry. The Tees is my river. Stay away from it if you wish to live!"

I walked away. I heard Walter Espec shout, "What of the spoils of war?"

Without turning I shouted, "What we took, we keep!" I saw my men waiting, "Get our men and our booty. We ride home. I will not breathe the same air as these cowards! I will be happier when my gates slam shut behind me and we are safe once more."

Chapter 9

Only one knight had fallen on our side. He had been with Walter Espec on the flank. I had never known such an unequal battle. All the way north, the young squires had been speaking of the battle as though that was the way they always ended. Gruff, plain-speaking Wulfric put them straight, "Let me tell you young gentlemen that we won so easily today for two reasons. The Earl has the sharpest mind since Alexander the Great and the Scots could not have fought worse if they had tried. Who in his right mind sends wild men with neither armour nor helmet across the open ground? Madness! And if you have that many men, you surround your enemies. You do not attack the centre held by mailed men. I will not say we were lucky but you will rarely fight such a battle again. Enjoy the moment."

Thus chastened, they took to regaling each other with their feats. Gilles still had the greatest prize; the standard of the Prince of Cumberland. Any honour the young prince might have garnered had been lost when he fled and lost his standard. He had sacrificed his men to make it to safety. I would not worry about such a foe.

We reached our homes before dark. Early August still meant long days and short nights. Soon, however, that would change. Our victory, whilst not complete, would ensure a better winter for us. The captured knights were all placed in my castle and messages were sent for ransom. The hauberks and arms were distributed equally. We now had many more horses as well as supplies we had captured. More importantly, our people had been able to continue to farm and to see to our crops. Harvest time was approaching and we would reap the rewards.

I left the next day with my men at arms and my archers. We would head for Carlisle. Sir Edward and my knights attempted to dissuade me. I would not listen, "If we allow King David the opportunity, he will form another army. His Islanders, Moravians and men of Lothian will be heading home. We killed ten thousand and more but there are still thousands more we did not kill. They will rise again. I must go to save this land from future incursions."

We went cautiously. I halted, briefly, at Sir Hugh's castle where I told him what had happened at Northallerton. He was relieved. After we had crossed the Tees west we rode with Aiden, Edgar and Edward far ahead of us to warn us of danger. It was fortunate that we did so for, on the far side of Brough, we came upon a company of Islanders marching with their Mormaer. There were sixty of them. I saw no point in risking a battle. They were too small a number to do any harm in my valley and they were heading home. The sounds of our horses clattering along the cobbles of the Roman Road were enough to disperse them. We saw them, high in the rocks and the trees, watching us as we rode by. Dick and his archers had strung bows ready in case of treachery but conflict was avoided.

I turned to Wulfric, "When we return, we will scour the forests from Barnard eastwards. I fear there will be others but they may not choose to return home."

"Many will see this as an opportunity to become bandits and take from a land riven with discord and conflict. The sooner the Empress reaches us the better."

I agreed with Wulfric but I knew that there was a war to be won in Normandy too.

We reached Carlisle Castle as the sun was dipping in the west. We halted and camped a mile to the east of the formidable fortress. We used a bend in the river which we could defend although Aiden and his scouts reported that there was no one between us and the castle. It was summer and it was warm. We ate well from the deer my men hunted but we were up before dawn. I wanted to be at the castle before they opened the gates. Wulfric had already asked me what I hoped to achieve. Before I had left Stockton I was not sure but the further west we went the clearer were my aims. I could do nothing about Durham and Northumbria. I did not have enough men to retake them and to hold them. What I did want was a guarantee for the security of the Tees and my valley.

"Gilles, unfurl the banner and let them see who we are!"

We rode down the road along which the Roman legions had marched. The flag of Scotland flew from the tower of the castle and the walls were manned. I heard the trumpets sound the alarm as we approached. We halted beyond crossbow range and I removed my helmet. "Dick, have your archers string their bows. You know what to do."

"Aye, lord."

"Wulfric, Gilles, take off your helmets and come with me."

We headed towards the eastern gate. Halting a hundred and fifty paces from the castle I waited. Prince Henry took off his helmet and peered over the ramparts. "If you have come to take the castle, Earl, then you need more men."

"If I had wanted to take it there are many men who would have wished to join me."

Just then we saw banners as more knights crested the rise to the northeast.

"Is this treachery, Earl? Have you brought more men?"

"I was going to ask you the same. These are naught to do with me."

Then one of the men on the ramparts shouted, "'Tis the King! It is your father, Prince!"

Wulfric growled, "Do we fight our way out, lord?"

"We will wait and see. I spy banners but few riders. We have Dick and his archers as our guardian angels."

We waited until the King and his twenty riders stopped less than fifty paces from us. He took off his helmet and urged his horse forward. "Earl, you have ridden quickly to reach here, as has my son. What is your purpose at this place? Do you come to give battle?"

"You have been soundly beaten, Your Majesty. The dead of Scotland lie over the north of this land. We have great numbers of knights to be ransomed."

"I know all of that but what is your purpose?"

"I would have your word that the lands of Cleveland, the lands of the Tees will be free from your raids and your warriors."

"I told you before, Earl, that my aim was to defeat King Stephen. I support my niece!"

"And yet you attacked my castle and I am a known knight of the Empress and her son. You can see my confusion."

He smiled, "I can." He looked up at the walls and shouted, "Come and join us, my son."

As we waited, I saw the device of the Redere amongst the men who accompanied the King. The knight glared at me. I made a note of the men around him. I guessed that he was a relative of the knight I had slain. Prince Henry rode over to us. It would not do for him to have to look up at a mere earl.

The King waited until he was present and said, "I have sent word that I wish to assemble another army, here at Carlisle."

"We lost but one knight. Do not worry, King David, what we did once we can repeat."

Prince Henry did not look happy. "Next time we would be stronger, Earl."

"So the knights we slew were not your best? I find that hard to believe. The men we hold for ransom seem to be men of substance. The arms and armour we hold are of the highest quality. I do not question your word but Scotland must, indeed, be a rich country if you can lose as many knights as you did and still have better to fill their ranks."

"My son, do not underestimate this man. He has a sound military mind and the Empress is lucky to have him and her brother as her generals. I said we were raising another army, my lord, in case you had designs on Carlisle."

I smiled, "Of course, I wish Carlisle, Copeland, Clitheroe, Skipton and Craven all returned to England but I am no fool. Until the Empress lands with her full force and we defeat Stephen the Usurper then we will have to live with this part of England under Scottish rule, but it will not last. One day, Your Majesty, I will come and retake this land. You have my word on that."

"They say that you are too honest for your own good, Earl, and I can see that now. You have more honour than sense too. I thought, coming from the East, that you would be able to be more pliant and amenable."

"I was brought up by a housecarl of King Harold Godwinson. Accepting Norman rule is as pliant as I get."

A thin smile played upon his lips. "Well, Aelfraed, Earl of Cleveland, and self-styled Warlord of the North, you have my word and that of my son that we will not attack your lands. From Barnard to Normanby, Norton to Yarm, you are safe from Scottish attack."

I looked at Prince Henry. His father nodded and he said, through pursed lips, "You have my word too, Warlord."

The King said, "However, I believe there are some of my countrymen who may take issue with you. Eustace Redere here, for example, is less than happy that you killed his brother."

I smiled, "Did I not do him a favour? Did he not inherit the title and the land without the need for ransom?" I saw the knight redden. "However, Baron Redere, should you wish satisfaction then let us test our blades on the field of honour. How say you?"

King David said, "There has been enough bloodshed and I would not have another of my knights slain by you, Earl!"

"In which case, I have no further reason to stay. Enjoy your sojourn in the castle. I will come for it one day. You have my solemn oath on that!"

I jerked Rolf's head around and headed back to my men. I saw Dick and his archers as they relaxed their arms. They had been ready to loose at the first sign of danger.

"Will he keep his word, lord?"

"I think he has little alternative. The flowers of Scotland were plucked in Yorkshire and the ones who remain are waiting for ransom. They will be impoverished. That is why William Redere's little brother is so annoyed. His brother must have gambled on victory against England and riches. He was riding a poor palfrey and his armour was old. I suspect we will have a little trouble from the likes of Redere and bandits but our main enemy will be the knights of Stephen. De Brus and Balliol will scurry back with tales of my words. Espec will ferment trouble too. We have one ally and he is an old and frail cleric. I will be happier when my ship returns with news from Anjou!"

Sir Hugh was delighted with our news. We spent the night at his castle. As we feasted, I suggested that he and his men at arms help us to scour the forests of bandits and the survivors of the battle. "Harvest time comes soon and then it will be winter. These men will become more desperate. It is best we rid the land of them now so that you may sleep easier this winter."

With our scouts out, we left early the next morning. We rode in groups of ten and swept through the woods and forests. When Edgar found the burnt-out farm and the dead bodies, we concentrated our search. It was not pleasant work, hunting men but we had to for the good of the people. We drove through the woods and flushed out groups of men. Most were the survivors of the first attack at Northallerton. They were the shaven-headed Galwegians. They were tough and hard to kill. It took most of the morning to slay the band of fifty who had taken up residence. The afternoon was a little easier for the other bands were smaller and they were the men of Lothian and of the Islands. I suspected they were the ones whose lords had died. There would be little honour returning home without a lord and brigandage was a better option.

We had done enough and I led my men back to Stockton. We arrived back after dark and I felt weary as we headed to the west gate. Even Wulfric looked tired. "I am getting too old for this campaigning, lord."

"As am I, but needs must."

"You have a castle and a home, lord. You should enjoy them."

"And I will, but only when I have heard from the Empress."

Alice took one look at Gilles and shook her head, "My lord, you must look after yourselves more. Sit now and I will bring you wine and food."

I smiled at Gilles. "She means well."

"She is right, lord, you do too much. Is there no other lord who could shoulder the responsibilities?"

"I am lucky to have loyal knights such as Sir Edward and the others but we have too few knights. I need more. The trouble is finding them. I have the power to make them but until the likes of you are ready then I have no one."

"Are there manors, lord?"

"Aye, Norton and Normanby. Both need a lord of the manor. Both need a castle. If the rebellion in Kent fails then Stephen will visit his wrath upon us and I need a ring of defences. You saw how poorly the enemy did when they besieged both here and Barnard Castle. We need to make all our manors as strong."

Perhaps it was the wine or the excellent food but the answer became blindingly obvious to me. I went to bed happy that night knowing I had a partial solution to my problem. I slept well despite my injuries. When I rose, it was the blow from the standard-bearer which still troubled me. Although my shield had taken the blow, my arm was both black and blue. In the days since the battle, I had had little chance to rest it.

I rose and ate with Sir John and Gilles. He knew the men of the castle better than I did and I questioned him about them. Of all those who followed me, I knew them the least well. John was, as I knew he would be, brutally honest. It was his way. After I had ordered Gilles to bring Sir Tristan and Sir Harold to me, I sent for John, my steward. I told him what I intended. For once he was in full agreement. I then spent an hour going through the affairs of the lands I controlled. Half of the ransoms had been paid already and the other half would soon be here. We had the finance to do what I wanted. He went away with a list of tasks and orders for both William the Mason and Captain William when he returned.

Tristan and Harold were both curious when they arrived. I saw it on their faces. "How goes the rebuilding of your manors?"

Both shook their heads, "It is heartbreaking, lord. We have done all that work building fine homes and the Scots destroy them both in an afternoon. Our wives are heartbroken. All their pots and linens are destroyed."

"I know, Sir Tristan. Tell me, both of you, and I wish an honest answer, do you each have a site at your manor where you could build a good stone castle?"

They looked at the ground and then it was Harold who spoke. "In Hartburn the answer would be no. We have no river such as you have here or at Norton and the high ground is not enough to build a castle which would be large enough to defend."

"The same is true of Elton."

"Yet both manors are productive and need a lord?"

"Aye, lord."

"Lord, speak plainly for I was brought up in Sherwood and I do not understand these games you play."

"I am sorry, Harold, but I play no games. You both have families and you need a castle where you can protect them. Is that not correct?"

"It is, lord."

"Then I have two plans. I speak with you first because I have others with whom I wish to share my ideas. I have powers I have not used. Until the Empress or her son are crowned then I shall use them. Normanby and Norton need lords of the manor. They are both perfect for stone castles. If you wish them then I give you those manors."

"And the alternative plan, lord?"

"More complicated, Sir Tristan. You would continue to be lords of the manor but your families would live here. I would give you each a tower for your wives and children. They would be safe and you would still be lords of Hartburn and Elton." They looked at each other nervously and I smiled. "I had a wife once. Go speak with your wives but I need your answer within the hour."

William the Mason had been waiting outside. He had his two sons with him. I remembered when my father had first given him work. The two boys had been quite young then. Now they were strong young men who were masons in their own right. "I wish you to build me a castle at Norton and another at Normanby."

William showed no surprise. "As large as this one, lord? Made from stone?"

"Not as large as this but in both cases, I want an outer bailey large enough for those who live in the manor to take shelter. Stone? Largely, but you may have to use wood too. I want them up by next summer."

"That is a lot of work, lord."

I nodded, "Hire as many men as you need. John will make the funds available to you."

"If you would allow my sons each to be responsible for a castle then I could supervise the two. The work would move on quicker."

"If you are happy, William, then I am too."

"And the lords of the manor?"

"That I do not know, yet, but they will work closely with you."

He nodded, "And thank you, my lord. Few lords would give a chance to two such young masons."

"You have never let me down, William."

Alice must have been waiting outside for she entered as soon as the masons had left. "Lord, you will need new clothes. I have taken the liberty of arranging for some seamstresses to make you new ones. Alf can make mail but that is all!"

I was distracted, "New clothes?"

"I went to wash those that you have worn on the campaign and they fell apart. I am having new ones made for you. I just came to tell you, my lord." It was not a matter for discussion. She had taken the decision and her tone told me that I would obey her in this.

"And I appreciate it, Alice. You will have to excuse my behaviour. I am more used to dealing with men than ladies. I apologise."

She put her hand to her mouth, "Oh, no, my lord. Do not apologise. I meant nothing."

"You are right to chastise me so. I deserve it."

Sir Harold and Sir Tristan entered, followed by Sir John, and Alice scurried away like a frightened mouse. I almost laughed. She had a good heart and it was a shame that her husband had been killed so young and on my service. Sir John, Gilles and myself had become her new family. My two young knights were confused by her hurried departure. Sir

John smiled. He was castellan and he knew Alice better than any. She mothered him as much as she did Gilles.

"Well?"

"Our wives are quite happy to stay here, lord, and we are too. Hartburn and Elton are close enough for us to manage them and to protect their people from here."

"Good. I will see John and Alice and explain the new arrangements. I think that Alice, in particular, will be happy. She likes the presence of the babies. Gilles!"

My squire ran in, "Yes, my lord."

"Fetch Erre, John of Craven, Wulfric and Dick, if you please."

"Should we go, lord?"

"No, Sir Tristan, this concerns you and Sir Harold." I had spent most of the night coming up with my ideas. Each person I had spoken to had clarified them but I knew this last part would be the hardest. Wulfric, Erre and Dick were used to my hall but John of Craven was not. Since he had entered my service, all had spoken of his honesty and his discipline. He had behaved heroically when the Scots had tried to scale our walls. He was a warrior in the mould of Wulfric. I saw his confusion when he arrived with the others. I think he thought he had caused me some offence.

"Two of you have served me since I first came to Stockton all those years ago. I would reward you. Wulfric and Dick, or rather Richard, I shall knight you at Martinmas."

"We need no title, lord."

"I know, Wulfric, but I need knights and you two have the qualities I need. It is not a request, it is a command." They nodded, "And you, Erre, have served me well. I would knight you too."

"I am but a common soldier, lord!"

"As was my father. Now I wish you, Sir Erre, and you, Sir Wulfric, to be lords of the manor at Norton and Normanby! You shall rule for me. William the Mason will build a castle at each site. You will need to hire your own men at arms but there will be silver for you to hire them. When the time is right, you shall pay taxes but, for now, the

Scots are paying for our men. Sir Richard, I need you and
your archers. You will have no manor but your archers will
become your company with your own livery."

They looked stunned, "What say you?"

"Lord, I would still fight at your side."

"And you shall, Wulfric, but I need the iron from the
Eston hills protecting. Until I hear from Anjou there will be
no campaign. We hold what we have. You hold on to what
we need. You will be at Normanby and you will have
Guisborough to watch. With your eyes upon it then De Brus
cannot use it. You see my reasoning now?"

"Aye, lord."

John of Craven asked, "Lord, what am I here for? You
are not knighting me nor making me a lord of the manor so
why am I here?"

"You are no longer a young man, John, but you are a
warrior. I have had good reports about you. With Erre and
his Varangians leaving for Norton, I need someone here to
help Sir John and to be castellan when we campaign. Sir
John's mighty arm was needed at Northallerton. With you
here, I know we can leave Stockton in safe hands. The men
of Copeland follow you already and the Frisian warriors
seem happy to serve with you.

His face broke into a smile, "Then I am honoured, lord,
and I accept, gladly!"

The easy part was telling them, the hard part was working
out, with John, the finances and the logistics of moving men
and horses to the two manors. Initially, it would mean we
had a smaller garrison at Stockton but that would not be for
long. Both Norton and Normanby, as well as the surrounding
area, had young men who wished not to farm but to fight.
Erre and Wulfric were the finest of teachers. The rest of
September was exhausting but in a different way from the
rigours of battle.

When the '*Adela*' hove into view at the end of September,
it seemed that it had been ordained by a higher power for at
the bow was my son, William. My ship had brought me the
perfect gift. "Come, John, let us go and see my son!"

Chapter 10

Although I was both excited and pleased that my son had come, I wondered at the reasons. He leapt from the ship as soon as the side touched the jetty and before the crew had tied her up. He put his arms around me and hugged me. There was power in those arms. My son had grown and was almost as tall as I was. When he finished growing he would be bigger.

"This is indeed an unexpected pleasure!"

He stepped back and took John's outstretched arm. "And for me. Good to see you, Sir John! I am happy to be in Stockton again."

"Is there trouble?"

He laughed, "There is always trouble, father, but I must speak with you. I can stay but one night and then I needs must return home." He took a step towards my castle and then stopping blurted out, "You know I am to be a father!"

"I know!" Despite my best efforts, I could not keep the disapproval from my voice.

He shook his head, "The Empress is happy enough, father."

We could not speak further for my son was greeted by my soldiers most of whom had served with him and they all liked him. Most had helped to train him.

Wulfric was in the inner bailey readying his horse, preparing to go to Normanby and he picked William up in a bear hug. "The cub is back! And growing! That wine in Anjou must suit you, young master!"

"It does although you have lost none of your strength either. Perhaps I should take back some English beer."

"It does not travel well." He mounted, "Do you stay long?"

"I return tomorrow."

"Then I will hear your tales the next time we meet." He turned to me, "I shall be back within the month, lord."

"If you need aught then send word."

"I will."

I could see that William was intrigued. I smiled, "After your news, which is of greater import, I will give you mine!"

Alice rushed up and curtsied, "My lord, it is good to see you. I will go and prepare a chamber. Sarah will fetch food and ale for you." She rushed out saying, "Such changes! Such news!"

William looked bemused and John said, "Alice thinks she is the mother to us all. If you were staying then you would get used to her ways."

The three of us were alone in my hall. I had dismissed the servant. "So, William, why did the Empress send you?"

"She would have sent a letter but feared that your ship might be captured or sunk."

"That could still have happened with you on board."

William looked at me and I saw that the boy had long since disappeared. Over four years of war and three years of Civil War had hardened him. "Then I would have perished but my message would remain a secret." I nodded. Alice and the servants came in with the food and ale. After they had gone, William continued. "The Empress and the Earl will invade next spring. They will land on the south coast. Kent supports our cause and the south and west are still loyal to the Earl."

"And what of me? I hear what you do not say. You speak of the west and the south. You talk of the east. What of the north?"

"Ranulf of Chester is an ally of Stephen but spies have told us that there is discord between the two of them. The Empress remembers that you and the Earl were close once and that he respects you. She wishes you to bring him to our side. He is a powerful Earl and the son in law of the Earl of Gloucester. If he could align with us then the balance of power in the north would shift."

I nodded, "That would make sense but King David says that he is an ally of the Empress. It was he took the Earl's lands in the north."

"And that is why she sends you. She has not entered into any sort of alliance with Scotland. His words are not the truth. He said he would support her in return for the historic lands of Scotland. She refused. She knows of the privations you have suffered and what the Scots have done to our people. You must convince the Earl that he should join us."

"And I will do so. I can see why the Empress sent you. Now eat and I will tell you our news." I told him of the siege and the battle. I spoke of the arrangement I had made with King David and I finished by telling him of my plans for the castles.

When I had finished, he raised his beaker, "My father, the hero of the north! Many say that had you led our forces in Normandy the war there would be over! I can only hope to be half the man that you are."

"You will be greater. And will you come to England with the Empress and the Earl?"

"I may. The Empress still has work for me to do and the Count relies upon me. Sir Leofric is a good castellan and runs La Flèche well. He can both manage and protect the manor. Besides, the Count and the Empress have given me a manor in Normandy. I am Baron William de Ouistreham."

"That is a fine manor."

"It will be but the castle there was reduced in the early days of the war. I must make my fortune in England and collect ransom. Then I will make it a fine castle."

"And the girl, Eliane, what of her? Will you marry her?"

"A little blunt, father, but to be expected. Eliane does not expect that. She is happy to be a lady and to bear my child."

"You said in your letter that you just wanted my permission. I give it to you."

"The letter was written in haste. Eliane and I have considered our position. I have told her she will have all the accoutrements of marriage without the title."

"She will be your mistress."

"A little blunt but yes."

"Your mother would not be happy about that."

"True and the Empress has also spoken to me. She thinks, like you, that I ought to marry her."

"And why do you not?"

"Who knows what awaits me? I am still young. I swear that neither Eliane nor my child will suffer. She will be accorded all that a wife would have save, of course, the title wife and lady."

"You have changed but perhaps that is my fault for leaving you alone in Anjou. Had you been here..."

"Had I been here, father, I would have been seen as Wulfric called me, the cub. In Normandy, I am known for my deeds and not those of my father. I am my own man and I like that. I am not you nor could I ever be." He stood, "And now I would like to visit with Sir Harold and Sir Tristan."

Sir John said, "Then you do not have far to go. Come, I will bring you to them."

I was left with Gilles who had hovered by the back wall during the time we had been speaking. He had known William in Normandy and he knew me too. "Lord, if I may speak?"

"You know that I like honesty, Gilles. Speak."

"I have spoken with those who have served you the longest: men like Wulfric and Dick. They tell me that your father was a great man and well respected but that you are nothing like him."

"That is true."

"Then I would take it as something in your family's nature that each generation changes. Your son is not you and you are not your father. Your father was the son of a peasant so he changed too. Accept your lot, my lord. Life will be easier. Your son is beyond your grasp. You must let him live the life he chooses or else face conflict and you would not wish that. You will have a grandchild; that is surely a good thing."

I smiled, "Words of wisdom from one so young. Thank you, Gilles, I will consider your words. I will visit the church and pray."

"And be close to your wife, lord."

"Aye, Gilles, the Lady Adela."

My church always brought me peace. There were always flowers or, in the winter, greenery on the tomb of my wife. I knelt before it and spoke to her in my head. I did not hear William enter but felt his presence as he knelt next to me. I suddenly sensed the spirit of his mother and I enjoyed a feeling of inner calm. Adela was happy. He was half her and half me. She had been a pragmatic woman and I had been lucky to have married her. William appeared to have inherited her pragmatism. I stood and left the church.

William joined me a few moments later. His eyes were wide. He said, quietly, "Mother was there. Her spirit, I mean. I know her body lies there but I swear that I heard her voice. She said she was happy for me. How can that be?"

"Your mother gave her life for this place and she loved both of us more than you can possibly know. I often come here and take comfort from her. I sensed her joy too. She loved you dearly, William, and would wish for happiness for you." I smiled, "And were Harold and Tristan happy to see you?"

"Aye, like Wulfric they cannot believe how much I have grown."

"We have you for but one day. Let us make the most of it. What would you do?"

"See Sir Edward, see Norton, walk Stockton and speak with Alf. Who knows the next time I will return here?"

The visit to the church had healed any rift there might have been and we spent the day doing all that he wanted. After a feast which Alice had lovingly prepared and when all my knights had left us, I gave William my message for the Empress. I also wrote a letter to her. When I gave it to him, he gave me a knowing look. "You are closer to the Empress than any man save her husband. Even her brother is more distant than you. That is strange is it not?"

I did not like deceiving my son but there were things he could never know for they would threaten the future of England. The Empress and I had a secret that could never be revealed. "The Empress made me her champion and the King ordered me to protect her. I fulfil an oath, that is all."

"And you do it with all the zeal of a crusader. It is to be admired. And you should know that I also took an oath. I swore to protect Henry, her son. He is young yet, but when he is old enough to go to war then I will be amongst his guards and protectors."

"Then I am happy, for Henry will be safe."

"He will be as safe as my child will be." My son gave me a knowing look.

The *'Adela'* left on the late tide. Captain William wished to sneak out and be down the coast before dawn. There were still pirates who preyed, at dawn, at the mouth of the river. This would be her last voyage before winter for she needed her keel stripping of weed and repairs to her masts. John, my steward, and Ethelred made sure that her holds were filled with trade goods. Normandy was our market now!

As I lay in bed that night, I wondered how much my son had deduced. Life was complicated. We all held secrets. I thought I knew my son's. Did he know mine?

The knighting of my three new knights barely interrupted the frantic work to get as much work done on the two new castles before the ground became too hard. Once we reached Yule, the ground would be frozen and mortar would not set. On one of my visits to Barnard Castle, not long before Yule, Sir Hugh had some interesting news.

"My lord, my scouts have seen many lords travelling twixt Durham and Carlisle. There are ongoing peace talks I believe. I made a point of crossing the trail of the Bishop's emissaries when they returned to Durham. I discovered that peace talks are at an advanced stage. I think that Stephen and King David will soon be reaching an agreement." My face must have shown my displeasure for he said, "Peace talks and a truce were inevitable were they not, my lord?"

I shook my head, "We had Scotland here in the palm of our hands. Had I had but five hundred more men I could have reconquered the land the Scots have stolen! We have wasted an opportunity."

"The peace you negotiated holds, my lord."

"I did not negotiate I demanded and I made it quite clear that I intend to take back Scotland when we have the rightful ruler on the throne once more." He nodded. "When the Empress and the Earl land again, I will be taking some of my men to join her."

"Will I be required, my lord?"

"I have put Wulfric and Erre in command of two castles so that I can leave a ring of defences around Stockton. You are vital to that defence. No, I shall not leave this land defenceless. I know that the Empress and the Earl must fight where they have their strength and that is far from here. You and my knights will defend and hold what we have bled for."

"You know that I will follow you anywhere, lord."

"I know and that is why I can go knowing that I leave my land in safe hands. The knights I leave will be a bastion against any predators."

"And who will you take?"

"Harold, Dick, Tristan and John. Those four knights, my archers and my men at arms are worth ten times their number."

"It will be strange not to have Wulfric with you."

"It will but I have begun to worry about Wulfric. Since Roger of Lincoln fell he has not been the same. He had what my father called the look of the berserker on his face. He was hurt because he recklessly charged the enemy. It was almost as though he wished to die. His last wound healed but, after Northallerton, he was weary. He is not finished as a warrior but I will give him a different challenge. He deserves a rest. He has served me well."

"Does he know he will not be going to war with you?" I shook my head. Sir Hugh laughed, "I would like to be there for the delivery of that piece of news."

After seeing his wife and new baby, we left to ride along the northern route to my home. It meant we passed close to Durham and I was curious as to the defences of Durham. Geoffrey Rufus had declared for neither claimant to the throne. He was trying that most difficult of tricks, sitting on the fence. There was always a danger one could fall off!

We met no lords but the farmers we encountered were unhappy. They were subject to bandits, brigands and Scots. They paid their taxes and received little in the way of protection. Times past, I would have offered them my shield but I could barely hang on to the manors within my own lands. I would help when at least one of my enemies was no more. Hugh and I parted and he returned to Barnard and I headed for Stockton.

Yule was as festive an occasion as any since my wife died. We now had two young families living within my castle walls and new men who had never had such a home before. Thanks to *'Adela'* and her bulging hold, we had wine and spices as well as wheat. Alice organised the cooks well. There would be the puddings laced with wine as well as rich cakes made with spices and the last of the fruit from autumn. She had Aiden and his hunters catching game to hang ready for the celebration.

Aidan came to me, "Lord, Alice wishes a wild boar. I know you allow us to hunt but wild boar is for lords of the manor is it not?"

"It is but you could hunt it if you wished."

"I would but Edward and Edgar are not experienced enough. I am loath to lose one of them to a boar. They are deadlier than the wolf."

"Then we will find one for Alice. It will be good to join my knights and squires in the hunt. Find us a boar and we will go the day after tomorrow."

My knights were eager for the hunt. Gilles had hunted with his father in Normandy but that had been deer. Deer rarely attack. A wild boar can attack with a body riddled with arrows and spears. They are hard to kill and therefore all the more delicious when eaten. We went to Alf to get some new boar spears. The spears he normally made were for war. A boar spear needed a small bar close to the end of the haft to stop the spearhead from penetrating too far. I had seen boars almost eat ordinary spears. If a man came within range of the tusks, he was as good as dead.

Aiden and his scouts had found a family of tuskers three miles upstream in the woods which bordered the river. It was halfway between my manor and that of Yarm. It bordered Sir Tristan's at Elton. Only the knights rode and that would only be until we reached the woods. We had brought two stable boys to watch the horses. With thick leather jerkins and gloves, we set off through the forest. Aiden was going to bring us so that we were downwind of the beasts. They had a great sense of smell. There was no snow but the ground was hard. That was a mercy. At least we would have a firm footing. We did not follow the trail but went in three loose lines. Aidan, Edgar and Edward led, then the four knights and lastly, the squires with spare weapons. I held my spear before me with both hands. I had hunted wild boar before. Harold had and he had the same grip as I did. Sir Tristan and Sir John held their spears one handed. They were going for the throw.

Aiden held up his hand and I knew that we were close. I relaxed and then tightened my grip. I would need firm hands when the beast was close. Aiden led his two scouts to the west. They would approach from upwind. They would make a noise. The animals would be driven towards us. I made sure that we were spaced apart and we waited. As with a battle, this was the hardest time. It was still and I could hear the squires breathing heavily behind us. It was nerves. It was like going into battle. The anticipation built within.

Then I heard the rustle of leaves ahead. There was a squeal and Aiden's voice shouting, "Huzzah!"

I said not a word for if my companions did not know that we were about to see wild boar then I had misjudged them. Four young boars raced towards us followed by a female and two males. One of the males was an old tusker. I allowed the four adolescents to run past me. It was the older males I wanted. Sir Tristan hurled his spear at the female. It glanced off her thick hide and she veered towards the young knight. His squire tripped as he raced to hand him another spear. It was lucky that Harold was there. He ran forward and rammed his spear into the side of the sow. It was not a mortal wound. In fact, it just scored a wound along her flank but it drove her away from both Tristan and his stricken squire as she hurried after her young.

Sir John had learned from Tristan's mistake and he changed his grip. I braced myself with my right leg behind me and, as the young male passed me, I lunged at the old boar. He had been hunted before and he swerved at the last moment. My spear struck him in the shoulder rather than the mouth or eye. He was powerful and I felt myself being pushed over. John was as strong as Wulfric. He had little skill with a boar spear but as the old male turned his head to eviscerate me with his tusk John rammed his spear through the side of the tusker's skull. It twitched and then life left his eyes. He was dead.

I turned and saw that the rest of the small herd had fled. It was good. There was another male to carry on and we would hunt him sometime in the future. The sow would heal and learn from her experience. "Is anyone hurt?"

Sir Tristan shook his head, "Just my pride and that of my squire. I have learned a lesson today."

We took some time to tie the beast to four boar spears. It would help us to carry it. Aiden and his two hunters emerged from the woods. They had a brace of game birds. They had not been idle!

"We have put the boar on spears. You two falconers help the squires to carry him. He is a big beast. You did well to find him, Aiden."

I smiled as they struggled to lift him. He would feed my castle! As we walked back, I anticipated the delicious roasts as well as the sausages we would make. Nothing would be wasted. His head would adorn the wall above my fire in my hall.

We marched triumphantly through my gates. The hunt was more than a way of getting food. It taught my squires and young knights how to fight an unpredictable enemy. The lessons learned could be translated to the battlefield.

Part 3
The Empress returns

Chapter 11

I had been eager to travel to Chester to see Ranulf de Meschines, Earl of Chester, but, after Yule, we had blizzards and storms which made life hard enough in the valley and would have made the high passes impassable. So it was that, as we headed over to the west, Stephen's emissaries were travelling to Durham to conclude the peace treaty. Thanks to the intelligence gleaned by Sir Hugh, we knew that Stephen had given away almost everything: Prince Henry was given the earldom of Northumberland and was restored to the earldom of Huntingdon and lordship of Doncaster. King David, himself, was allowed to keep Carlisle, Westmorland, Cumberland and Lancashire north of the Ribble. Stephen had only hung on to Bamburgh and Newcastle. He had bought off the Scots with half of the Earl of Chester's lands. All that we could have won had been given away. King David had lost the battle but won the war.

I had with me my four knights and their squires, Philip of Selby and half of my archers and my eleven men at arms. Deaths and knighthood, not to mention my garrison in Anjou, had taken their toll. The eleven were more than enough. We took three servants too but left our warhorses at home. I did not think that we were going to war. We were going to find allies.

The blizzards had long gone and, once we crossed the top of the col across, the snow thinned and we made better time. I was not worried about enemies: there were too many of them but as the Scots were just interested in the lead mines to the north of us and the land before Chester had few people, I was confident we could reach the Earl safely. No one with any sense would be out at this time of year. What I did not know was how I would be received. He had sided with Stephen. Even though he was married to Maud, the Earl of Gloucester's daughter, he had decided to take the opportunity to ingratiate himself with Stephen. I was disappointed. I had thought better of him. There were many such men who had taken Stephen's offer of money and titles.

I sent Ralph of Wales and Walter of Crewe to scout ahead. They could both pass for natives of the area. I wanted to avoid any conflict before we reached Chester. It was with some relief that we saw the huge castle and my two scouts returned to tell me that they had entered the city without incident. We might not have such an easy time. We rode through the outer gate without too much trouble. I think the guards there were half asleep or perhaps the cloaks we had wrapped tightly about us hid our identity. We rode through the narrow streets of the busy city. We passed the cathedral and saw the castle with its fine keep. When my banner was unfurled and our cloaks opened, armed guards rushed to the gate. A sergeant at arms asked, nervously, "What is it you seek, my lord?"

I had fought alongside many of the Earl's men and they knew me. More importantly, they knew my reputation. "I am here to speak with the Earl. I come in peace." He looked beyond me at my men. I said quietly, "If we came for war, sergeant, then you would be lying dead with arrows in your body. You know that. Let us enter. I promise you that your master will not be harmed."

He nodded and stood aside.

We rode through the gate into the castle. It had a large square keep and a huge bailey. We rode up to the keep and I dismounted. My men remained outside with the horses. I knew not what reception we might receive. The Earl himself came to meet me. He was flanked by his half brother, Sir William de Roumare, and his wife, Maud. I was happy to see that she was smiling. She had always liked me. The Earl and his half brother looked worried as though they feared I would draw my sword and slay them all.

I smiled, "My lord, I am here on an embassy."

"From whom, my lord?"

"Is this the place for such discussions, my lord?" I saw him hesitate, "I told your guards that you would be safe. Do you fear that an old friend will turn violent?"

Maud snapped, "This is Aelfraed, husband! You will be safe!" She came next to me and put her arm through mine. "William, see to the Earl's men." She walked into the keep with me. "Tell me, my lord, have you heard from my father or the Empress?"

I said, quietly, "I have, my lady, and I have travelled here at their behest."

"Good." She spoke equally quietly, "I have told my husband that he has sided with the wrong ruler but..."

We had reached the Great Hall and she let go of my arm and clapped her hand. "Food, wine, hurry! We have a distinguished guest."

I was seated between the Earl and his wife. His half brother faced me. I could see the discomfort in both men's faces. When the wine came, Maud poured me a beaker. "I hear, my lord, that you were at the Battle of the Standards?"

"I was."

"Then let us toast a hero, for the Scots would have been at our very gates had you not done so." The two knights were forced to accede to her request. "Tell me, Earl, who led the men at the battle?"

"It was the Archbishop, Thurstan himself, who led us, my lady."

For the first time, Ranulf smiled, "I fear you are not being totally truthful. Thurstan is a brave fellow but he has no more idea of dispositions for a battle than my wife here." I smiled as she giggled. "I hear that it was you."

I did not answer his question directly. "Sadly, my lord, I had no power. If I had had the command, I would have followed King David to Carlisle and defeated him once and for all." I paused, "Stephen has allowed King David to keep the lands he has taken."

"That is a lie!"

I said quietly, "Careful, Ranulf. I promised you that I would not harm you but do not insult me. When have you ever known me to lie?"

"Then you have been misinformed."

"Prince Henry has been given the earldom of Northumberland and restored to the earldom of Huntingdon and lordship of Doncaster; King David, himself, has been allowed to keep Carlisle, Westmorland, Cumberland and Lancashire north of the Ribble. I have no reason to lie."

"None save that it would bring me into the Empress' fold."

"Which is where you should be, lord. You swore an oath to King Henry to uphold his daughter's claim."

"Stephen was crowned!"

"More shame on those that did so. We all took an oath to see that the Empress and her son would rule. Now is the chance to make amends. The Empress has allies in Kent who are making advances. This year sees the return of your father in law and the Empress."

I could see that I had surprised the two men. Maud poured more wine. "It is as I said, husband, my father will return. Join them."

Just then the door burst open and a dishevelled looking messenger threw himself to the floor. "My lord, I apologise for the interruption but I bring grave news."

I looked at Maud. She said, behind her hand, "He is in the service of the Baron of Congleton."

"Rise then for you look like a worm wriggling there! Speak!"

"I have come from Windsor, lord, and there was an announcement that King Stephen has concluded a peace treaty with the Scots. All of your lands north of the Ribble as well as Doncaster, are to be given to the Scots. Prince Henry has been given Doncaster and he is there now looking at his new lands and manors."

Ranulf was roughly the same age as I was but he behaved, sometimes, like a spoiled child. He hurled his beaker at the messenger and began to beat the table with his hands. "I have been betrayed! That bastard! I will kill him! He has deceived me for the last time!"

Maud put her hand on mine and shook her head. She said quietly, "He is often thus. He will calm soon."

His half brother said, "The Earl was right, brother. He did not lie."

I could have taken offence at that but I chose to ignore it. "You say that the Prince is at Doncaster?"

The shaken messenger looked grateful that I was not hurling things at him, "Aye, lord. He arrived there three days since. He came directly from Durham."

I wondered how he had got by my castles and then realised, that in winter, he could do so with ease. Maud asked, "Why do you ask, my lord?"

I shrugged, "I just thought that if we could get hold of the Prince then we might be able to exchange him for the lands Stephen the Usurper gave away."

The Earl of Chester suddenly looked interested, "Could we?"

"When I chased him back to Carlisle, he had but one household knight with him. He may be guarded but they will not be the best of guards. It could be done. However, my lord, if you did that then you would be rebelling against Stephen for he has signed a peace treaty. Are you willing to do that?"

"By God I am! You and my wife are both right! I should never have broken my oath. I have been punished by God for that act!" His wife jumped up and kissed him. Then he looked at me, "Earl, will you come with us? You have the best men at arms in the land and this is the sort of thing you are used to."

"Not exactly used to but I will come with you. The Prince and I have unfinished business."

"It is ninety miles to Doncaster. If we took spare horses we could be there in two days." He suddenly seemed to realise that the messenger was still in the room. "Go and thank your lord. I will reward him when time permits." The messenger bowed and left. "I am sorry that I ever doubted you. I was seduced by Stephen's generosity."

"It is easy to be generous with another man's goods, titles and lands. He has done the same to you; giving your lands and titles to an enemy. He seeks to cling on to power no matter what it takes."

The food was brought in. I said, "My knights, they are being fed?"

Maud shook her head, "Of course. How rude. William, fetch the knights of the Earl of Cleveland and see that his other warriors are well looked after."

I felt happier with my knights close by. It was important that they knew what we were about. I told them the news and Dick said, "Doncaster? I know the area. It has fine woods for hunting but the castle is a strong one. It would not fall easily to a conroi such as ours."

I shook my head, "I had not planned on assaulting the castle. The Prince will want to inspect his lands. He will be abroad and there we can take him. Philip's archers should be in their element in the woods and forests."

We spent the rest of the evening discussing plans. It was decided we would take my men along with the Earl, his half brother and ten of his men at arms. The two brothers soon drank more than was good for them and, after my knights had retired, I was left with Maud.

"Do not misjudge my husband, my lord. He has many good qualities."

"Self-control and loyalty do not appear to be among them."

She shook her head, "You are the perfect knight. My father told me so. He wished he could be more like you. Look how long it took him to declare for his sister. It is another reason why my husband joined Stephen. He wanted to do as you did but lacked the self-belief. You see problems, which would be impossible obstacles to others, as challenges to overcome. You were being your usual modest self earlier. It was you who led the forces which defeated the Scots. You did that despite fighting alongside men you despised. It is no wonder the King had you as his champion and you continue to serve the Empress even though she is far away."

"It was the way I was brought up. You cannot change your nature. I fear the Earl will be ever thus." She nodded. "The sooner your father comes here the better."

"Amen to that but fear not, Aelfraed, the blood of the Conqueror runs in my veins too. I may be a woman but I can fight... in my own way!"

As we headed east, it was as though winter had disappeared and spring was trying to burst forth. The skies were bluer and the air felt fresher even though the ground was still hard and a vicious wind blew from the east. The skies gave us heart as we headed into the biting breeze. We would stop but once at Glossop Castle. The Baron there, William Peverel, was a friend of the Earl. It was halfway and we would be weary when we arrived.

"I know not this Baron. Upon whose side does he sit?"

"He says Stephen, but as I did that too, it will not be a problem."

"And how will you explain me?"

"I will say that I have persuaded you, as my friend, to travel and meet with King Stephen and settle your differences."

"And will that be believed?"

He laughed, "You are the only one who sees things as either black or white. The rest of us see shades of grey and accommodation. He will believe us."

The castle was set against the high hills which were the east-west barrier. The Baron greeted us warmly enough and the Earl was correct. He seemed to accept the story that I was considering speaking with Stephen. It helped that he knew me not. I had never fought with him. That, in itself, was revealing for he had never fought alongside King Henry nor the Earl of Gloucester. He had not earned what he held. He was, however, generous with his hospitality and the two brothers, once more, ate and drank more than my knights. We were on campaign and we would be frugal in what we drank. My knights and I retired early leaving the Earl to carouse with his friend.

We had not told him our plans save that we were heading for the London Road as we believed that was where Stephen would be. The Baron left with us for he was on his way to his castle at Nottingham. We parted at the Dunford Bridge. My knights were alert as we rode the road to Barnsley. We did not want to alarm the Prince. My banner was furled and we rode beneath the banner of Chester. As far as all knew, the Earl was still a loyal supporter of Stephen.

While my men rode like professional men at arms, the Earl and his half brother had to stop, frequently, to empty the contents of their stomachs. I saw Dick's look of disapproval. He was the most recent knight. He had earned his title and could not understand the behaviour of those who were, apparently, his betters. Tristan and I had been brought up with other young men like that and we were not surprised. I reflected that, of my knights, only Sir Tristan and Sir Hugh were noble-born. I had been lucky with them. Those whom I had made noble appreciated their position. Perhaps that was why I had such loyalty amongst my men.

We approached Doncaster towards dusk. Leaving me with my men in the woods a mile from the castle, the Earl and his brother rode towards the castle. The Prince's banner flew from its keep. They would visit with the constable there and send word to us to capture the Prince when the opportunity arose. As it was late, we knew we would have to spend a night in the forest for it would have looked suspicious had one of the Earl's men tried to leave during the night.

I saw my knights looking at each other and, finally, Sir Harold spoke for them all. "Can we trust the Earl, lord? He has changed sides remarkably quickly. I thought we would have had to persuade him and use many arguments but he came to our side as soon as you arrived."

I nodded, "Whose banner do we follow, Harold?"

"The Empress, of course."

"And why is that?"

Poor Harold had been brought up as an outlaw in Sherwood forest and I saw the confusion on his face. "She is the rightful ruler of England, lord."

"However, if I was not Earl then whom would you follow?" I looked at Tristan, "Tristan's father behaved the way I believe you would have done. He sided with Stephen, at first, for that was the safest route for his family and the easier act." I held my hand up, "I am not criticising, Tristan.

Your father is now on our side but it took a wound to you to do so."

He nodded, "You are right."

"And so it is with the Earl. He chose the safe option and the loss of his land is the same as a blow to Tristan was to his father." Understanding lit their faces. "However, others may not have the same motivation. Expect treachery."

I saw Dick nodding, "My time among the outlaws taught me that. Some men smiled and then tried to knife you in the back. The men I trust I see around this fire. All others have to earn that trust. I know what you say, lord, but this Earl has not yet earned my trust."

"And yet I have been ordered to bring him into our camp. I will watch him, carefully, Dick. Doubt not that."

It was a cold cheerless night in the forest and I was glad when dawn broke. I was no longer the young man who could lie in the woodlands and not feel it. When the Earl and his men left the castle and headed towards us, I knew that something was wrong. We had stayed within the woods to avoid observation.

"What is wrong, Ranulf?"

His face was red. "We have been thrown out of the castle! That young cockerel demanded that I pay him obeisance as he was now my lord. I refused!"

His brother said, "We were guarded during the night. Harsh words were spoken before we left."

I shook my head. Once more the Earl's lack of self-control was hurting us. I took a deep breath. I owed it to the Empress and her brother to do my best with this volatile earl. "It does not change things. We wait here. Dick, send four archers to the south road and four to the north road. We will watch this one. When the Prince emerges, we will take him."

William de Roumare said, "He plans to head back to Scotland in the next few days."

The Earl said, "How do you know?"

"When you were cursing him and spitting fire and brimstone, I was speaking with the servants. They told me that the Prince had heard that the Earl of Cleveland had left his castle and he feared for his life."

"Then we can take him." I turned to Edgar, "We will make a camp in the forest. Set guards."

"Aye, lord."

My archers scouted the woods and made sure that we were not discovered. The Earl found the waiting the hardest. He seemed like a pot on the fire constantly bubbling and threatening to spill over onto the coals. His half brother was much calmer and more thoughtful. On the second morning, we received unwelcome news. Henry Warbow rode in. "My lord, King Stephen has entered Doncaster with knights and men at arms."

The Earl became agitated, "What does this mean?"

"I suspect it means that William Peverel sent word to Stephen the Usurper of our presence. Stephen is a clever man. We might take others in with the ruse that I was ready to negotiate but he would know better. Add to that the fact that my absence from Stockton has been noted and I see treachery."

"Does it not spoil our plans?"

"Of course not! They still have to travel north sometime. I cannot see either the Prince or Stephen happy to stay in Doncaster. Either they come to seek us or they travel. We continue to watch."

Henry Warbow brought us news the next morning that the Prince, escorted by Stephen, had left Doncaster and was heading north. "He is going home. How many men does he have, Henry?"

"There look to be ten Scots and Stephen has twenty men with him."

"We have more than enough to take them!" The Earl was quite excited.

"It would seem to me that he would have more men than that."

"Where is your spirit, Aelfraed? I can do Maud's father the greatest favour. I capture Stephen and then the Empress can be crowned Queen."

This was the foolhardy Earl once more. "We will head north, Ralph, take the archers and try to get ahead of them. We will follow and attempt to trap them between us." I had a picture of the land in my mind. They would head for Pontefract or Wakefield. Both had castles and lords loyal to Stephen. After that, it was a short distance to York. There they would be safe.

As we rode north towards the road, I said, "A better place to ambush them would be north of York. They have to head towards Piercebridge and I know the land well there."

"No, Earl, we will take him as soon as we see him."

I did not reply. I had the majority of the men at arms and I would decide when we attacked. Within a short time, we had reached the road and made good time along it. My archers would be able to ride across country and make much better time. Ralph of Wales knew his business. He would keep them closely watched and send a messenger to me when the time was right for an ambush. Pontefract was a couple of hours from Doncaster and I suspected that the Prince and Stephen would stop there for refreshment. As we neared the castle, I slowed us down. "What is the problem, Earl? Why do we stop?"

"Yonder is a castle. We cannot ride through it. We must wait until we see our prey move north and then skirt the castle."

"Why not skirt it now and get ahead of them?"

"We have men ahead of them. What if they choose to turn around and head back? This could be a ruse. He may be visiting his nearest neighbour." I could see that the Earl was not used to thinking such things through. He just reacted. "Send one of your men to the town. He can return here when he sees which way they go."

"John. Ride to the town." The Earl gave him a copper coin. "Buy yourself a beaker of ale."

I put my arm on his shoulder, "If you are questioned tell them that you are on your way to Barnsley on an errand for your master and make sure you leave by the west gate." He looked at the Earl who nodded.

William Roumare said," You are a cautious man, my lord."

"It is how I have survived so long surrounded by enemies. If you do not think, you die."

I could feel the Earl's impatience. He fiddled with his mail and with his sword. He strode around like a caged wolf. I shook my head and said to his brother, "He is wasting energy."

"It is his way. He is a man of action."

"Better to save your action for when it will do the most good; on the field of battle."

John returned a short while later. He reined in next to the Earl. "I have found out where they go! They are riding to Tadcaster where they will spend the night."

"Excellent!"

"How did you find out, John?"

"I was in the inn and when two of the King's men entered in livery, they began to talk about it."

"That is convenient." I was suspicious of such happenstance.

The Earl shrugged, "Sometimes men are careless. We are wasting time. We can catch them at the River Aire. They will have to catch the ferry at Fryston. We ride!"

I let the two brothers lead their men off. Something about this did not smell right. I rode next to Dick. He was the master of ambush. I told him what we knew. He shook his head, "I am sorry, lord but it is just too much of a coincidence for two of Stephen's men to go into a tavern and tell the whole world their plans."

Harold asked, quite reasonably, "But how could he know that the Earl has defected and that we pursue them?"

"I can think of two reasons: the servant who brought us the news and William Peverel. Both could have told Stephen. It is known he pays well. I fear that this is a trap. Warn the men. We may have to run from our foes this time." I now regretted sending my archers ahead. They would be watching for somewhere where they could spring an ambush upon our prey. I hoped that they did not fall foul of whatever plan the Usurper and the Prince had concocted.

The Earl and his men were now half a mile ahead of us for they were eager to catch our prey when they tried to cross the ferry. Just after the small village of Brotherton, there was a wood which closed in with the road as it descended towards the river. The Earl was so concerned with catching Stephen and Prince Henry that he failed to keep a close watch on the undergrowth to the side of them. Suddenly arrows, spears and stones were hurled at the column of men. Four men at arms fell in the first volley. It was a trap. I heard a horn sound and knew that Stephen and Prince Henry would be returning to deal with the enemy they thought was me.

"Dick, take Tristan and go right with half of the men. John, take Harold and go left with the other half. Leave your squires with me!" I spurred Rolf. "Draw your swords, squires and keep tightly to me."

My plan was simple. The ambushers needed to have their attention on the road. That would enable my men at arms to catch them unawares. I had no doubt that Ralph of Wales would be bringing my archers back for they would have heard the clamour. I drew my own sword and pulled my shield tighter to my body. Even as we approached, another three men at arms fell. The Earl, his brother and their squires were fighting desperately but they were assailed on all sides by men wielding axes and billhooks. Horses and men at arms fell for they were overwhelmed by sheer numbers.

Beyond the ambush, I saw the banners of the Prince and Stephen as they rushed back to catch the prize that they hoped was me. I put them from my mind. I veered to the right and brought my sword down on the back of the neck of the crossbowman who was levelling his weapon at the Earl. My sword tore through his aventail but he was dead already. The blow from the heavy blade had broken his neck. Gilles had learned well and he leaned to the side to sweep his sword at the unprotected head of an archer. Blood, pieces of bone and brains splattered the trees. I heard cries from my right and left as my men at arms and knights fell upon the ambushers.

The Earl and his brother were the only two survivors who remained on their horses and I saw Prince Henry and Stephen as they raced to finish them off. I spurred Rolf who responded magnificently. I left the squires in my wake. Their horses could not keep up. I fended a blow from a billhook with my shield. The Earl and his brother had both been struck and their horses were struggling. I shouted, "Clear the way! Earl, fall back!"

I was less than twenty paces from them but they managed to pull their weary mounts to the side. I did not slow up but went directly for the Prince and Stephen the Usurper. It was a move they did not expect. They were riding boot to boot and I aimed Rolf at the narrowest of gaps. Their horses both pulled away. I swung my sword horizontally at Stephen as I punched as hard as I could with my shield at the Prince. My punch caught him just as his horse veered and he tumbled from his horse. My sword smacked hard into Stephen and he pulled away to the right. I saw the men at arms coming towards me. There were too many for me and my squires. I had bought the Earl enough time and I pulled my horse to the left. I slashed at the two men at arms' horses as I turned. The blade made them both baulk. At the same time, I saw the next two were plucked from their saddles by invisible hands. It was my archers.

When I had completed my turn, I was astonished to see the Earl and his brother still in the middle of the road, "Retreat! Back! Do you want to die?"

They seemed to see the column of men behind me and they put spurs to their horses. I felt something strike my back but I did not turn around. I kept yelling, "Fall back! Fall back!"

Had my archers not arrived when they had done then it would have gone ill for us. As it was, the unhorsed Prince and the foiled ambush made them form a defensive line. We left the woods and when we were half a mile from them, I halted the remnants of our conroi. I was relieved to see that I had lost none of my own men. The Earl and his brother looked shocked. I saw my archers as they emerged from the woods. They, too, had avoided losses.

I nudged Rolf next to the Earl while I waited for the archers to catch up with us." Are you hurt, Ranulf?"

He shook his head, "Just my pride. My armour and my gambeson saved me from hurt. The tears look bad but I am whole. You were right about the trap but how..."

"There will be time for that later. We must get home. We will have to abort this attempt. Do you have any allies other than Peverel? We shall need shelter and it should be close by."

The Earl thought and then said, "Svilentone. It is a small manor. I gave it to one of my men at arms who had served me well when I was given the manor of Doncaster. There is no castle but he has a hall."

"And you trust him?"

"This time I can say with certainty that I can."

Chapter 12

This time the Earl was proved right. His former man at arms, Harold of Brotton, had lost an arm in the service of his lord. He had the same look about him as Edgar, Wulfric and my older men at arms. He had a homely wife and four strapping sons. He had made the hall easy to defend for the animals slept on the first floor and there was a ladder to reach the second floor, where they lived. He was happy to give the animal quarters to my men and we enjoyed the safety of his home in the company of his wife and sons. We ate a frugal meal but we were just grateful for the sanctuary.

After we had eaten, his wife and his sons were discreet and went outside to see to their animals. We needed Harold's local knowledge.

"How did they know, Alfraed?"

"I am guessing your friend William Peverel." I sighed for I wanted neither to ask my next question nor hear the answer but I knew that I had to ask. "When you were drinking at the Baron's castle, is it possible that you told him what we were about?"

His guilty look and the sudden look of surprise on his brother's face gave me the answer I had expected.

"Then we know how Stephen found out."

"But William was a friend!"

"This is war! You have no friends! All that you have are the men that you can rely on and with whom you can stand shoulder to shoulder." I turned to Harold, "Is that not so, Harold?"

He nodded, "The Earl is right, lord. Many would like to be Earl of Chester. It is amongst the greatest manors in the land. I know this William Peverel. He is both greedy and ambitious. He has eaten up many manors since King Stephen was crowned."

"And that means that we are in a trap. We are safe here because this is a small farm. He will not look here. There will be a hue and cry but they will search the main roads and the larger castles. This will be our last night indoors until we reach your castle. I am afraid that our trap has been turned on its head." I shook my head, "The night of drinking has cost you much. Especially the brave men and squires who fell. Tell me, Ranulf, was it worth it?"

His head drooped as he took in my words and felt their impact. "I am in your hands. How do we escape?"

"Tell me where your lands will be safe. Which castle do we need to reach?"

He studied the fire and William answered for him, "That would be Merpel. It is further west than Glossop. That manor also belongs to William Peverel!"

The Earl said, angrily, "I should burn it around his ears!"

I snapped back, "Do what you will but let us get home first. I do not wish my men to suffer the same fate as yours. I value them a little more!"

He calmed a little and nodded, "I deserved that. My brother is right. Merpel has a lord of the manor and a castle. It is more than ten miles from Glossop. So long as we can avoid Peverel's garrison, we will be safe."

"Then let us get some sleep." I turned to Harold, "This may go ill with you."

"I know, my lord. Perhaps we will leave and begin again."

The Earl looked concerned, "Where would you go?"

"I know not but it would need to be somewhere where the King cannot find me."

The Earl seemed bereft of ideas. I said, "It is a long way, perhaps sixty miles, but I have farms and manors which I would give you in payment for your services. If you could get to the Tees, I will reward you."

Sir John said, "You will be safe there. They are good people and you can trust them."

The ex-man at arms said, "I will speak with my wife. Thank you, lord. It is both a kind and generous offer."

"No. Thank you, Harold. Had you not provided us shelter then who knows what our fate would have been?"

We rose before dawn and were ready to ride as the sun peered from the east. Harold and his family approached us. "We have decided to take you up on your offer, lord. There is a farmer two miles away who will buy my animals. I will tell him that I have decided to return to Chester. We often speak of it and he will believe me. We will buy horses and, perhaps, the journey might take just two days."

Dick said, "If you ride hard, just a day."

"They have a woman with them. It will take two. I would ride to York and break your journey there. The Archbishop is a good man and you can trust him. When you get to Stockton, take the ferry and ask for John, my steward. Tell him I sent you. He will, no doubt, ask you about these others. Describe us and what we said. He will believe you. I will return home when my business here is concluded."

"Thank you, lord. I will not forget this."

We headed west. We had not been on the road long when the Earl said, "Why do you care so much about men like Harold? He is a one armed farmer. How can he possibly help you?"

I shook my head, "The day you stop worrying about men like Harold is the day you lose. The men who fight for us deserve our protection once their days of fighting are over. There is a bond between a leader and his men." The look of bewilderment and lack of understanding on the Earl's face made me despair. He did not understand.

We kept to greenways and the forests. We used the skills of men like Dick and Harold as well as my archers to live off the land and to remain hidden. We made forty miles the first day and reached a small deserted farmhouse in the high fells. I reckoned we had another ten miles or so before Glossop. I wanted us to skirt that castle and so we would take a detour north. We would be crossing land without paths and without houses. It was desolate land even in summer. That would suit us.

Rolf apart, our horses were showing the effects of the journey. The Earl's and his brother's, in particular, were finished as horses. They could not be used in war again. I thought that they would be lucky to reach Merpel let alone Chester. We kept the two of them in the middle of our column when we rode. I assigned Long Tom and Rafe to watch them. We were all weary when we mounted our horses the next day. We had less than half a day to reach the relative safety of the Earl's castle at Merpel.

Ralph of Wales and my archers were a thin screen ahead of us finding the best route through the boggy and sometimes rocky route we had chosen. When we left the poor and barren land, I saw, ahead of me, a green and verdant valley. We found a trackway and the road became easier. We were less than a mile away from safety when disaster struck. We saw ahead of us a line of men at arms and knights. They were between us and the distant castle of Merpel. We were so close we could see the banner flying from the hall. The standards of the men awaiting us showed that they were the men of William Peverel. Had they anticipated or had Harold of Brotton been captured and forced to tell of our plans? It made no difference for the moment. We had been seen. We had to break through them.

"Tell me, Ranulf, is Peverel with them? You know his banner."

He peered ahead, "I do not see him."

"Then we charge in a wedge. Dick, take half of the archers to the right and, Ralph, the other half to the left. When we charge, I want you to make life hard for those on the flanks."

"You are going to charge, Aelfraed? They outnumber us. Why not negotiate?"

"Simple, these are not the only enemies. I have no doubt that a rider is already heading east to fetch the rest of the men who are seeking us. I mean no disrespect, Ranulf, but if Stephen can rid this land of me then he will be a much happier man. He knows he cannot buy me."

Perhaps I was tired and had not chosen my words wisely for he looked angry. "You go too far!"

"Let us get through this line and reach your castle and then we can discuss my rash words. Keep close. Rafe, Long Tom, you know what to do?"

"Aye, my lord."

We cantered towards the waiting men at arms and knights. There were forty of them. Eight knights, four squires and twenty-eight men at arms. I had time to count

them as we rode towards them. I suspect they had thought
we would either turn or negotiate. As we thundered towards
them in three lines, I saw someone hurriedly shouting orders.
He was moments too late. We were cantering now, not quite
boot to boot but certainly closer together than the
disorganized line which rumbled up the slope towards us.

They had formed in a single line and were now trying to
advance towards us. I aimed Rolf at the knight who had been
shouting orders. He held a lance and I saw that he was
unused to such a weapon for the head wobbled alarmingly up
and down. I pulled my shield around a little tighter. He
intended to aim for my sword side. That suited me. I saw the
look of triumph in his eyes as he punched with his lance. I
moved my shield horizontally across my body and angled it.
The tip of the lance slid along the shield and opened his
body. I swung my sword at his middle, just above his cantle.
There was no finesse in the stroke. It was pure brute force.
Added to the weight of my horse it meant a massive force
struck his middle. I did not break his mail but I broke many
parts of his body. Blood erupted from his mouth and he fell
from his horse. His squire was a brave youth. He looked too
young to be a squire but he came at me with his short sword.
I smashed it from his hand, "Yield, boy! Or die!" I saw him
consider the question. "You have done your duty but your
lord is dead. You are too young to follow him."

His head bowed and he offered me his sword. "I yield."

"Good. Give me your sword later! Stay by your lord until
my men return."

My knights were equally skilled and, along with my
squires, we punched a hole in their line. It was a single line
and I reined Rolf around to attack the survivors from the
rear. My archers had slaughtered the horses of the men at
arms on the flanks and were now racing in with their short
swords to finish them off. Three men at arms galloped east
while the two squires and two knights who had survived
surrendered. They were now the ones heavily outnumbered.

"Get the horses and the mail from the dead knights. Well
done, Dick. Cover our retreat to the castle in case there are
any others close by."

We made it into the castle before dark. The Earl sent two of the garrison to Chester for help and I breathed a sigh of relief when Dick and the archers brought in the last of the horses and the booty. We had found sanctuary. The question remained would we have to battle our way out of it?

John of Merpel was older than I expected. During our stay there I found that his sons had gone on a crusade for they thought Merpel held little for them. They had perished and now the old knight lived in his castle with half a dozen retainers. All were as old as he was. It was my father all over again. They added little to our numbers but it meant we had plenty of room in the small motte and bailey. I inspected the defences with Dick, leaving my three knights to question the prisoners. They did so separately.

"The walls are made of wood, my lord, and can be fired. A ram or even a log will break down the gate. Added to that we do not have enough men to man the walls of the outer bailey."

"Then we will fall back to the inner wall when they breakthrough but we make them bleed for the outer wall. We have seen the other side of this coin, Dick."

"Aye, lord, and it always seemed to go our way."

"We keep four archers in the inner bailey along with Sir John's retainers, the Earl and his brother."

"You would not use the Earl on the walls of the outer bailey, lord?"

"I fear his nature. He might do something rash. I hope that Tristan and the others can elicit information from our prisoners. It might help me to know whom we face."

We had finished our tour. Oswald and Gurth stood at the gate to the outer bailey. "We will get you relieved in a couple of hours. Keep a close watch although I do not think any will come before morning." We headed back through the deserted buildings of the outer bailey. None live there any longer. The handful of servants who remained with the old baron lived in the inner bailey. I pointed to the buildings as we passed them. "We will have kindling in these. When we fall back from the outer walls, we fire them. It will delay the attack and stop the enemy from using them."

"I will get my archers to do that. They like making fires!"

We stopped at the main gate. There was just one gate in. The ditch, however, showed signs of neglect. It was not deep enough to stop determined men nor did it have any traps. It was too late to do anything about that. I hit the gate with my hand. It seemed solid enough. "This is where we have to hold them. It is our archers who will save us."

"My men have but a quiver left for each of them. They used many on the road."

That meant twenty or so arrows for each man. Luckily, my archers could also handle themselves in combat. There were plenty of spears and shields in the armoury. When Sir John's sons had lived here it had had a bigger garrison. I looked up at the gate, Raymond of Le Mans and Leopold of Durstein were standing watch. "Make sure you patrol the whole of the inner bailey."

"Aye, lord. That will not take long. Your keep at Stockton is bigger."

"Aye, lord and made of stone."

I laughed, "I think we are being tested!"

As we walked towards the hall where I could smell the food which was being prepared, Dick said, "Do we go home now, lord? We have done what the Empress wished. The Earl is an ally."

I stopped and spoke quietly, "He is an ally but this latest foray means he is not a confident one. The wind may change and he will defect again. I would stay here until I am sure." I shook my head, "Like you, I would either be in Stockton or with the Empress. I have not heard yet that she has landed in the south. When she does so I will join her. We will stay with the Earl until midsummer at the latest."

I saw Dick smile in the light from the hall, "You are assuming we will survive this battle, lord."

"Let us say I am hoping. I do not think that our work is done but if we are to fall here then let us make it one which Stephen and our foes will remember."

Sir John was being a gracious host as we entered the hall. The majority of my men were still busy either looking after their animals or sharpening weapons. My own sword needed an edge. Gilles was busily turning the wheel to sharpen it. Even William Roumare was preparing for battle but the Earl had broached a jug and was in his cups already. I could see he was feeling sorry for himself. I sighed; it was like caring for a spoiled child. Before I could deal with him, I needed to speak with my knights. The three of them had been speaking with their prisoners. Edgar guarded the last, a squire, who looked to be no more than thirteen summers old. I recognised him as the squire who had surrendered to me.

"Edgar, arrange the sentries."

"Aye, lord."

"Dick, go and make sure the men eat and rest. I will speak with this young warrior." I saw the fear on his face despite his stiffened lip. He expected the worst.

"Where is the sword you promised me?" He pointed to it. My men had placed it in the corner. I picked it up to examine it. "What is your name?"

"I am Richard, sir. Richard son of Alfred. I was squire to Sir Ralph of Buxton. "You slew him, sir. I was an orphan and so I have no master." He looked up at me. "And there will be no ransom for me."

I liked that he did not beg. This boy had courage. "And what is your expectation?"

He continued to look at my face. "That you will either make me a slave or you will have me killed." He hesitated, "I would prefer to live, lord. Life as a slave would be hard but it would be life and that is better than the unknown which is death."

I balanced the sword in my hand and then tossed it and caught it. "Do you not believe in heaven, Richard?"

"Of course, lord, but, if it is all the same to you I would wait a while before seeing it."

I nodded, "There may be a third choice I could make but we will see. Firstly, you surrendered to me and gave me your sword." I flipped it over to hold it by the blade. "You know what that means?"

"That I am yours to do with as you please and I will not try to escape."

I flipped the sword back so that I held the hilt again. I nodded, "Good. Now I have a few questions, none of which will threaten your honour or your word. When you have answered them, I will make my judgement." He nodded and I saw hope enter his eyes. "Who commanded this conroi?"

"Sir Walter de Langeais, Sir Ralph's elder brother. You slew him, my lord."

"And who commanded him?"

"Baron William Peverel gave him his orders and I think the King was there too."

"Do you know what your lord was told of his task?" He hesitated, "Come boy, I am not asking for secrets. I need to know the purpose of your conroi for there was not a large number, was there?"

"We were told that we would be trapping a traitor; the wolf of the north! Sir Walter was promised a larger and richer manor than Buxton. My master was promised Buxton. We were to hold you." He paused, "We sent a rider to the Baron when we spied your column."

I nodded. It was as I had thought. They had expected us but how? I doubted that this youth would know much more. If Sir Ralph had been forced to use an orphan as a squire then he was not a rich knight nor an important one. I looked at the armour the boy wore. It was leather studded with a few pieces of iron. His sword was a short one and his horse was of poor quality. I flipped it again and held it by the tip once more.

My silence encouraged him to speak, "Are you the wolf of the north, lord?"

I looked at him and saw honesty in his face. "Some call me that."

"They say that you roast children on your sword and that you use the forces of darkness to win your battles!"

I laughed, "They are tales to frighten children. You saw me fight this day. What do you think?"

"I think you are a fierce warrior and it would take a brave man to stand against you. They also say that you were King Henry's champion."

"That I was. And it is why I still fight for his heirs. Now, young Richard, what to do with you." He stiffened his back as he prepared to hear my judgement. "You have two choices."

His eyes widened, "I have choices, lord?"

I nodded, "You can either choose to serve me for I need someone to help my squire or when we get to Chester I will let you go free."

"So I would live, my lord?"

I nodded, "Despite what people say of me, I do not make war on orphans. It is your choice, Richard. You are almost a man and can make your own decisions. I do not attach any conditions to my offer. You have given your word that you will not escape and I will hold you to that."

"Then I will become your man. I know not Chester and who knows what would become of me. At least this way I have life and you seem like a fair master, lord."

I handed him his sword. He grasped it as though it was Excalibur itself. "Good, then give me your hand we will seal the bond." I clasped his arm. "Now go and ask for Gilles, my squire. Tell him you are now my retainer. He will tell you about your duties. When he sees you have your sword, he will understand."

"Thank you, lord. I was frightened of you."

"As you should be but now you will serve me! Fear me no longer. Go, for I have others to see!"

Eventually, my three knights emerged with the other three prisoners. "Have they given their words?"

Harold nodded, "There will be a ransom for them." He looked around, "The one who was here will have no ransom."

"I have dealt with him."

I saw on the face of the surviving squire that he thought I had slain him. I smiled. He would think he was seeing a ghost soon. "I will speak to you when we have eaten. You all did well today."

The Earl of Chester seemed oblivious to the action around him. He ate and he drank as though we were safe. I knew that we were not. Our enemies would follow us and try to destroy me and my men. The Earl of Chester was a political animal. He would make arrangements. Everyone knew that the Warlord would not. I sat next to Sir John. I had fought alongside him when his sons were alive. We had been together in the army which had garnered over five thousand head of cattle from the Welsh. We spoke of those days together.

"Those were the days, my lord. King Henry and his son knew how to cow the Welsh. This King Stephen has lost all of the land which the Earl of Gloucester had gained. I have lived long enough. I grow weary of this life."

"Do not say that, old friend. The Empress and her son will need doughty warriors like yourself. Your arm can still wield a sword."

"Aye, but the saddle is not so easy these days. I fear the next battle shall be my last." He lowered his voice, "I wish you well in your endeavours on behalf of the Empress. I swore an oath to her father as did many others." He flashed a look at the Earl who was oblivious to it. "The breaking of the oath was almost as hurtful to me as the loss of my sons. I tell you now that I will oppose this King Stephen no matter which way my lord and master bends."

"Well, for now, he bends towards the Empress but tomorrow will see if that is to be. I fear that we will be attacked."

"And I am only sorry that there are but seven of us to die with you."

"Do not bury us yet. I have good warriors." I turned to Harold, "Well, what did you learn?"

"You were right, lord. It was William Peverel who betrayed us!"

The Earl roused himself, "I will pay him back!"

"Let us just get back safely to Chester and then we can make plans for our future. What else did you learn? Do we know who will be coming here?"

"The two knights both said it would be King Stephen for Prince Henry has returned to Scotland. He went to Lincoln first. They believe that the King ordered the knights of Lincoln to escort him back to Carlisle."

Sir John chuckled and looked twenty years younger. "The new king must think highly of the Scottish Prince. Lincoln controls the Great North Road. A man who controls that city and York controls England!"

The ghost of an idea came to my mind but I left it there. We had the problem of escaping this trap. When that was done, I would resurrect my thoughts. "Tomorrow we rise before dawn. My plan is to use most of my archers to make them bleed while they take the lower gate. We fall back to the keep and use the weapons from the armoury." I turned to the Earl, "When do you think your forces will reach us?"

"Tomorrow at noon would be the earliest." He smiled, "My wife can be very forceful when she wishes. She gets that from her father."

"Aye, the Earl of Gloucester knows his own mind."

Sir William said, "And it is rubbing off on my wife too. She has changed since meeting your wife."

I arranged with my three knights to share the night watch. I did not want to be surprised. It was a trick I had often used. The Earl seemed to think that such tasks were beneath him. I took the middle watch. I did not mind the broken sleep. It had been hard enough anyway. My mind was beset with all sorts of problems. How could I defend my castles against Stephen and fight for the Empress? Where would she land and would she be opposed? If the Earl was typical of those who might support her, how could we rely upon them?

I found Henry of Langdale and Cedric on watch. "How goes the night?"

"Quiet, my lord. The castle has a good aspect. You can see far to the east. These old castles do have the advantage that there is but one gate in."

Cedric grumbled, "Aye Henry, and but one out."

"You are a miserable old codger! When has an enemy got the better of the Earl? I do not think this will be my grave." Suddenly he stopped and peered east. "Lord, I saw a movement."

I whistled and Gilles appeared. He was sharing the watch with me. He had younger eyes than either Cedric or me. I pointed, "What do you see?"

He looked for a moment and said, "Horsemen. They are leading their horses from the woods."

"That would be a mile away. Go, Henry, wake the garrison and have them stand to arms but do it silently. I want no noise to alert them. I want every man hidden beneath the ramparts."

"Aye, lord!"

My enemies were trying the same ruse as me. The question was, would we be able to deal with it? I had a short time to plan.

Chapter 13

Gilles having identified our enemies, it became much easier to see them. There were many of them. Their numbers were hard to ascertain as they were mere shadows. There were men on foot as well as horses. They came steadily down the slope. Dick and my knights were the first to reach me. They had done as I asked and kept below the ramparts. "They are coming from the east. Spread yourselves out along the ramparts." I looked and saw Sir John climbing the steps. "Where is the Earl and Sir William?"

Harold snorted, "He took some rousing. Dick told him to guard the keep and the prisoners."

I nodded and noticed Richard was there. He was unarmed, "Gilles, find a shield for Richard. We cannot have my new retainer being slain because he was unarmed."

"Aye, lord."

"You two stay with me and fetch my banner. If the sun rises on us this day, we will show our enemies that we do not fear them."

When I looked back, I could make the enemy out a little clearer. They were less than two hundred yards away. "Lord, they are mounting."

"Thank you, Cedric. Pass the word for the archers to be ready but wait for my command."

Henry of Langdale said, "Lord, there are men with axes running towards the gate."

We had placed spears by the ramparts the night before. They were in plentiful supply. "Use the spears."

The three of us hefted a spear each. I said to Sir John, "It is your castle feel free to join us."

I saw that his men were not in the keep but had joined him on the ramparts. "Couldn't leave you alone, lord, although we have annoyed the Earl by leaving him all alone in the keep."

They were truly oathsworn.

He shook his head at my offer of a spear. "A sword will suffice. I will leave the throwing of spears to you young men. My men and I will use our swords as we always did. A sword is the weapon of a man."

I nodded, "Ready?" My two men at arms nodded. "Archers, now!" I hurled my spear and struck the man at arms who was crossing the ditch. I struck him between his shoulder and his head. He spiralled into the ditch. My two men at arms slew two more. Arrows began to pluck the men with axes from the track down which they ran. My archers were aiming at shadows but they struck flesh. I picked up another throwing spear and hit a knight who was urging on his men. It struck him in the knee and as he fell on the ground an arrow ended his cries for help.

Someone amongst our enemies took charge and the next men at arms who advanced came under the cover of their shields. None of us had targets. The gate would not hold out for long. "Sir John, come and join me. Gilles, Richard, I want you behind me. Cedric, you are in command. When the gate is breached run back to the keep."

"Aye, lord."

As we stood twenty feet from the gate, I heard footsteps coming down the steps from the ramparts. The knight's six retainers had left the wall to join us. They placed themselves on either side of Sir John and me with Gilles and Richard standing behind guarding the standard. We were ready.

Sir John said, "This is fitting. This will be the end of all things and I could not wish for better company. King Henry's champion and my oathsworn."

I heard the axes as they smashed against the gate. It was well made but it would not last long. I shouted, "Prepare to retire to the keep!"

I heard a ripple of replies. None of my men was foolish enough to try to be a hero. They knew I did not approve of such acts. We fought together and my men obeyed orders. I saw the flash of an axe. They were almost through. "Retire!"

The sound of footsteps thundering down the wooden walls drowned out the noise of the axes. Two axes sheared the bar holding the gate and the knights and men at arms burst in. I held a spear still and I hurled it at the huge knight wielding the axe. It struck him in his chest and he fell to the ground. Not dead, he was out of the fray. I drew my sword and shouted. "The Empress and Henry Fitz Empress!"

The eight of us were a solid line and our enemy came at us piecemeal. Sir John may have been aged but he had not lost any of his skills. He took the blow from the sword on his shield and then jabbed with his own, ancient weapon towards the eye of the man at arms. It takes a brave man to keep his eyes open and the man at arms closed them as the sword entered his skull. I brought my sword over as I blocked a sword strike and struck the knight before me in the middle of his helmet. My sword was sharp and my arm was strong. It split the helmet and the skull.

I saw more men entering the shattered gate. "Fall back but keep the line."

The experience of the old knight and his ancient warriors showed as they moved back alongside me. We were just slowing up the enemy to give my men the chance to reach the keep. Once they did so then their bows would wreak havoc on the enemy. Inevitably, it was the man at arms on the extreme right who fell. Two men came at him on his sword side and his reactions were not quick enough. He died. The man next to him was then assaulted by three and he was struck by an axe and a sword; he died quickly.

"Wheel right!" It was a hard manoeuvre but it swung the end man at arms further from danger.

An enemy man at arms took advantage of my distraction and moved towards me. I barely blocked the blow but a short sword darted out and Richard slashed the thigh of the man at arms. "Thank you, Richard! First blood." The enemy were reforming for another attack. "How far, Gilles?"

"Forty paces, my lord."

"Are the others safe?"

"Aye, my lord!"

"Run! We will stop them at the gate."

As we prepared to run, a spear was thrust into the side of Sir John. His men at arms slew the killer but I could see that the knight was badly hurt. I moved towards him. He shouted,

"No, Earl! Save yourself and the young warriors." He raised his sword to me in salute. "It has been a privilege to serve with an old-fashioned warrior! King Henry's Champion! My friends, let us go out in a blaze of glory!"

The four of them hurled themselves at the men at arms who climbed the hill to get to them. I could hardly tear my eyes away from such a brave gesture. Gilles grabbed my arm, "Come, my lord, or their gesture will be worthless!" We ran up the slope to the gate which was still open.

As we entered the gate, I saw the last of the retainers slain around his lord. The men of Stephen and Peverel had killed all six. The old man was happy and his retainers had been oathsworn to the end.

As I stepped through, Edgar said, "It was a good death, lord. Let them come now and I will show them that we too know the meaning of loyalty!"

The gate was slammed shut. Unlike the lower gate, this one had extra beams laid across it. I ran to the gatehouse. Already my archers were carefully picking off the enemy. They were conserving their arrows for we had few. The Earl and his brother were looking fearful. I shook my head, "A brave man lies dead before these walls. Stir yourself, Earl, or you will lose your life as well as your land. We fight this day and we fight together!"

The men who heard me shouted and banged their swords against their shields. My men were a throwback to an earlier time when honour and loyalty meant more than coin and reward. I was lucky and I knew it. He picked up his sword and his shield and joined me.

I reached the centre of the gate. Dick and Harold were there. "I have sent John to the east tower and Tristan to the west. We have alternated archers and men at arms. We are down to ten arrows each."

"Well done, Dick! This is not over yet!"

I hefted my shield around as I saw the crossbowmen begin to loose their bolts. My archers hated crossbows and crossbowmen. The ten the enemy had brought all died. I looked to see who was leading this conroi. It was not Stephen the Usurper. It was Baldwin Fitz Gilbert. I had met him before. He was a ruthless man. It did not matter for we were all warriors. We would ask no quarter and, certainly, we would not give any.

I turned to Dick. "How many do you estimate?"

"Until the dawn breaks, it will be a guess but I have counted at least eighty. Of course, forty warriors lie dead and they will be feeling a little more nervous about the assault. Even the old man had teeth enough to bite. They will not relish taking you on, my lord."

"We must keep them from the gate. I have no doubt that they can use shields to scale the walls but we can deal with that. We have spears aplenty!"

Baldwin Fitz Gilbert halted his attack. We were going nowhere. The only gate out was the one on which I stood. He had no crossbows and no archers. It would be down to brute force to gain access. For my part, we had to buy time. If Maud, daughter of the Earl of Gloucester, had aught to do with it then she would be moving heaven and earth to reach us.

I saw the first thin line of light in the east as the sun began to rise. Baldwin Fitz Gilbert had made up his mind. He formed his men at arms into an old-fashioned wedge and they moved towards the gate. There was no drawbridge but the bridge into the castle would only accommodate six men abreast. They had a wall of shields before them. Arrows would be useless and Dick ordered his men to save them for softer targets. Sir John had been old fashioned enough to have piles of stones along the wall. We picked them up and hurled them down onto the advancing mailed men. A sharp arrow can fail to penetrate a mail hauberk. But a stone dropped from a height can crush a skull even if it is protected by a helmet.

The men who did not throw a stone hurled a javelin or a spear and, at thirty paces distance, they caused mortal wounds. The first attack fell back leaving ten wounded and dead men. There was another debate and more orders were issued. The sun began to peer over the eastern hills. Each moment of daylight brought us hope. "Gilles, Richard, fetch ale for the men and see if there is any food left from last night."

This was partly to keep up my men's strength and partly to keep my two young warriors occupied. Waiting was harder than fighting. They raced around the ramparts with food and the last of Sir John's ale. It filled a hole, as Wulfric was wont to say. By the time the sun was above the hills, they had decided upon their plan. They attacked simultaneously all along the wall. They wanted to divide our efforts. I turned to Gilles and Richard. "Stand either side of me and keep hurling spears and stones. If you see a finger on the wall then cut it off. If you see a face then ram your dagger into it!

"Aye, lord!"

My archers used the last of their precious arrows on the lightly armed men who approached the walls. They were not the main threat but an arrow aimed at mail was a wasted arrow. When their missiles were gone, they drew their swords. The enemy had not had time to build ladders and they were using shields to raise men to the ramparts to fight us. We had done so ourselves and the walls were not high. The knight who was raised close to me had an axe which he swung as soon as he was in range. It was the wrong weapon. The momentum took the blade harmlessly across my face and I darted forward with my sword. It tore into his eye and I twisted as I pulled it out. He fell screaming onto the men below. Gilles and Richard hurled a rock and a spear to injure two more of their men.

The next attack saw two men raised. I could only fight one but Gilles and Richard worked together. They both jabbed at the two men with their spears. They were safe from the enemy swords and the distraction allowed me to sweep my sword across the throat of one of the men. The dark blood spurted and he seemed to almost choke on his own blood before falling to the ground. The second man had to fend off two spears and my sword. He could not block all of them and Gilles' spear rammed into his eye. He too joined his comrade in the ditch; dead.

We had had success all the way down the line and the enemy withdrew. More of their men had fallen but they still outnumbered us and I had no doubt that reinforcements were heading this way. It would be a race to see who reached us: Maud or the enemy! This latest attack, however, had cost us men. I saw, in the inner bailey, men being tended to by the servants of Sir John. Our supply of spears was exhausted. Sooner or later, if they were determined, they would breach the walls.

As they gathered for another attack, I wondered what else I could do. Then, from the north, I heard a horn and a cheer from the enemy. Maud, it appeared, had lost the race. If there were warriors to the north then they were the enemy. Baldwin Fitz Gilbert certainly thought so for he began to cheer and organise his men for another attack. It was only when Gilles spied the banners of Chester and of Gwynedd that we knew it was Maud, the wife of the Earl of Chester. She had shown skills of which Caesar himself would have been proud. She had confused our enemy and used a clever ruse to get close.

"Men at arms, to the gates! Relief is at hand! Archers, hold them on the walls!" I rushed down the ladder to the bailey. Two of my men took away the two bars which held the gates in place. The forces of Baldwin Fitz Gilbert had heard the trumpet and our sudden appearance discomfited them. We rushed directly at them. Baldwin must have realised that the relief force was not his own for he shouted for his horse. As I blocked a blow from a man at arms, I dropped to one knee and rammed my sword upwards into his middle. His body tumbled over my shoulder. As I stood, I saw Baldwin and five knights mount their horses and gallop out of the gate.

Leaderless the men at arms threw down their swords and asked for mercy. The four remaining knights looked ready to continue fighting. I took off my helmet and pointed to the body of Sir John and his retainers. "Do you really wish to die? Your leader has fled and there has been enough death here this day!"

The sound of the hooves of the relief force drew closer and the leader of the knights said. "We yield and ask for ransom!"

I put my shield in my scabbard as the Earl's wife, Maud, led in the Earl's men and a contingent of Welsh led by Cadwaladr ap Gruffyd, the brother of the Welsh King. Maud galloped directly up to me. She saw the body, draped in a cloak, and said, fearfully, "Is that my husband? Am I too late?"

I shook my head, "Your husband and his brother are in the keep. He is safe. Thank you for your timely arrival." She was too worried about her husband and she galloped off to the keep.

Cadwaladr dismounted and took off his helmet. He smiled, "The last time I saw you, Earl, you were chasing us from the battlefield. Things have changed for now we fight on the same side."

I laughed, "You are right, for war makes strange bedfellows. Tell me, why did you approach from the north?"

He shook his head, "The Earl's wife is a shrewd one. She said that the road from the west passed through a wood and we could be ambushed. She said the north road was a better one and she was right. We made as good a time and we arrived without hindrance."

"She is a force to be reckoned with. The blood of the Conqueror runs through her veins." I turned to my knights and men at arms. "Come, let us bury this brave knight and his oathsworn and do them honour. Then we will look to ourselves."

There was a small chapel next to the keep. I saw a grave there and assumed it was his wife. There was, as yet, no stone. I would find a stonemason and have one carved. We dug the seven graves and laid the seven men in them with their arms and covered them with stones and then earth. I was no priest and there was none nearby and so I gave them a warrior's farewell.

"Lord, take these seven heroes and welcome them into heaven. They died on the side of right, they kept their oath and they died with honour. Give them peace for they have earned it." I allowed a few moments' silence and then said quietly. "You were a throwback to an earlier time, Sir John, and I am glad that I met you."

We went into the keep where Maud had organised Sir John's servants and they had prepared the last of the food. She threw her arms around me in a most unexpected manner. "My father always said that you were his rock and he could rely on you to hold against the greatest of odds. You have saved my husband and brother in law. I am in your debt."

I said quietly, "Your husband, my lady, is too reckless."

She nodded, "I know and he needs me. I shall stay by his side for a while. I have sent for food. We will fortify this castle. We have retreated before this Stephen long enough. Now we take back. I will persuade my husband to besiege Glossop. This Peverel needs punishing. He has behaved without honour."

The force of nature that was Maud of Gloucester organised the whole of the forces available to the Earl. I felt that we could return to Stockton, for the Empress had still to land in England and the Earl was now on the Empress' side. I decided to wait until the Earl had committed to the capture of Glossop before we returned north. The ransoms for our prisoners were paid promptly. Despite the fact that he had done little to earn the money, honour demanded that the Earl and William received their share. I gave most of my share to my men at arms and archers. I knew I would have had nothing without them.

Young Richard got on well with Gilles. Once his initial shyness and fear of me wore off, he began to ask me questions. "My lord, why did you not keep all of the ransom? You are Earl and it was yours by right."

"True, William, but I only have that right because of the men who fight for me. Besides, I have coin enough in my castle vaults. I do not fight for what I can make. If I wanted riches then I would fight for Stephen the Usurper."

"I am glad you did not kill me. I would like to follow you."

I smiled at the honesty of his words. "We shall see how far that service takes you. I have need of another squire. If you impress me then that may be you."

He looked at me so earnestly that Gilles had to hide his smile, "I swear that I will be the most diligent and hardworking of all of your men, my lord!"

It was May when we set off to besiege Glossop. It was the strangest army with which I had travelled. The Earl and his half brother had their wives with them and there were servants and other followers. I was used to being surrounded by warriors only. This time the Earl listened to my words and advice. He did not assault the castle with all of his men as he had planned. We surrounded it and made sure that nothing got in or out. It fell within the week and we took great quantities of arms, hauberks and ransom.

It was as we were eating one night, just the Earl and his brother, their wives and me, that the Earl came up with an idea. "You have inspired me, Aelfraed."

"Have I, my lord?"

"You and my wife. You have both demonstrated that subtlety and cunning can achieve more than a force of arms."

"Sometimes."

"You are right, Aelfraed, sometimes. I have a plan to take Lincoln Castle without losing a man."

He had even me interested now. "Lincoln Castle? It controls the heart of England and Stephen would have it well defended."

"Normally he would but I have learned from the garrison here that some of the garrison soldiers of Lincoln are still with Prince Henry in Scotland and there is just a small garrison commanded by the constable."

His half brother said, "Even so, brother, it is still one of the most powerful castles in England. How would we gain entry?"

"Through our wives. Hawise, is not your cousin, Agnes, the wife of the constable?"

His sister in law said, "She is but I have not seen her for some time."

"I have heard that she had a son six months since. It would seem a timely opportunity for you to visit. If, after a few days, three knights were sent by your husband to fetch you home it would not arouse any suspicion, would it? The three knights would be us, in disguise, of course. Once inside we could capture the gates and the castle would be ours. Your men could wait by the river and the castle would be taken."

I was dubious. There are many 'ifs' in there. However, it was the ghost of an idea which I had had myself. I disliked using women to such an end. "William and you would be putting your wife and Lady Hawise at risk."

Maud of Gloucester put her hand on mine, "I do not think there is a risk. We are women and the Constable will not be suspicious." She looked at Lady Hawise, "Are you willing?"

"Of course. It is exciting and I crave such excitement."

I shook my head, "Is there madness in the air? Tell me, Earl, who would go with the ladies?"

"They would have to be your men. I thought your two squires for they showed great courage at Merpel and perhaps your two older men at arms, Edgar and Raymond of Le Mans."

"My men?"

"Do not forget, Aelfraed, that I lost the men I would have sent when I recklessly pursued the Prince. I have paid the price. And to be honest, your men are the best I have ever seen. I know that I would be more confident with four of your men watching over our wives than any other. They are loyal and, more importantly, they are good at this sort of thing. Did you not capture Durham with such men?"

I could not argue with that. "I will ask them, Ranulf. I will not send my men into such danger without giving them the chance to back out."

"I do not understand that but they are your men. Ask them now for we must strike while the garrison is depleted. If we leave then we leave tomorrow."

"Whom will we take?"

"It will have to be your conroi for I want the world to think that I remain here. My new squire will parade in my

hauberk and we will leave my standard here at Glossop.
Cadwaladr can command in my absence."

"You have thought all this through then?"

"You did not think that when we waited to take Glossop
my mind was idle, did you? You are right about my nature,
Aelfraed, it is restless and I put that restlessness to good use.
We will keep this secret. I have learned my lesson and my
tongue will no longer be so loose. William Peverel was a
harsh lesson to learn for it cost me good men!"

"Then if you are determined, I will speak with my men."

I went to find my knights and the four men and boys who
would be used for the ruse. I explained what it would entail
and asked, "Well? Shall I tell the Earl that you will have
none of this foolish and madcap idea?"

Edgar smiled, "To be honest, my lord, I thought that this
was one of your ideas. It sounds like one to me. Besides, I
like the Lady Maud; she has courage and if she is willing to
go into this lion's den then I would be honoured to protect
her."

Raymond said, "And I agree. I cannot wait to tell Wulfric
what he missed. He will be madder than a shaken wasp's
nest!"

I looked at Gilles and Richard, "And you two?" Their
faces gave me the answer and I shook my head, "I blame
myself for all this madness. You need to shed my livery.
Find livery from the garrison here. As escorts to Lady
Hawise, you will need to be well-armed. That will be
expected." They nodded. I turned to my knights. "We ride
tomorrow but this will be a secret. The Earl will not tell
others what we are about. Tell the men to spread the word
that we return to Stockton. I do not think there are spies here
but if there are then this will put them off our trail."

Chapter 14

It was a two-day ride to Lincoln. My men could have made it in one but we had ladies with us and they were riding as though at their leisure. We kept them in sight but they appeared to be travelling alone. They spent the night at Sheffield. In those days, it was still a motte and bailey built of wood and the lord of the manor and his wife were honoured to be offering hospitality to two such honoured guests. We slept in the fields.

We parted with the ladies and their escort a mile and a half from the castle which we saw on the hill. There was a wood to the south and west of the large area of common land used by the town to graze cattle. It was a good place for us to wait.

We had a whole day and a night to wait and to worry. I did not fear for the ladies. Chivalry demanded that they be treated well but my men were a different matter. When we approached the castle the next day, would we see their heads atop the gate? As much as I wanted to get there as early as possible, we had to make our arrival as plausible as possible. We would arrive towards dusk. That would allow Dick, my knights and my men to close with the gate and await my signal. We wore the cloaks we had taken from Glossop. I left my shield with my men and took a plain one. We headed towards the gate before it was closed for sunset.

When we reached the gate, we allowed Sir William to do the talking. He was the eldest of us and his greybeard made him seem less threatening somehow.

"What is your business, my lords?"

There were just two guards at the gate and had we wanted to we could have disposed of them easily but this was a well-made castle. There were four more sentries in the two towers above the gate. There would be more sentries on the walls. We had to be subtle. I saw that all of the guards wore the royal livery. This was a royal castle. The Constable was a royal appointee. Stephen had appointed Eustace de Aumale to the castle.

"We have been sent by William Roumare to escort his wife home. She is visiting here with the wife of the Constable."

"Just three of you?"

"We are enough, believe me."

The Sergeant at Arms said, "I would want a bigger escort, my lord. We have heard that the Wolf of the North is loose in these parts. There are rumours that he is sacking castles to the west of us. He has taken Glossop and Buxton or so the story goes."

"We saw him not but thank you for your concern." William spurred his horse through the gate. I was not certain we had been given permission but they did not try to stop us. We were in. The hardest part of our plan had succeeded. When we entered the outer bailey, we dismounted. The two guards there directed us to the stable. The two stable boys unsaddled our horses and we headed for the gate leading to the inner bailey. As we did I saw, by the burning braziers, that there were just ten sentries on the outer walls. We had decided that we had two tasks: take the armoury and inner bailey and then secure the gate.

As we approached the gate at the inner bailey, there were just two guards. We strolled towards them and as we did so we heard the watch announce that the gates were closed. The two men crossed their spears. "I am sorry, my lords, but the watch has sounded the closure of the gates. You will have to spend the night in the barracks yonder. There is a kitchen there and beds aplenty." He pointed to a stone building attached to the outer wall. Darkness had now fallen and only the lights from the braziers showed where men stood. In the recesses of the inner gate, we were hidden from view.

I moved to the left of the Earl as William said, reasonably, "We need to tell my Lady Hawise and Lady Maud that their escorts are here to take them home."

The guard turned, "Alan, go tell the Constable that the escorts for the ladies are here and they will spend the night in the barracks."

As Alan turned, I grabbed the other sentry and hit his head against the stone wall of the gate. He slumped to the ground, unconscious. The Earl had his dagger at Alan's throat. "One word and you die!"

I had short lengths of rope concealed about me and I trussed up the unconscious guard and handed some to William to do the same to the second. The Earl said, "We will not gag you but if you raise the alarm then I will kill you." The man looked defiantly at the Earl who smiled as he said, "This the Wolf of the North, the Earl of Cleveland!"

The man shrank back in terror. "I will say nothing. Spare me, my lord!"

"Then remain silent!" I hissed at him.

We finished tying them up and entered the inner bailey. We had little time to delay. We hurried to the Great Hall in the keep for that would be where we would find the Constable. As we entered the keep, Edgar and Raymond of Le Mans appeared. Edgar got directly to business, "There are just six guards in the keep along with the Constable. The two squires are with the ladies and acting as page boys. Two of the guards are at the armoury. The other four are on the battlements."

"Then that is where we will go. Earl, go with your brother to the Great Hall. Hold the Constable. We will deal with the other guards."

Drawing my sword, I followed Edgar down a corridor to a chamber at the rear of the keep. I heard the two guards. They were playing dice. Edgar and I stepped into the antechamber and our swords were at their throats before they even knew we were there. "No heroics! The castle is taken!" They might have thought of resisting had not Raymond of Le Mans appeared. "Tie them up and meet me at the Great Hall. Raymond, you guard the armoury."

I guessed that the other four sentries would be on duty on the battlements. We needed to eliminate them first. When I reached the Great Hall, the Constable was being tied up by Ranulf. Maud smiled when she saw me, "I knew you would succeed, Earl."

The Constable suddenly recognised me, "The Warlord of the North! God save us! We were told you were dead."

"Many men have said that and yet I still walk this earth." Turning to the Earl I said, "We have the armoury." Edgar appeared, "Now we shall secure the keep and I will let my men in. Come, Gilles and Richard, we need you."

The advantage we held was that the sentries were keeping watch beyond the keep. They were looking out to the town and the lands around the castle. There were others charged with securing the entrance. They would not be suspicious of someone coming from below. I used Gilles to peer around the corner of the door to the battlements. He pointed to the right and held up one finger and then did the same for the left. I pointed right to Edgar and Gilles and I tapped Richard on the shoulder. We went left. The guard was leaning out looking down at the ground. The first he knew of my presence was when my sword pricked his neck. I put my finger to my lips. He nodded. Richard took the man's sword and tied his hands behind his back before securing his feet.

There were two sentries left. We moved towards the one nearest us. As luck would have it, he was using the garderobe. A man with his breeks around his ankles does not resist. We let him finish his business before trussing him up. Edgar and Gilles had taken the other. With the keep secured, I led Edgar to the main gate. The guards were still tied up although I could see that they had tried to escape their bonds. One of them shrank back as I approached! He was terrified of what I might do. We undid the door and using the torch which burned in the guardhouse signalled for our men. They were less than a mile away but, even so, it took some time for them to reach us. As they neared the gate, I heard the alarm shouted from the outer walls. There were still four sentries who had not been captured. It mattered not, for the hooves of my knights' horses were clattering over the drawbridge.

Dick looked relieved to see me. "The Earl was right then? We pulled it off."

"Aye, there are four guards still at large. Have them taken and tied up."

"What do we do then?"

"I am not certain but we have the castle and we will not relinquish it without a fight!"

By the time dawn broke, the Earl, or rather his wife had made the decision about the garrison. She was practical. She knew we had not enough men to hold them and would not countenance murder. We disarmed them and let them go. The Constable and his wife were kept as hostages. It was as simple as that. The castle was strong enough to be held by my men. William, escorted by four of my men returned to Glossop, to fetch the Earl of Chester's men. Once they arrived then our work was done.

We took our share of the treasures of Lincoln. There were many fine weapons. We found a hauberk for Richard and a better one for Gilles. The Constable had a brand new mail hauberk which the Earl appropriated. I know not how but the smith had managed to make it shine like silver. For me, it was too bright. We also found and took four warhorses. Dick did not have one yet neither did Gilles. Although he and Richard were just squires, one day they would need a warhorse. The treasury was divided between the Earl and me. I shared my half with my men, equally, and he gave a quarter to his brother.

I was happier when, four days after we had taken it, the Earl's men arrived to take over the duties of the garrison. The Bishop of Lincoln had visited with us. Maud was superb, she won over the cleric using her father's name and the peaceful manner in which the castle had been taken. I do not think we could have taken the castle without her presence. It was from the Bishop that we learned that the Empress and the Earl of Gloucester had landed in England. We discovered that the Empress was being besieged in Arundel Castle. It was the home of Queen Adeliza, the widow of King Henry.

That news helped me make up my mind. "I must go to the aid of the Empress."

Neither the Earl nor his wife was happy about that. "Aelfraed, it is an almost impossible journey. You have to travel through Stephen's territory. The enemy will know you are abroad and every man will hunt you."

"I have waited four years for the chance to fight alongside the Empress and your father, my lady. Any who try to stop us had best bring a large army!"

She nodded, "I cannot stand in your way, my lord, but I shall miss you. Your coming was as the start of an avalanche. We are gathering speed and soon my father and his sister will have recovered what Stephen has stolen."

We had plenty of spare horses, courtesy of the garrison. We were well supplied with food, arms and arrows. Our only problem was the almost two hundred miles of hostile territory we had to travel. We took a western route to avoid London. London was loyal to Stephen. The further west we went the more chance we had of meeting allies. What we would not do was seek hospitality anywhere. I wanted to be invisible. We would not use the Great North Road but smaller side roads. It would be just as quick for my small company. There were less than thirty of us. I left my servants with Maud in Lincoln. It was not fair to risk them. We would fend for ourselves.

It was unknown land for us all. Ralph of Wales led my scouts. They did not range far ahead, just a mile or so. We managed to reach Burton before we were spotted. We had made almost seventy miles unseen. It was unfortunate for we were ready to camp but the handful of hunters who spied us headed back to the castle we could see in the distance and that determined our action. We headed further west. We rode for ten more miles and were then forced to halt. We found a clearing in a wood. Our horses were in no shape to move on.

We had just lit our fires and were cooking the game which my archers had caught when our outlying sentries galloped in. "My lord. Men at arms and a knight. They are hard behind us!"

"Stand to! Arm yourselves!"

I drew my sword. There was little point in running, even if it had been possible. The knight, his squire and twenty men at arms rode in. He wore no helmet. Had we wished we could have slain them with arrows but I respected the gesture of peace.

The knight dismounted and held out his hand, "You are Aelfraed, Earl of Cleveland and King Henry's Champion."

I nodded, "Do I know you?"

"We have never met but I have heard of you. When my hunters reported your livery then I knew who it was. I am Alan de Dinant, Baron of Burton."

I recognised his name then, "You are the knight who defeated the champion of the French King at Gizors."

He nodded, "King Henry gave me the manor as a reward. Come, you shall stay with me this night."

I shook my head, "Our horses can go no further. We have ridden eighty miles this day."

"That is quite a feat and yet you were willing to fight me with exhausted men."

I pointed to the woods and whistled. My archers emerged, "Not quite."

He laughed, "Your reputation is deserved."

"Tell me, whose side are you on?"

"As I was not a baron when the King made you all swear an oath to the Empress, I am not honour bound to support either contender. I serve myself. England and Normandy are not well served by Civil War. I look to my own lands."

"Then you are lucky for I swore the oath twice and I must restore the Empress and her line to the throne."

"Then I wish you well. Fear not, my men will not tell any that they saw you but I would keep away from Northampton. It is filled with the supporters of Stephen. Wallingford Castle is held by Fitz Count, Lord of Burgavennu. He supports the Empress. There you would find an ally."

"Thank you. Farewell."

"Farewell and may God be with you."

After hearing the news from the Baron, I decided to leave early and head for Wallingford Castle. I had been trying to work out how to cross the Thames. The only fords were well to the west, Wallingford would afford us the opportunity to be safe while we crossed. Once again, we made our way through the small twisting lanes and tracks used by locals. We were spotted more frequently but our numbers prevented any from interfering with us and we now moved quickly for Wallingford was close.

We were close to Brill when we hit trouble. There was a castle nearby; it had been a palace in Saxon times and Stephen must have fortified it for there were banners hung from its walls. Although we skirted it, I fear we were seen for we heard a horn sound. I knew that we were close to the River Thames. It was perhaps ten or fifteen miles away. I took a chance. "Let us outrun them. Dick, order the archers to guard the rear. Sir Harold, take the squires and find the river!"

I did not know this area at all and we were now relying on the sun to guide us. We had to keep heading south. We could not afford the luxury of reading the occasional signpost. There had been few enough of them anyway. After a couple of miles of the chase, Rafe caught up with us, "Lord, there are twenty or so men following. They are gaining on us."

"In that case bring your men through us. Ride ahead and we will ambush them. You and the archers choose the spot."

"Aye, lord."

The archers were lighter than we were and their horses could go faster. Unlike many lords, I made sure my archers had the same horses as my men at arms. We would reap the reward this day. Soon the archers came through us. The last one, Ralph of Wales, said, "They are whipping their horses, lord! They will surely kill them!"

"We will lead them to your ambush." When they had passed me I said, "Draw your weapons and prepare to turn and charge them. When I give the word, flee and we will draw them to our ambush."

In situations like this, the worst thing that a leader could do was to panic.

Alan son of Alan was at the rear and he shouted, "Lord, they are forty paces from me."

I turned and saw that they were gaining on us but their horses were lathered. "Turn and charge them!"

My men were prepared and the column split in two as we wheeled around. Suddenly they found themselves being charged. They did not expect it. I rode directly at their leader, a knight. Rolf was galloping hard and he was very responsive. I feinted to go shield side of the knight and as he tried to turn his weary horse, I pulled Rolf to the right. Standing in my stirrups I brought my sword across the knight's neck. He tumbled to the right pulling his horse down with him. The next two riders next to him were thrown from their horses. Dick had slain a man at arms and I shouted, "Fall back!"

I continued my wheel and galloped up the road to our waiting archers. The fallen horses delayed them and they dropped back to sixty paces behind us. I saw trees ahead and knew it would be a good ambush site. I glimpsed my men hiding there. As I passed Ralph, he gave a whistle. I rode forty paces and shouted, "Turn and face them!"

I wanted their attention to us. Angered at the loss of the knight and three men, they came hard towards me. They passed the ambush without even knowing it was there. My archers released at less than twenty paces. No one can survive that. The first twelve all died and the ones at the rear, seeing their comrades slain turned tail and headed back to their castle. Their departure meant we had time to rest. We collected the horses, hauberks and arms as well as the few coins they had with them and then headed for the river and Harold. When we reached the three of them, they were with ten men at arms. I recognised the livery of Sir Brian Fitz Count. We had reached friends and we would sleep safely that night.

Our greeting and our welcome were as warm as I could remember. The Baron had been holding out for as long as I had. The difference was that he had been assailed many times by the forces of Stephen the Usurper. He had, however, a strong castle and a fine position. He was the most westerly of the Empress' supporters. He guarded a valuable crossing of the Thames.

He threw his arms around me when I dismounted. He was a huge bear of a man. "I have longed to meet you, Earl. This is an honour. We face enemies here but you face Stephen and the Scots as well. You have a reputation as a doughty fighter."

"And it is good to meet someone else who did not bend the knee to this Count of Blois! I have much to tell you and much to ask too."

"We will eat first."

Edgar said, "Lord, is there a healer?"

"Someone is hurt?"

"Stephen the Grim and Oswald suffered wounds."

I was annoyed with myself for failing to check on my men. The Baron said, "Aye, Father John in the chapel. He is a good man with a needle!" I must have hesitated for the Baron put his huge arm around me and said, "Come, let the priest do what he must. You can do nothing by worrying and we have much to speak of."

I went, reluctantly, with him. He was a man of prodigious appetite and he could both talk and eat, Poor Tristan who faced him spent the entire time wiping morsels of food from his face. When I told him of the attack he nodded, "Stephen fortified the old palace at Brill and he uses it as a base for a column of men at arms who prey on any who try to cross the Thames. You did well to emerge with your lives."

"We handled them roughly and I think that other travellers will be safe for a while." He nodded. "What news of the Empress?"

"She is still in Arundel and Stephen prosecutes the siege. I think if the King's widow was not in the castle, he might have tried harder. It is, however, a powerful castle. It will not be easy for him to take it."

"And the Earl of Gloucester?"

"He is in Bristol. The Empress needs to be reunited with him."

"How many men do you have, Baron?"

"A sound garrison but not enough to relieve the siege."

"I was not thinking that but we are the foremost thorns in Stephen's side. If we took our conroi towards Arundel with banners and standards, he might think we led an army that would relieve the siege. You are surrounded by enemies here. It would not take much to spread the rumour that the

Baron of Wallingford and the Earl of Cleveland have raised an army to rescue the Empress. If it failed we could retreat back to your castle. It is but fifty miles. We could be there in half a day."

"By God but you are a man after my own heart! Are your men fit to travel?"

"Aye, but our horses will need a day or two to recover. We rode them hard."

"Then we will leave the day after the morrow. That will give us time to spread the rumours. It will be good to see our banners together. The Usurper will shit himself!"

Even without our deception, word would have spread that I had reached Wallingford. My banner was flown from the tower and my men strode around with their distinctive liveries. They were free with their words and spoke of rescuing the Empress. After speaking with the Baron, I had discovered that Stephen had had to spread his forces thinly. He would find it hard to keep up the siege and send a force to defeat us. I began to believe that our presence alone might raise the siege.

When we left we used the main roads. We did not want to be hidden. The Baron left plenty of men to guard his castle and when we rode we took the horses we had captured and spread them around the column as spares. That and the fact that we rode with more distance between us than was normal meant that observers saw a huge army snaking its way south. Ralph of Wales and my archers rode ahead of us to ensure that any prying eyes were too far away to count men. They just measured the distance on the road which we occupied.

We had reached the tiny manor of Lurgashall when we met our first opposition. We were thirteen miles from Arundel but, more importantly, we had passed the crossroads with the London Road from Arundel. We had cut the Usurper's lines of communication with his heartland and his supporters. Crossbowmen used the manor to try to ambush us. Our archers sprung the trap and Edgar and his men flushed them out and slew them but two riders escaped and headed south. That did not worry me. We wanted Stephen to know we were coming.

We entered the manor house. We had been ready to rest our horses for the final push and this seemed as appropriate a place as any. The lord of the manor and his family had fled but conveniently left food cooking. We ate a hot meal. I summoned Dick, "Send a couple of scouts south. Let us see what is ahead."

The Baron was in a much better humour with food in his stomach. "There is nothing which tastes finer than a meal taken from another! This venture has proved interesting, Earl. I had thought that we would have met opposition on this road before now."

"Stephen is now beset on all sides. The Bishop of Ely is stirring up unrest in the east. The Earl of Chester and his Welsh allies have Lincoln and much of the land to the west. With the Earl of Gloucester in Bristol, the Usurper knows not where to go."

"Think you that the tide has turned?"

I shook my head, "It has taken four years to subdue Normandy and we both know that Stephen has bought many of the barons. They may have no honour but they will fight to hold on to the lands and titles which the Usurper has given. My unborn grandchild may be married before this war is over."

"That is cold comfort, my lord. I would have expected more optimism from you. The world knows that you are the most loyal supporter of the Empress just as you were of her father."

"I have seen too much betrayal for optimism. We have a Bishop of Durham who watches and waits. Even the Earl of Gloucester's son in law was on the side of the Usurper until Stephen gave away the Earl's lands."

We were preparing to ride the last few miles when my archers rode in. James son of Robert and Will Red Legs had ridden hard. "My lord, King Stephen comes!"

"Does he come for war?"

"No, lord. He has a strong escort, that is all."

The Baron clapped me on the back, "By God, Cleveland, you were right! He comes to talk!"

"Before you think this is over, wait until we speak with him. He may come to ask for our surrender. He may have taken the castle."

"No, lord. Arundel is too big a nut to crack. He will have to wait it out and starve them into submission."

In that, I agreed with the Baron. As we had discovered, it was only the wooden castles that could be taken by assault. The rest needed lengthy sieges or deception as we had proved at Lincoln.

The Baron and I gathered our knights to meet with Stephen. As the most senior noble, it would be me who would speak with the Usurper. He arrived with a retinue of a hundred. Half were knights and the rest men at arms. I doubted that he could have left many knights at the siege. This was a ploy to cow us. He wanted us to think he had more knights than he did. We had done the same. This was a war of deception as well as bloody battles.

He halted ten feet from me. Neither of us dismounted although we both took off our helmets to show that we were here to speak and not to fight. We both knew, however, that one false move from either side could result in a bloody encounter. As I stared into his eyes, I wondered if I should break the convention and fight him. I was certain that I could defeat him. Even as the thought entered my head it disappeared. I could not behave so basely.

"Well, Earl, what brings you this far from your river? Have you come to gloat about the trick you used to gain Lincoln?"

"No, nor did I come to compliment you on the trap you set for us on the Great North Road. We have come to fetch Empress Matilda, the rightful heir to the crown of England."

"Is this all that you bring? This motley crew of brigands?"

I smiled, "It is all that you can see although we managed to capture Lincoln with just six men. If I were you I would worry about that."

"So you did come to gloat!"

"Relieve the siege and allow the Empress to leave!"

"I cannot do that."

I shrugged, "The Empress is safe enough in the walls of Arundel. It is to be a battle then or perhaps I will use my men's skills at night. Will you sleep easy at night knowing that my men of the woods, my archers, are wandering abroad?"

For the first time doubt filled his face. Stephen came from Blois. Archers there were rare. They preferred the crossbow. The skill of my archers was known not only in England but Normandy and Blois. They were hated and feared. I had fine knights and men at arms but the weapon most of my enemies feared was my archers.

"I do not wish my cousin harm."

"You have a strange way of showing it."

"If I let her leave the castle to your protection, would you persuade her to return to Anjou?"

I laughed, "England waits for four years for her to return and you want me to put her on a boat back to her husband? I think you have been eating the mushrooms which make a man mad!"

Even as I had been speaking, he had been looking at the faces of my men. He saw no doubts there. He had a garrison to subdue and two of his most resilient enemies before him. If we attacked and he lost this battle, it might mean he would lose the war and with it his borrowed crown. He nodded, "Very well. I will allow you, Earl, to fetch the Empress but I want her far to the west and away from London!"

I could see why he wished that. If the Empress was in Wallingford then the people of London might rise up in support. I thought it unlikely but I understood his reasons. I cared not. I had what I wanted.

"And the Baron here can travel back to his castle unmolested?"

He nodded, "You have my word."

"Good, then you have my word that we will not slit your men's throats this night!"

I saw that I had angered many of the knights who were close to their leader. Stephen smiled, "It is good speaking with you, Earl, for you never change. You have a steel stake for a spine and you never bend. Come, let us go else we will not have reached Arundel before dark."

I shook my head, "We will come on the morrow. I have promised you safety for tonight. I feel safer here."

"You do not trust me?"

"I have no reason to doubt your word but some of your men are as treacherous as vipers. I would not trust them as far as I could spit. We will stay here and travel in daylight to Arundel."

He nodded and turned his horse to lead his men away. I had made no friends that day but I cared not.

The Baron was ecstatic, "We have won!"

"When the Empress is in Bristol with her brother then we will have won. I will not count my winnings while I still sit at the table."

He nodded, "That is, perhaps, wise. I will wait here tomorrow until you are safely in Arundel."

"No, my lord, ride tomorrow for your castle. You have many enemies and some may try to take your refuge. The Empress will need that if she is to take London and the east."

"You have a cold and calculating mind, Earl. It has been a pleasure to serve you."

Chapter 15

Even though we had been promised safe passage, I kept my scouts out as a protective screen. We reached Arundel unmolested. Stephen waited there and he rode with me to the gate. I took off my helmet. The Empress appeared on the ramparts and I shouted, "My Empress, I have permission to escort you and your retinue to your brother, the Earl of Gloucester."

Stephen shouted, "You have my word that until you are safe with your brother then you shall be unmolested."

"We will be with you shortly!"

As we waited Stephen said, "I have told you before, Earl, that I only mean the best for England."

"Then abdicate and give the crown to your cousin. England suffers from this civil war."

"I cannot do that."

"And yet you can give away a huge part of England to the barbarians from the north. I am sorry but I do not believe you. You are a bad leader. I have fought alongside you and know that you are no coward but, I am sorry, you are no king."

"Then there is no more to be said. We will meet on the field of battle."

"I have no doubt about that. And when we do then God will decide who has behaved with the most honour."

"Sadly, Earl, we both believe that."

The Empress emerged with her knights, her women and Henry Fitz Empress. Her young son had grown. The Empress and her women rode horses rather than riding in a litter. I was pleased it would make for a quicker journey. Despite the words of Stephen, I did not wish to risk her on the road for too long.

She offered me her hand to kiss. "Ever the white knight, you come to my rescue each time I need you."

"I swore an oath, my lady, and I do not break such oaths. Come, Empress, let us away. We have far to travel if we are to get to Bristol."

She leaned in towards me, "We go to Gloucester. I have forces gathering there."

"It is further to travel."

"I know, but it is where my brother has gone. We were under siege but we still received messages."

I turned to Dick, "Have four of your archers ride to Gloucester and warn the Earl that we are on our way. Give them spare horses so that they reach it in one day."

"Aye, lord."

Young Henry nudged his pony next to mine. "Judith and Margaret both said that you would come, lord."

I nodded to the two women; both were keepers of secrets. They smiled. "They are wise women, my young Lord Henry."

"You fought the Scots and defeated them?"

"I was part of the army."

"Did you slay many?"

"Our army slew ten thousand, lord. They will not trouble your northern lands for some time."

"Will we have the crown soon, Earl? Mother says that you will know such things."

I glanced at the Empress who gave a shy smile, "You have a way of making things happen, Aelfraed. You took Lincoln with three knights."

"That was the Earl's plan and we would not have succeeded without the courage of Lady Maud and Lady Hawise."

"As ever, you are too modest. And now you have travelled through the heart of the enemy's lands and raised the siege."

"It was a bluff but Stephen is stretched. It is good that you and your brother have arrived for we have the opportunity to finally defeat Stephen. With Lincoln in our hands and the peace with Scotland, we can shift the balance to us." I waved my hands at the knights who followed her. "With knights and your brother, the enemy can be brought to heel. There are many in the land who vacillate. It will not take much to bring them on our side."

Henry piped up, "And I will fight at your side, lord!"

I looked at Matilda who gave the slightest shake with her head. "That is indeed an honour, my lord, but first you must be tall enough to ride a palfrey. This is my new squire, Richard. He is but six years older than you. When you are his size then you can fight with me."

"But I am the son of an Empress!"

I laughed, "And Gilles is but the son of an archer. It matters not." I tapped my heart. "It is in here that decides if you are a warrior or not. These two young men have both stood with me and faced overwhelming odds. There will come a day when you do so too. Be patient and I promise you that I will keep you close when we fight your mother's enemies. But you would not wish a warrior to watch over you when he could be fighting, would you?"

"I suppose not. Then will you teach me how to become a great champion like you?"

"When time allows, I will. Richard, Gilles, tell the young prince what the job of a squire entails while I speak with the Empress."

Young Henry dropped back and I nudged Rolf next to the Empress. "You wish to speak of those I can trust and those I cannot?" I nodded. "These are dangerous times. I am grateful that my father's wife offered me sanctuary. I fear it would have been the tower otherwise."

"The Bishop of Durham has his own interests at heart. He supports neither Stephen nor you although if either of you appeared outside his walls then he would join you. The Archbishop of York wishes to support you but Stephen was anointed and he must support the anointed one. Old Thurstan will guard your borders against your uncle who used the lie that he fought for you." I shook my head. "He did not. He took your land and killed your people."

"And Ranulf, Earl of Chester?"

"I confess I do not know. It was a bold move to take Lincoln but he joined Stephen quickly enough when he was crowned and only switched sides when he had lands taken from him."

"You paint a black picture."

"There are bright spots. Cleveland and the Tees are safe. Edward and Wulfric guard it. Wallingford is well protected by Brian Fitz Count and will be a good base to attack London and the Thames Valley. When Stephen's heartland is threatened, we shall see the resolve of his supporters."

"I hope so."

Young Henry laughed at something Gilles had said and we both turned. "He is a fine young boy."

She nodded, "He takes after his father. I hope he proves to be as valiant. I fear he will need all of his courage if he is to wrest the crown from my cousin."

"There are things we can do to make what we hold safer. Your Majesty needs strong castles. Sir John of Merpel died because he had an old wooden castle. When King David came to Stockton, we lost barely a man and he lost many. We must have more archers. Crossbows are of no use. My archers are feared more than knights. Your people can use them. These knights are Norman or Angevin and they are good fellows, but if we are to win back the crown then the people will look to English knights and English men at arms. It is why it was so important to have the Earl of Chester on our side."

She nodded, "I can see that. Now that my brother has committed himself to our cause, we can begin to win back the land as well as the hearts and minds of our people."

Lowering my voice, I asked, "I am curious. Why did he not commit earlier?"

"He and my husband had a falling out and there were those who encouraged my brother to claim the Dukedom." She shook her head. "I am sorry, Aelfraed. You cannot be in two places at once but you are the one who can talk to both my husband and my brother and mediate. I tried but I failed. I am just a woman."

I heard a tut from Margaret behind us and I smiled, "My lady, you are the strongest woman I have met. There is steel in you. Your grandfather would be proud of you. The fact that you could not mediate is not a criticism of you but rather your husband and brother."

The journey passed quickly for we had much to say and our eyes spoke even more. The Earl of Gloucester and Sir Miles Fitz Walter met us forty miles from Gloucester and escorted us the rest of the way. It was the end of our precious time together. From now on we would be under the scrutiny of everyone. I cherished those hours and miles I had with the Empress.

The army which gathered at Gloucester was nowhere near the size of the army which had faced and defeated the Scots. It was, however, man for man a better army. Once we were in the Earl's hall, he greeted me like a long lost brother, "Aelfraed the hero of Northallerton! Gods but I wish I could have been there! We would have chased those barbarians all the way back to their highlands!"

I nodded, "Sadly, those who were with me would have none of it. They slunk back to their own castles with their loot!"

"We are together now. This is Sir Miles Fitz Walter, the High Sheriff of Gloucester. He is a firebrand just like you. He and the High Sheriff of Hereford, Sir Pain Fitzjohn, are my two rocks. Now that you have joined us there will be no stopping us. I have great plans to conquer this land."

"I will do all that I can to promote the cause of the Empress and young Henry."

The Earl of Gloucester rubbed his hands together, "I would suggest a strike now while the Usurper is distracted by Arundel. If the Earl of Chester can mobilise his forces in the north then we may well trap Stephen between us. Then we prepare our forces. You two can lead the men we already have. I will send a messenger to Ranulf." The Empress stood all the while listening to this. Henry was by her side. I could see that she was becoming increasingly agitated.

"Am I to stand here while you make these decisions, brother? I bring a hundred and forty knights. What do you bring? Where were you when I was trapped in Arundel? It took the Earl here to come hundreds of miles through hostile land to rescue me."

The Earl of Gloucester reddened and stormed off. Sir Miles turned to follow and I said, "Sheriff, you have a choice to make here. Do you follow the Earl or the Empress? I know you hold your office through him but we owe our duty to the Empress and her son."

He nodded and returned to us, "The Earl can be a little...."

"Overbearing?" I ventured.

He shook his head, "You might say that, lord, for you know him but I cannot." He dropped to his knee, "I serve you, Your Majesty, as I served your father. Command!"

She held her hand for him to kiss, "I did not object to my brother's plans but I did not like the way I was treated as a piece of furniture!"

I smiled, "I think he was just enthusiastic. I will speak to him. So, shall we prepare to attack along the Thames Valley, Sir Miles? Sir Brian has a mighty castle and if we can build on his success, we can work our way towards London."

He nodded, "I will get Sir Pain and organise our men." He looked nervously at the Empress, "And who will lead this army, Empress?"

"Why King Henry's champion, of course, Aelfraed, Earl of Cleveland."

He raced off and I bowed. "I will find your brother then while you settle yourself into your new quarters." I turned to my knights. "Find quarters for the men. I will take Gilles and Richard with me."

"Aye, lord."

I mounted Rolf and we rode after the Earl. He had been heading for his men. When I reached his camp, I found it being packed up. I recognized Reginald, Earl of Cornwall. "Where is the Earl?"

Sir Reginald looked embarrassed. "It seems we are returning to Bristol. The Earl wishes to hunt."

I shook my head, "This is not well done, my lord. We should be fighting Stephen and not each other."

"I know. I will try to persuade him to return. When he calms down, he may be more amenable. He likes not being spoken to that way; not least by women."

As I rode back, I reflected that I had fallen out with the Earl myself for being outspoken. The Earl liked men who agreed with him. Gilles asked, "Will we campaign then, lord?"

"We will."

"And you will lead the army?"

"Aye, but it will be smaller than it should be. Still, it will be more men than I am used to."

When we reached the Earl's Hall, Sir Pain and Sir Miles were in conversation with the Empress. They looked up expectantly. "Your brother has gone to Bristol. We will have to undertake this expedition without him."

Sir Miles shook his head, "We cannot leave the Empress undefended."

"You are right. We will take but half of the knights you brought. The rest can remain as your protectors."

"But that will leave you perilously short of men."

"What we have are superior to our enemies. I will use my discretion. My aim is to move quickly. Sir Miles, Sir Pain, I only take mounted men. We move quickly. We forage for our food and we take castles in which we will stay. We take those castles which lie between here and Wallingford and then use Wallingford to bring the enemy to battle. We leave the day after tomorrow while Stephen is still at Arundel."

I saw that I had stunned them but they both nodded their agreement.

The messenger who arrived that night put an end to those hopes. He dropped to his knees before Matilda. "Empress, King Stephen has lifted the siege and moved north."

"Where to?"

"I know not. He left with his army."

When the four of us were alone I said, "This complicates things. He could be anywhere. Perhaps he goes to Lincoln to retake his castle?"

The Empress said, "But that does not change our plans, Earl. If we attack down the valley, it means we will have less opposition."

"Perhaps. However, I cannot think of a better strategy. We still leave at the appointed time."

In the end, it took longer to prepare the retinue of the two Sheriffs. My men were chafing at the bit but the two Sheriffs did not have enough horses. I even gave them some of the ones we had captured. We were about to leave when a messenger arrived from Sir Brian Fitz Count. He dropped to his knees before me, the Empress was still within. "My lord, The Earl of Chester has been visited by King Stephen."

Even before he uttered his words, I knew what was coming. "Gilles, fetch the Empress, Sir Miles and Sir Pain." I smiled at the messenger. "Wait until the Empress arrives. This news should be heard by her too. Rise"

The three of them came together. Young Henry was with his mother. I nodded to the messenger, "Empress, the Earl of Chester has joined with King Stephen. Lincoln is back in the hands of the enemy." He seemed uncertain what to say and just said, "I am sorry."

The Empress was ever gracious and she smiled, "You are the messenger only and not the turncoat. Go into the kitchens and have some food. When he had gone she said, "You seem prescient, Earl. Did you know?"

"Let us say that he is a hard man to understand. Lady Maud will not be happy." I shrugged, "It changes nothing."

"It does for me, Earl. I shall send Henry back to the Count with Judith. It may not be safe for him here any longer."

"I will not go! I want to fight alongside the Earl!" Henry stamped his foot and crossed his arms.

I knelt and held his shoulders in my hands, "And you shall but I said before you are too small yet to fight, but I promise that when you are big enough I shall send for you and you shall serve alongside Gilles and Richard." He pouted. "A good soldier follows orders." I saw his lip quiver and then he nodded. He did not trust himself to speak and rushed away to Judith who stood with arms outstretched.

I turned to the two Sheriffs. "We ride now with however many men are mounted. Our enemies think that this will discomfit us and make us afeard. It will not. My lady, I leave you here with your knights and those men of the two sheriffs who are not mounted. Send news of this to your brother. He is pig-headed but even he may come to our aid." I saw Margaret and Judith smile at my words.

The Empress came closer and kissed me on my cheek. She whispered as she did so, "Take care, my love. There will be other battles."

As I stepped away I said, "I have never run away from a battle yet. When a man begins to do that, it is time to hang up his sword."

My scouts had already found us a good route and my conroi led the column as we headed east towards Wallingford. There was a castle at Stanford. It was held by the Earl of Derby. I had fought alongside Robert de Ferrers at the Battle of the Standards. Stephen had seen fit to make him an Earl after the battle, the Earl of Derby. Although he had lands in Warwick too, our scouts had reported that he was at Stanford. I knew not why. It was a wooden castle and guarded the road from Gloucester to Wallingford. I doubted that they would expect us to strike at such a target and I wanted to make a statement to Stephen that even his closest allies were not safe from the wrath of the warlord.

I knew much about the castle before I arrived. I had not wasted time while my sheriffs had been gathering their forces. I knew that they had no natural features to use and the mound was just the spoil from the ditch. It was a large structure and could hold over a hundred men. I had almost two hundred men under my command. My plan was simple: I would surround the castle and cut it off. The nearest manor house was at Serengford but it was not fortified. I had but twenty extra archers and I gave Ralph of Wales the captaincy. He led the archers off and disappeared from sight.

Despite the fact that I had many illustrious knights with me, I kept my household knights and my men at arms close by. We managed to get within a quarter of a mile before we were spotted. I saw the standard flying; the Earl was at home. I saw them hurriedly pull up the bridge from over the ditch. That did not worry me over much. There were many houses nearby and I would use their crude doors as a makeshift bridge. The important fact was that they were trapped. Henry Warbow approached us from the east. "Two riders were sent for help, lord. They are dead."

I turned to Sir Miles. "Have ten of your men at arms go to the east end of the road and watch for enemies. I do not think there will be any but we need my archers."

We dismounted and Gilles and Richard took the horses to the field which had a convenient gate. They would graze. I gestured to the two Sheriffs. Come, we will see if the Earl of Derby is in the mood to surrender."

I had no archers yet and so I halted well beyond crossbow range. I took off my helmet, "Robert de Ferrers, Earl of Derby, I call upon you to surrender this castle to Empress Matilda, heir to good King Henry and rightful ruler of this land. What say you?"

In answer, a crossbow bolt flew from the walls and landed twenty paces from me.

"You have allowed yourself to be deluded by a moment of glory, Earl. This is not Northallerton. Prepare to die!"

I turned my horse around, "How do we attack this, my lord?"

"We use archers first and then my men at arms and knights."

Sir Pain said, "We are not cowards lord! We know how to fight."

"Have you assaulted a castle like this before, my lord?"

"No, but we are warriors all."

"Then let my men and I show you how we do it and next time we assault a castle you can do as we do now. I do not want to waste men on a fruitless attack. We will get this done."

"Yes, lord."

"Ralph, in a moment I want the walls clearing of defenders."

"Aye, lord."

"Edgar, fetch the doors from the houses. We will use them as a bridge."

"Aye, lord."

"Dick, the knights will lead."

"Of course." He turned, "Leopold, fetch me an axe. I may not be as big or as ugly as Wulfric but I fancy I can wield an axe as well as he."

The wait worked in our favour for the defenders on the outer wall watched as we prepared. They would be nervous for we moved with purpose. Eventually, we were ready, We moved towards the ditch and the walls. Those within the castle would have wondered at the small number of men who approached. I turned to the two Sheriffs. "Have the knights ready to follow when we breach the gates. We must move swiftly and take the second gate before they close it."

"Aye, lord."

I turned to Gilles and Richard. "Leave the standard here. You will follow the men at arms. I want each of you to have two spare spears."

"Aye, lord." Gilles showed me that he had already anticipated me and he raised his two weapons.

"Good. This day we may get more weapons for you!" I turned, "Ralph, clear the walls! Edgar, fill the ditch!"

My men worked as one. The defenders were suddenly assailed by fifty arrows and then another fifty. Any face which peered over the walls was struck. Edgar and the men at arms raced forward and skilfully made a bridge as I led my knights forward. My men at arms then tucked in behind the five of us. John and Dick carried axes. We ran across the crude bridge. It was barely stable but we made it. Our archers ensured that no crossbow or javelin came our way. Harold, Tristan and I held our shields above the heads of Dick and John as they began to hack at the gap between the gates. It was a single bar that held the gate closed.

Dick said, "It is weakening, lord."

"Ready, then we will push!" They both made one last strike and then I said, "One, two, three!" We hurled ourselves forward and the weakened bar gave way and we spilt inside. The Earl had been naive. He had no men waiting behind the gate. "Spears!"

Our squires gave us spears and we raced up the slope towards the main gate. The defenders were trying to reach it too but they had left it too late to descend. Had I been the

Earl, I would have ordered the gates closed but he kept them open. Tristan and Harold were young and they were fast. Along with John and the squires, they raced to the gate. Too late someone gave orders to close it. I was twenty feet away and I hurled my spear. It struck the man trying to close the gate in the chest and he fell backwards dragging the gate open. I saw Gilles and Richard as they raced ahead and thrust their spears into two men who raced to help their fallen comrade, and then the inner gate was secure.

I turned and yelled, "Come! The men of Stockton have secured the gate! Now secure the keep!"

There was a roar and the two Sheriffs raced up the slope with their men. They were eager for some honour and glory too. I reached my two squires as they, along with Harold and Tristan, fought off the knights who ran to kill them and then close the doors. Richard had no mail and was an easy target but he was young and he was lithe. He sidestepped the sword which found not flesh but fresh air and he rasped the edge of his short sword behind the knee of the knight. The hauberk did not cover that part of his leg and when the tendons were slashed, the knight fell. I reached him and put my sword to his throat. "Surrender to my squire!"

"I yield!"

"Richard, Gilles, hold the prisoners here."

The Earl of Derby realised he and his men were in grave danger and I heard a horn sound. A dozen men made it into the wooden keep before the gate was slammed shut. Those who were without yielded as we flooded up the hill. Sir Miles and Sir Pain led their men to the door. This time there were no archers to clear the walls and crossbows claimed the lives of seven men before the two sheriffs ordered their men to take cover.

I shouted, "There is no hurry! Do not waste lives." I turned to Gilles, "Go fetch Ralph and my archers."

Dick and my knights gathered around me. Dick grinned as he gestured with his bloody sword towards Richard, "A feisty cockerel that one and fast too. That was a clever blow."

I nodded, "I am glad that I made him my squire. I see now that something stayed my hand."

"It would have been easy to slay him."

"You are right, Harold. A cool head is needed in such situations."

There was a strange silence in the castle. Save the occasional moan from an unattended wounded man it was deadly quiet. We were waiting. The bodies with the bolts in them were a salutatory lesson. The men of Hereford and Gloucester had been too eager. They had thought the battle won. I heard feet as my archers ran through the gates. Dick shouted, "'Ware crossbows!"

Ralph nodded and they took shelter alongside the buildings. "Edgar, shields!"

My men at arms stepped out and with overlapping shields made a narrow shield wall two shields high. Bolts thudded into the shields but the men behind them were safe. Ralph and eight archers ran from shelter and hid behind the shield wall. Edgar took command. He peered over the top of the shield. The only target was his eyes and it would take a lucky strike to hit him.

"Now!" Five archers released their arrows. I watched as three men fell from the tower. "Now!" The second four released theirs. Two men fell and then a line of heads appeared as they thought my men had finished. "Now!" All nine released at once. I heard cries and saw four crossbows and their owners fall to the bailey. The ramparts were emptied of targets.

Ralph turned to me, "Clear, lord!" The rest of my archers ran to stand behind their comrades and all of them knocked an arrow.

"Sir Miles, Sir Pain, the walls are cleared. Take the gate!"

With a roar, the men of Hereford and Gloucester raced up the slope towards the gate. There was no ditch here but the gate was a man's height above the ground and they had pulled up the ladder. Sir Miles ordered the bodies of the dead crossbowmen gathered and they made human bodies into steps as they ascended to the gate and then began to hack and chop their way through the wooden door.

I heard a cry from the top of the tower. "We yield! The Earl is dead! Mercy, lord! Do not visit your vengeance upon us!"

"Sir Miles, hold. You in the tower, come out with palms showing and no helmets." I turned to Ralph, "Watch them for tricks."

Dick said, "Another castle taken! And with few losses. This will hurt the enemy."

I shook my head, "Not yet but it is a start. We now have a line of supply to Wallingford. We begin the fight for England here."

Chapter 16

We had many prisoners and I sent them back to Gloucester with an escort of Sir Miles' men. The treasure we shared. My share was a horse and suit of mail. After the hall was emptied, we had the bodies of the enemy dead placed in the ditch around the castle. It was a crude grave. Then I ordered the castle and its walls to be burned. When we rose the next morning, the wooden remnants of the castle looked like blackened teeth. Our men pulled them down into the ditches and it was as though the castle had never been. If the family of Robert de Ferrers wished to rebuild their castle, they would have to dig up the rotting corpses of the Earl and those who had fallen.

We left after noon and marched to Wallingford. Our messengers had kept Sir Brian informed of our progress and we were greeted as heroes.

"Now, with your men, Earl, we can begin to destroy the enemy around us."

The four of us were seated in his Great Hall. We had a strategy to plan. "Had the Earl of Chester not defected then I would have agreed but we cannot count on his men and until the Earl of Gloucester stirs himself then our four conroi constitute our whole army."

"You are not suggesting that we sit on our backsides here behind my walls? I have done that for too long as it is." Sir Brian was a man of action.

"No, my fiery friend, we do not. We use our men judiciously. Of the four of us, I am the one who knows Stephen the best. He prefers to buy men rather than fight warriors. I have no doubt that the Earl switched sides |because of new titles."

Sir Brian nodded, "I have heard, from defectors, that was the case. So how do we use this to our advantage?" He swallowed half a beaker of wine, wiped his mouth and said, "Earl, you know me to be a bluff soldier. I do not use subtlety. You will need to explain in clearer terms."

I smiled, "You are honest, Sir Brian, and that is what we need. I propose that we head north to Oxford. It is but fifteen miles away. It is a rich city. The churches there are the ones which were endowed richly. We take the city and hold it to ransom. By taking the money from Oxford, we deny it to Stephen and enrich the Empress."

Sir Miles questioned, "Will it not make an enemy of the Church?"

"Which church? There are factions within the church already. The Pope himself sides first with Matilda and then Stephen. The churches in Oxford are the result of rich guilds and noblemen endowing them. The Church does not see their gold but its clerics live well. Besides," I smiled, "I am the Warlord and the Wolf of the North. It is expected of me."

"You gamble with your soul, my lord."

"No, Sir Pain, for I am not foresworn. When others broke their oath to King Henry then they put their souls in jeopardy. I believe that any sins I commit against the Church will be forgiven. I do not do it for gain."

"Even so, when judgement day comes, my lord, you might face hell!"

I waved a hand around as though encompassing England, "And this is not? But you need not worry, Sir Pain, your soul will be safe for you are carrying out the orders of your lord. I gamble just my soul."

Sir Brian said, "Know you, Earl, that my wife's uncle is the Constable at Oxford. Her father was Gilbert D'Oyly who built the castle there."

"You can stay here if you wish. I would not drive a wall between husband and wife."

He smiled, "No, lord. There will be no problem but I wanted you to know my connection. There is no treachery in this castle."

"I know, Sir Brian, and I appreciate your honesty."

We left three days later. Again I just took mounted men. The rest we left at Wallingford as a garrison. Sir Brian came with us and we had over a hundred and fifty knights. The banners alone would cow the city. The gates of the castle were closed to us. It mattered not. I had the castle surrounded. I sent my men at arms into the churches. The clergy had fled into the castle and they were empty. They gathered the treasures from within. There was gold and there were relics. I had them brought to the main gate.

The city had no lord of the manor but a Governor and a Constable. The four of us rode to the gates and dismounted. Taking off my helmet I shouted, "Sir Nigel D'Oyly."

A knight appeared, "I am he. Sir Brian, I am surprised to see you here."

"And why is that? I serve the rightful heir of England and you support the Usurper. Your only surprise should have been that it took me so long to come here. This is the Earl of Cleveland. He commands this battle."

My name was known in these parts but not my device and I saw the priests crossing themselves when they heard my name. "You are far from home, Earl."

"England is my home and Matilda my Queen."

"What do you want?" He pointed to the relics and the treasure. "Are you brigands who come to desecrate churches?"

"You know me not, Sir Nigel. I had my men bring these here to show you what we could do. Your priests and monks can take them back to their churches when we have gone."

"You would leave?"

"We will leave when I have done what I came here to do."

"Which is?"

"You will surrender to us. You may keep the castle and keep the town if you swear allegiance to the Empress and pay taxes not to Stephen but to the Empress."

I had surprised Sir Nigel. "I will come down and speak with you. Do I have your word that I will not be harmed?"

"Of course. I said that I came here with peace in mind."

He disappeared from the walls.

Sir Miles was surprised, not to say shocked and he asked, "Why does he come down to speak with us?"

Sir Brian laughed, "Simple, Sir Miles, he wishes to negotiate and does not want others to hear. You are clever, Earl. You threaten and yet no blood is spilt."

"Perhaps. The negotiations are not over yet."

The Constable came outflanked by a richly dressed man and a priest. Sir Nigel had taken off his helmet. The seven of us were out of earshot of all, including my men.

"What do you propose, Earl? We could agree to your terms and, when you leave, refute the truce."

"And then I would come back, raze your castle and your town and slaughter everyone within the manor," I said it calmly and dispassionately. The priest crossed himself.

The richly dressed man said, "I am John of Oxford and master of the Guilds of Oxford. Tell me, Earl, if we agree to this, what is to stop King Stephen attacking and punishing us?"

"The same thing which stopped the Scottish Army at Northallerton and helped King Henry defeat the French and the Flemish in Normandy; me. I will protect your town and if Stephen the Usurper comes then I will defeat him."

The priest pointed to the treasures we had taken, "And if we agree, we get to return these to the churches?"

"I gave you my word and I am never foresworn." The three of them looked at each other. "I need an answer now."

Sir Nigel nodded.

"Good, then you need to send the first taxes to Wallingford by the end of the week."

"Is the Empress at Wallingford then, lord?"

"No, Sir Nigel, but Sir Miles will ensure that the money is safely taken to the Empress."

He nodded, "You are an interesting man, Earl. I had heard much about you. You are not what I expected."

"I never believe what I am told about any man. I judge with my eyes. I am not afraid to be judged on my actions." I looked at the priest, "In this world or the next."

We returned to Wallingford. Sir Brian said, "I am almost disappointed. That seemed too easy."

"We have poked one of the rat's holes. He will strike somewhere else. We have to be ready to respond. I want the three of you to send out scouts to find the enemy. Stephen will react to this and when he does we must respond equally quickly."

One of the treasures we had taken from the Earl of Derby
was the hauberk his squire wore. It fitted Richard and I felt
happier having him better protected. When we had been in
Gloucester, I had used some of the ransom we had received
to buy new surcoats for my men. I had learned that my livery
and my device sometimes gave me an advantage. Now that
our reputation was spreading in the south, I wanted to exploit
it. I also had a new warhorse. This one had belonged to the
Earl of Derby. It was an unusual golden colour and reminded
me a little of Scout. I could not give him the same name as a
horse which still lived and so I called him Copper for his
coat seemed to shine like burnished Copper. Leofric also
rode a horse called Copper but he was in Anjou.

We spent a day or two in Wallingford repairing shields
and sharpening weapons. It allowed the scouts to ferret out
the enemy and his intentions. As I had expected, Stephen
reacted angrily to the loss of Oxford. He sent columns of
men to capture the Empress' castles at South Cerney and
Malmesbury.

The others appeared worried by such action. "It was to be
expected. Sir Miles, you and Sir Pain head to Malmesbury
and try to recapture those castles. I will go to Trowbridge. I
fear that is Stephen's goal. He is heading towards the Earl of
Gloucester." I sent two of Sir Brian's men as messengers to
the Earl and to the Empress warning them of the danger.

"And what of me, my lord?"

"Prepare to be attacked. This raid may be a ploy to lure us
away from Wallingford. Stephen has to retake Wallingford
before he can take Oxford. Be vigilant."

I split the Empress' knights into three. They were eager
for more treasure. Many of them, I knew, had accompanied
the Empress in the hope of riches. Although not mercenaries,
they had a mercenary attitude to war. I cared not so long as
they fought on my side. I knew their leader, Raymond of
Rouen. I had fought with him in Normandy. He was an old-
fashioned knight. His squire, Alan, was the same age as
Harold and I had asked the knight why his squire had not
been ennobled.

He had shrugged, "In Normandy, there are too few manors. My own is small. You are lucky here in England, my lord. I hope to gain a manor here and then I shall knight Alan. He deserves it but it is useful having a squire who is the equal of a knight. I never fear for my back."

The other Normans had a similar attitude to Sir Raymond. It made them hungry. I hoped that the Empress would reward them wisely. Stephen knew how to dispense such favours. We headed south and west towards Trowbridge. The evidence of the passing of the army of Stephen was evident everywhere. Houses and farms had been burned. Animals had been slaughtered and their butchered remains littered the countryside. Stephen was attacking the heartland of the Empress. I wondered if the Earl of Gloucester would now stir himself to defend his lands.

Having a wholly mounted force meant that we reached Trowbridge in less than a day. The army of Stephen had the motte and bailey of de Bohun encircled. We reached the hamlet of Whaddon before dusk. It was a small manor and had not been burned. It was, however, deserted save for a swineherd. He told us that his lord had fled to the castle when the forces of Stephen had arrived.

"Tell me, swineherd, how is the castle defended?"

"There is a river, the Biss, around the south and west sides. The north and east have a ditch."

"And where will the camp be?"

"T'other side of Hilperton. It is a small farm on the main road."

I turned to my household knights and Sir Raymond. "Then that means the forces of Stephen will be on this side of the castle. We try a night attack."

Sir Raymond was dubious, "A night attack? Is that not dangerous? We will not know friend from foe."

"That is why I will attack first with my own household knights. You and your knights will form up at Hilperton. When the alarm is given, you ride and attack the camp. We will have slain the guards and, I hope, captured Stephen. If we take the head of the snake then the body will wither and die. We use the password 'Adela'. The response is 'Maud'."

He nodded, "You take a great risk, my lord."

"And if we win then a great reward."

I gathered my men. We did not wear cloaks nor did we encumber ourselves with spears. My archers took their bows but they were not strung. It would be knife work. I divided my men at arms and archers between my knights. I had two men at arms and three archers with me as well as my two squires. We left our horses with Sir Raymond at Hilperton where we gathered after dark. We left them silently. We were less than a mile from the enemy camp.

Ralph of Wales, Long Tom and Rafe went first; they were silent. Edward the Fair followed them as a precaution. They would take care of the sentries. Five of us wore hauberks, carried shields and held swords. We would deal with men who were armed more heavily. I heard nothing but I saw the dead sentries as we passed them. Three of them had had their throats cut. Ralph was stringing his bow at the edge of the trees when I reached him. He pointed to the fires and the tents. I nodded.

The army had arranged itself with their lords closest to the houses and their ordinary warriors closest to the woods and the insects. I recognised some of the banners but the one which was missing was that of Stephen. I paused to take in the camp. I could not see all of it but there appeared to be fewer men than I was expecting. The day's fighting was over and meals were being cooked. I pointed to the campfires. Ralph and his archers drew back their bows. I raised my sword and led my four men, with weapons drawn, towards the fires.

Four men fell with surprised looks on their faces as the arrows descended in the dark. Another three fell to the next flight and then we were amongst them. A man at arms reacted quickly and he picked up his axe. I hacked across his body with my sword. Freshly sharpened, it cut his arms through to the bone and he fell spurting blood. Shouts erupted all around us as the alarm was given. Panic ensued. I ran towards the tents of the knights. Arrows still descended and struck men who had little idea where the attack was coming from. Gilbert of Basildon came out of his tent flanked by his two squires. I had fought alongside him once. That meant nothing now and he shouted, "Cleveland! You treacherous dog! I might have expected this."

I left the posturing to him and I ran at him. He swung his sword at head height. It was a slow and clumsy blow. He had never been a particularly clever fighter. I had time to angle my shield and to thrust at his face with my sword. His sword slid harmlessly down my shield while he had to react quickly to block my sword. It was not totally successful for it flicked his helmet from his head revealing his coif. Henry of Langdale and my two squires fought with his squires. Sir Gilbert was forced to step back and he found himself in the entrance to his tent. When he tried to swing at me again, his sword became entangled in the tent. I thrust at his middle this time and scored a hit on his mail. Links were severed.

He was hampered by the tent while I was outside and had freedom of movement. "Yield and you shall live!"

"Never!" He stabbed at me but it was a predictable strike and my shield was there to block the blow.

I pulled my arm back. "Then die!" Wulfstan had always told me that I had the quickest hands he had seen and my right hand darted out and my sword struck him between the eyes. There was neither helmet nor nasal to protect him. He was dead instantly. I turned and saw that my men had slain the Baron's men.

I spied papers in the tent. "Gilles, you and Richard guard this. We have much to learn. The rest of you, with me!"

I ran towards the next tent. I saw Harold was there already with his men but they were being attacked by eight knights and men at arms. Henry of Langdale had picked up an axe and he hurled himself at their backs. His mighty blow sliced through the mail and back of one knight and knocked a man at arms to the ground. As they turned, I darted in and stabbed a knight in the groin. He fell writhing to the ground.

Ralph and the archers had their short swords and seaxes in their hands. In close combat those double weapons were deadly. The archers were without armour and could close with mailed knights. I saw Ralph hamstring one knight who, as he fell, had his throat slit by a second archer. The sound of horses approaching was like thunder and men began to throw down their weapons and shouted, "Mercy! I yield!"

Sir Raymond reined in next to me. "You did not need us, lord."

"I did. It was your horses which made them surrender." I pointed to the tents, "But this does not seem like a huge army and where is Stephen I wonder?"

As we rounded the prisoners up, the gates of the castle opened and Sir Henry Bohun emerged to greet us. "The Earl of Cleveland! I might have known you would come to our aid."

"Where is Stephen?"

"The King? He and the majority of his army left this morning and headed east."

I turned to one of the prisoners. "Where has Stephen gone?"

The young knight gave me a smile, "He goes to capture Wallingford! He knew you would take the bait and come here. King Stephen can outwit a wolf any time!"

Sir Raymond said, "So it would seem."

"I think not, Sir Raymond. Sir Brian has Wallingford well defended. He will hold out. We rest and leave at noon. Send a rider to the Earl of Gloucester and tell him the news."

I returned to the tent of Sir Gilbert. My squires guarded it still. Gilles pointed to a box of coins. "The Baron was a wealthy man."

I examined the coins. There were some with the face of Stephen but many bore the image of the King of France and the Count of Flanders. Here was a true mercenary. "Guard the chest, Gilles." I was more interested in the papers. "Richard, fetch me a light."

I began to read. They were messages from lords and barons. Here was evidence that Ranulf, Earl of Chester, had indeed gone over to the side of the usurper. It also showed that he had spies for one letter spoke of Nigel, Bishop of Ely who was fermenting rebellion against Stephen's rule. Alarmingly, there were letters from Prince Henry in Scotland hinting that when he became king, he might switch the allegiance of Scotland from Matilda to Stephen. Stockton was in danger.

"Richard, gather these papers. You are to guard them."

"Are they important, lord?"

"They are. We might have missed our prey but these are as valuable as the coins which Gilles watches."

We left the prisoners with Sir Henry and headed back to Wallingford. I was concerned for there had been no word from the Earl of Gloucester. A rider found us as we headed for Wallingford telling me that Sir Miles was also going to Wallingford and the Empress had sent men with him to help relieve the siege. Our news had reached the right ears.

Sir Raymond rode next to me. "Do we try the same trick with Stephen?"

"If we can then we do but he has campaigned in enemy lands before. I will be surprised if it works with him. We may have to give battle here."

"How many men will he have?"

"The prisoners spoke of two hundred knights. There could be a thousand men at the siege."

"Even with Sir Miles, Sir Pain and the men the Empress sends, we will be outnumbered."

"In total numbers, aye, but we will have more knights and we have Wallingford. Sir Brian knows how to defend and he knows how to attack. If he gets the opportunity then he will sally forth. This will be a battle of wits as well as arms."

We reached Wallingford after dark. We could see the fires of those besieging the castle. They lay to the south of the castle and to the west of the river. We made a camp and placed half of our men on watch. I would not be caught out by my own trick. When dawn broke, we were tired but unharmed. I sent out scouts to find Sir Miles and Sir Pain while I went with my household knights and Sir Raymond to scout out the enemy positions.

It was a mighty host. Stephen had anticipated relief and dug ditches to the west of his camp to prevent us from attacking that way. With the river on the other side, it would be a costly venture to attack him. He had also encircled the castle so that there was no way that we could deliver a message to the defenders. I was confident that Sir Brian had prepared for a siege. He would be well provisioned. When I reached our camp, I set Edgar and the rest of the men at arms and archers digging ditches and embedding stakes. Until the rest of our forces arrived, we could be attacked and overwhelmed. Stephen had the advantage.

Sir Miles arrived first. "We have retaken South Cerney. Sir Pain had more trouble at Malmesbury and he lost more men. It will take him a day or two to reach us."

"Until he does, and until the men the Empress has sent reach us then we have to be on the defensive. We make our camp a fortress."

As I walked the lines with my squires, Richard asked, "Why will it take so long for men to reach us from Gloucester, lord?"

"They will have many men on foot. You are used to travelling at the speed of a horse. They will come and they will be needed. If the Earl of Gloucester came then we could end this war once and for all."

"Why does he not come, lord? The Empress is his sister."

"I know not, Gilles, but when this is over then I will visit with him. I served his father too long to allow this petulance to jeopardise his father's legacy."

I had the men dig a deep ditch and line it with stakes we cut from the nearby woods. We had time to sharpen them and fire harden them. When our reinforcements arrived, I breathed a sigh of relief. Although still outnumbered, we could now face them and meet them blade to blade. We watched as the enemy built rams and towers. They took time but they would be effective. It was infuriating not to be able to attack them while they were being built. The ditches and the stakes made any attack risky.

I was riding the defensive lines in the mid-morning when I saw knights leave the camp of the enemy and ride towards us. I recognised the standard of Stephen and also that of the Earl of Derby. I had slain the Earl and I wondered who had claimed his title. My household knights and my squires closed about me. Dick shouted, "Archers!"

I smiled. My men were protective of me. I was not worried for they had two ditches between us. Stephen took off his helmet and I took off mine, "Earl. We are meeting more frequently these days."

I nodded, "The pleasure is all yours."

He laughed, "I forgot when we met at Arundel that I had to thank you for defeating the Scots for me. I had thought that you would have sided with my cousin's uncle."

"I defend England and I defend my valley against all who would harm them."

He nodded and gestured to the knight who had the livery of de Ferrers. "This is the cousin of the Earl of Derby. He would have words with you."

I faced the young man. He took off his glove and hurled it across the ditches to me. "I am Walter de Ferrers and I am here to challenge you to mortal combat. You have killed my cousin and I demand satisfaction."

I picked up the glove and laughed, "Is this some kind of joke, Usurper? Do you find boys to do the work you should do?"

Stephen shook his head. "This is not of my doing, Earl. I have spent the last few days trying to dissuade the young knight from this folly but he will have none of it."

"You purport to be king. Order him."

"You and I both know that once someone begins this course of action, it must be pursued to its logical end. I cannot have him leading his conroi off on some wild goose chase to fight with you. We will do this properly. You have the choice to accept or decline."

Stephen was clever. He had distanced himself from the offer. If I declined then it would weaken our men and if I accepted, the young man might prove successful. I guessed that the young knight had proved himself in the tourney.

I walked to the glove, picked it up and threw it back across the ditch to him. "Very well. Reluctantly, I accept the challenge but I urge you, young man, to reconsider."

"You are old and no longer King Henry's champion. You will die by my hand."

"And what will that gain you?"

"Honour and glory!"

I shook my head. He wanted to make a reputation for himself. He would be the knight who slew King Henry's champion. It was no wonder that Sir Alan de Dinant lived a quiet life. There would be many who would wish to fight and kill the man who defeated the French King's champion. "Where and when?"

He pointed to the area between the castle and the river. "There and then both our armies will see my victory and your death! Noon when the sun is at its zenith!" I looked at the place. It was flattish but there was a gentle slope that led to the River Thames.

I nodded, "Noon it is then."

I turned my horse and rode back to our lines. Sir Miles, Sir Raymond and Sir Pain had all seen the interchange but heard nothing. Only my squires and household knights knew what would ensue. When I told them, Sir Pain said, "Decline the offer. There is nothing to be gained from the combat!"

"And that is why Stephen has put him up to it. If I decline then our enemies see it as a victory and they hope that my wounds and my age will make me weaker. If not then they have lost but a reckless young knight. Either way, they win. It is my fault for placing myself close to their lines. I had forgotten how clever Stephen the Usurper is."

I would have to fight the young knight. Stephen too was gambling but the odds were in his favour. He could not lose no matter what the outcome. The best outcome for me was my survival.

Chapter 17

I ordered Gilles to saddle my new warhorse, Copper. I had no doubt that the young knight would bring a warhorse and I would not risk Rolf. I had not ridden my new warhorse over much but as the horse of the Earl of Derby, I felt that fate decreed that I should ride him. Gilles put an edge on my sword. "Richard, go and put an edge on my spear."

"You will not use a lance, my lord?"

"A long spear is as good as a lance and easier to handle. Besides, you can put an edge on a spear. I would not make the young knight suffer. He is brave. I have seen splinters from lances kill a man in days. I would either just defeat him or kill him swiftly."

As my squires dressed me, I thought about the young knight. He may have done well in mêlée and the tourney but they were different from combat to the death. I had done both. He had been badly advised. Stephen had gone down in my estimation. I had thought him honourable. This was not. Perhaps I brought out the worst in him.

The final preparation was for my helmet to be polished and my mail given one last coat of oil. Although I wore my surcoat, I knew that when Walter de Ferrers struck at me with his sword he would cut through the surcoat. I wanted his sword to slide off my mail and not to cut into it. The tip of my sword had been sharpened too so that a thrust had more chance of penetrating my enemy's mail. Such were the margins which would determine success or failure.

Richard had groomed Copper so that he shone. The young Ferrers had made a mistake choosing noon. The sun in the south made my horse shine like molten gold. It would seem like an omen. My warhorse himself was eager for combat. I did not think that the Earl had ridden him for some time. Once in the saddle, I leaned forward and stroked his forelock, "Today we begin a friendship which will last a lifetime." I was taking a chance riding a horse I barely knew but it felt as though it was meant to be.

Copper whinnied and raised his head. I took it as a good omen. I took Gilles and Richard with me. They had spare weapons with them in case my own broke. Wooden bridges had been laid across the newly dug ditches and the sharpened stakes removed. There would be a truce for the day.

As I passed the main gate of the castle, Sir Brian leaned over. "What is happening, my lord?"

"Young de Ferrers has challenged me to a fight to the death."

Sir Brian shook his head, "Has the young man a death wish?"

"I think someone has put him up to it."

"Go with God."

It was not a large area in which we would fight. It was, perhaps, fifty paces long but only thirty paces wide. With the river at one side and a ditch at the other, it would need close control for a rider to stay in the saddle. I saw Walter de Ferrers and his squire as they crossed the ditch towards us. I let him pass for he wanted the eastern side. It was his first mistake as it meant he was facing the sun. The three squires took their horses and spare weapons and stood close by the ditch. They would also have to be careful to avoid being knocked into the ditch during the combat. A whirling warhorse could be as deadly as any sword or spear.

I rode to the western end and waited. He was the challenger and it was up to him to initiate the combat. I watched him as he began to build himself up for the fight. He kept pulling back on his reins to make his horse rear. It evoked a cheer from his own men each time he did so. I wanted my horse calm and so I stroked his mane and spoke quietly to him. I kept my eyes on young Ferrers. He had a proper lance and not a long spear such as I held. It would strike me before my spear could hit him. However, it was much heavier. The combination of his posturing and rearing was sapping energy from his arm. The longer he did this the more tired he would become.

Perhaps he realised he was becoming tired for he suddenly put spurs to his horse and hurtled towards me. I set Copper off and kept my spear levelled on my cantle. He had

decided to attack my shield side. That suited me. I saw the
tip of his lance wavering up and down. He made a second
mistake when he leaned too far forward. I remained upright
and held my spear slightly behind me. Although he was
aiming at my head, his wavering lance meant that he hit my
shield as I raised it. The lance shattered. I punched with my
spear the moment his lance hit my shield. I aimed at his
middle. My spear slid above his cantle and beneath his
broken lance. The sharpened head struck him hard in the
stomach and the head must have severed some of the mail
links for I felt it grate before it was torn from my hand. It fell
to the ground.

I wheeled Copper around and was able to turn faster than
the young knight who was travelling far too fast. He barely
managed to stop his horse before the river. I drew my sword
as I cantered up. He turned his wild-eyed horse's head
around and saw that I was closing with him. He panicked a
little and drew his sword as he spurred his horse. This time I
had the choice of which side to attack and I pulled Copper to
the left so that I met him sword to sword. I swept my sword
just above his horse's head. I saw him raise his sword to hack
at my head. Bringing my shield across, I held it before me.
The knight's antics had made his horse skittish and when my
sword came towards its head, it pulled to the left. The result
was that my sword struck him hard in the middle again while
he hit fresh air. Worse, he overbalanced and tumbled from
his horse.

I turned Copper towards Gilles and Richard. Sir Walter's
squire ran to help his knight to his feet and to grab the
rearing horse. He would have difficulty. As Richard held
Copper, I dismounted. "Gilles, you had better help his squire
with his horse."

"Aye, lord."

Richard asked, "Is it over, lord?"

"It should be but I fear the young man is too pig-headed.
He is brave but he lacks control." Richard helped me to
tighten the strap on my shield. We used it loose when
fighting on horseback but held it tightly fastened when on
foot. I nodded my thanks and headed back to the knight who

was now on his feet having shrugged off his squire. I noticed that he had not tightened his strap. That was the third mistake.

His fourth was to run at me. I had hit him twice in the middle. Those blows sapped energy and he now wasted even more. He was, however, a strong knight and his blow, when he struck my shield was a powerful one. I took some of the force from it by stepping to the side and angling my shield. I held my sword slightly behind me to disguise my strike. He was going for power and was attempting to bludgeon me to death. He swung at me a second strike, this time backhanded. It meant I could not angle my shield but I was able to bring my shield up across my body. The length of my shield absorbed the blow for me but I saw that it had hurt the knight as it jarred his arm.

He stepped back expecting a strike from me. I kept my sword behind me. "Use your sword, old man!" Taunting me was a desperate measure. It demonstrated his lack of experience.

I said nothing. I noticed that his shield was hanging a little loosely from his arm. He had not tightened his strap and the blows had made him tire. Mine was still held tightly to my body. I knew what he intended next for he raised his sword high above him and swung from behind his back. He would take my head. Instead of stepping back, as he assumed I would, I took a step towards him and lifted my shield as I stabbed at his middle. His sword hilt hit my shield and I heard the gasp from him as his knuckles struck it. Then the tip of my blade began to sever the already weakened links. I kept pushing and the sword tore through the hauberk and the gambeson. He hurriedly took a step back. Pulling my sword back I saw blood upon it. Equally damaging for the young knight was the fact that his hauberk was now split and a length of severed mail hung down.

I spoke for the first time. "I have first blood and you are wounded. Let us end this now for you are brave but this will not end well."

In answer, he ran at me. It was a double mistake. It made him bleed faster and his trailing mail tripped him. I stepped to the side as he lurched towards me. He fell and rolled onto his back on the slight slope leading to the river. I stepped above him with my foot on his right arm. I cut the fastenings on his ventail revealing his young face and put my sword to his bare throat. "Yield!"

On the castle walls, Fitz Count's men were cheering. I saw De Ferrers' squire hang his head but the young knight said, defiantly, "Never! Kill me! I die with honour!"

I raised my sword, "You are a brave young man but a foolish one." I brought my sword down and stabbed him in the palm of his right hand. I turned the sword as I pulled it out. I wanted him incapacitated for some time. "Live and have children. Learn wisdom."

I stepped away and lifted my sword.

I walked to the side where Stephen and his army watched. "I have defeated your young knight. He needs a surgeon......"

"My lord! Watch out!"

Gilles' words made me turn around. Walter de Ferrers was running at me holding his sword in his left hand. I swung my sword backhanded. His sword flew from his hand as my blade struck it. Left-handed he had no power. I pulled back my shield and hit him so hard in the face that he fell unconscious at my feet. "Brave and yet treacherous. Just like your master!" I sheathed my sword and waved for his squire. "Come, take your knight home. Gilles, Richard, help him to put the knight on his horse."

I was lauded all the way back to our lines. Sir Brian leaned over and shouted, "You should have killed him, my lord. He will hate you for the humiliation you have heaped upon him."

"It is why I hurt his right hand. He can still be a lord but he can challenge no other. I will live with his hate."

The enemy in contrast to the cheers from my men were malevolently silent. Stephen had gambled that he could not lose from the encounter but the sparing of the young knight had been unexpected. Soon his men would speak of it and would begin to doubt both themselves and their knights.

I crossed the ditch, followed by my squires and the defences were reinstated. The truce was over and the siege resumed. The castle's garrison was in good heart and we would soon have more men from Gloucester. I was more confident now than I had been.

I dismounted in the heart of my camp, "What now, my lord?"

"Now, Sir Miles, we prepare for a night attack from our enemy." Both he and the Sheriff of Hereford looked at me quizzically. "They will think we celebrate. Their tower and their ram are not ready. They were close enough for me to see that they were still being constructed. It was as they intended. Stephen is clever. In Normandy, he used a night attack on the French once. They will think we will be relaxed. Have the men make much noise this night as though we feast. I want half of the camp standing to as soon as it is dark. They will come across their ditches and it will be knife work this night."

Had we been in open country then I would have had my men lay traps but we were so close to the enemy and the ground so open that was impossible. I waved my household knights and my leaders of archers and men at arms over. Pointing to my standard I said, "They will make for us with their best warriors. Stephen tried to get rid of me today and tonight he will use assassins. Have our men rest now. Tonight, we play drunks. Before dark I want our men to pretend to drink. I want much cheering about the fight today. They will expect it. Dick, I want you and my knights to do the same. You will stagger around as though drunk and retire early. It will encourage them."

Dick grinned, "They will come thinking that we are unable to move because of drink and they will slit our throats."

"Exactly, and their very silence will work in our favour for the noise of any who die will be taken as our deaths."

I went to my tent with my squires. "Put an edge on our swords and daggers. Then the two of you will sleep. Tonight you must be alert. We will have to wait within for those who come to kill us."

Gilles nodded, "Aye, my lord. Come, Richard. I will show you how our lord likes his sword sharpening." Gilles would keep young Richard occupied rather than dwelling on the morbid thoughts of death.

I took off my own mail and gambeson. Some of the blows I had taken had been hard ones. I used some of Father Henry's ointments. They would make my aching injuries less painful. Then I lay down on my bedding and closed my eyes. I doubted that I would sleep but I would need my rest. I had made it sound easy to the others but I knew that waiting to be killed by shadows in the night would test the nerves of all of my men. Harold, Dick and the others who had been brought up in Sherwood would find it easiest but even they would worry as they lay in the dark feigning drunkenness. They would need senses that they rarely used now.

Gilles and Richard returned. I heard them enter my tent but they made not a sound. I smiled. Gilles would be gesturing for Richard to lie and to sleep. I felt my cloak being laid upon me, "Thank you, Gilles, but I am just resting."

"Aye, my lord."

Despite myself, I dozed. However, I was awake before dark. Wrapping my cloak around me, I went out into the camp. It was like a midsummer fair. I smiled as Dick and Harold came up to me as though drunk and shouted, "Hail, the Knight of the Empress!" The drunken cheer went up from my men and Dick winked at me. I passed around my camp and was cheered by all. Sitting next to the pot of food, I fed myself and then picked up a wineskin. Leaving the stopper in, I held it to my mouth and mimed drinking deeply. I pretended to put the stopper back in and wiped my mouth. I repeated that a number of times and then staggered back to my tent.

Poor Richard started when I entered, "Are you ill, my lord?"

I smiled, "No, Richard. I was a mummer! Now go and eat and then become as drunk as you can as quickly as you can."

Richard looked confused. Gilles said, "Just do as I do, Richard!"

It was dark when they returned and the noise from the camp had diminished as men fell to the ground in a drunken stupor. Or so I hoped the enemy would believe. We were hidden in our tent and we could prepare. We wrapped my spare hauberk in bedding and placed it across the tent entrance. Any assassin would assume it was a squire protecting his knight with his body. Then we dressed for war. We donned our gambeson and our mail. We would not wear helmets for we would need to hear. We stuck our spare swords and daggers in the ground at the sides of the tent. That would be where we would sleep. Then we used straw wrapped in our bedding to simulate our bodies. The helmets made a fair imitation of a head. Gilles went to the candle and snuffed it out. We sat in the dark recesses of the tent and we waited with our swords in our hands. We sat close together. It was getting colder at night and wearing mail seemed to make it even colder. The proximity of our bodies slightly offset that. Waiting was hard. I think young Richard found it harder than any.

I was convinced I had heard something outside but when there was no alarm I relaxed again. Then I smelled something. It was a human smell. It was not one of my men. I nudged my two squires. They gave the barest of nods. We had sat in the dark so long that we could see clearly. A hand came through the tent flap and a knife slashed down on the mail. Immediately four men raced into the tent and leapt at the three bundles of bedding. Even as they hacked and slashed at them we were on our feet. I thrust my sword through the side of one assassin. I pulled it back and then hacked the right arm of a second. Richard and Gilles both had swords and they killed the two men at arms each with a single blow. The man whose arm I had severed moaned as he began to bleed to death.

Grabbing my shield I led my squires from the tent. We moved through my camp. I could now hear grunts and moans as men died. Then there was a shout from Sir Miles' camp to my right and the sounds of sword on sword. Silence disappeared. As the alarm spread so did the cacophony of noise. The sneak attack was over and now it would be a battle.

"To me!"

My men came from where they had been fighting with the unarmoured killers sent to slay us in our beds. Stephen had stolen the idea from me. My archers formed a line behind my knights and my men at arms. The archers would struggle to see targets; it was night but any flesh which could be seen would be hit. There was a roar from the dark as the first wave of men at arms and knights rushed at us. They were hampered by their own dead men who lay haphazardly in their path. One knight was so eager to get to us that he failed to see a body and as he tripped, Sir John brought his war hammer over and used the spike to impale the knight.

A man at arms thrust his spear at me. I stepped forward and punched with my shield. I deflected the head and brought my sword diagonally across his neck. With the weight of my body behind it, I broke the man's neck. I quickly stepped back as a sword swung at my head. It missed and Sir Tristan's blade darted out and severed the knight's arm.

"Lock shields!"

My men squeezed together. Sir Tristan's shield overlapped mine and I tucked mine behind Sir John's. We held our swords over the tops of our shields. The enemy ran into the wall of wood, leather and steel. We did not strike. We had no need. Their weapons struck our shield and some of us were lucky enough to have a warrior pressed onto our blades. They came at us in a mass; they were a jumble of men eager to get to us. We were an unyielding wall. There was a brief moment of almost stillness as we stood face to face. Dead men were pressed against some of us. The man at arms who faced me spat at me. Suddenly a dagger came over my shoulder and pierced his eye and his skull.

Gilles shouted, "Do not spit at my lord! Barbarian!"

That simple act of spitting seemed to inflame my men. Edgar shouted, "Forward! Kill them!"

I should have given the command but my men had taken enough insults. I stabbed forward with my sword. The dead

man at arms was still before me but my sword scored a hit
on the cheek of the man behind. Sir John's war hammer
swung high and crushed the skull of the hapless warrior in
the second rank. My archers and the squires pushed into our
backs and the enemy before us fell to the floor. I saw a face
beneath me and I stabbed down, skewering the man. The
enemy fled. We rushed after them. When we reached the
ditch I yelled, "Hold!"

We spent the rest of the night despatching the dead. The
wounded knights had been carried to safety by their squires.
There would be no ransom. As dawn broke, we saw the
charnel house that was our camp. I sought out Edgar. "Find
wood. I want a mangonel building. It need not move."

He did not question me. He just said, "Aye, lord." He and
my men could knock one up in a couple of hours. The
difficulty was always in making one with wheels. I did not
need that. The enemy had set sentries. They stood two
hundred paces away. They had shields before them for they
respected my archers. I summoned Dick and Ralph. I gave
them instructions.

Sir Miles and Sir Pain joined me along with Sir
Raymond. "You were right, lord. It was well that we
prepared. It was an attack in force."

"Did any of you lose large numbers of men?"

"One or two but the enemy suffered more. It was not their
knights. They had neither mail nor helmets."

I nodded, "Stephen is clever. He sent assassins who could
use knives and would profit the most from our deaths. He did
not risk his knights. They were to attack later."

"What now, my lord?"

"We eat and we watch. I have set my men to work. If my
plan succeeds then we can build on the success of yesterday
and last night. I want to buy us a day or two. By then our
reinforcements should be here and we can attack them."

By noon, Edgar and his men had finished and they
brought the mangonel to the edge of the ditch. Dick and the
archers brought sacks with them. Intrigued, Sir Miles and the
others joined me. I nodded to Edgar. He reached into a sack
and brought out the head of one of those slain the night

before. He placed it in the mangonel and released it. The enemy ducked behind shields. By the time Edgar had sent the third one, they knew what we did and they advanced.

"Ralph!"

My archers began to release their arrows. A couple of men dropped to the ground and the rest retreated. It took an hour to send the grisly trophies back to them. I turned to the others. "Now we watch. I hope this has taken the heart from them."

Sir Raymond said, "How so?"

"I do not think that Stephen will have let on to his men their losses. We sent eighty heads back to them. They now know that we killed that many of their men. It will make them worry that they may be the next." They did not come again.

My sentries who watched in the night woke me. "Lord. We can hear noises from the enemy camp."

"I will come."

I had one in four of all my men on watch. If an attack came again then we could repel it. However, an attack would mean that I had misjudged my enemy and that was a dangerous thing to do. My squires followed me and we walked to the ditch line and the sharpened stakes. I could hear the sound of men but it was not close. I turned to Alan son of Alan, "What do you make of it? Are they moving towards us?"

"If they are then they are being clumsy about it but I think they are preparing for something."

"A dawn attack perhaps? I will watch with you. Richard, go and find us food and ale."

By the time dawn began to break, I saw what the noise had been. They were breaking camp. The siege was over and Stephen was retreating. Without fighting a battle or losing men, we had outwitted and defeated Stephen. It was a small victory but it was a victory.

Chapter 18

We spent a few days clearing away the enemy defences. I sent Sir Harold and Dick with twenty men to find Stephen. I wanted to know that he had retreated. I went with Sir Miles and Sir Raymond to meet with the Empress at Gloucester and to decide upon our next course of action. The Empress was delighted with our success. I saw that she desperately wished to embrace me as I descended but it would not have been seemly.

"Earl, you and my warriors have served me well. I will reward you. You shall be Prince Bishop of the Palatinate!"

I shook my head, "I am sorry, Empress, but until it is captured that is not yours to give. Besides, your brother might resent my elevation. It is better that we are both earls."

She nodded, "As ever, you are wise. Then I give you the manor of Azay in the Loire. The Baron there died. It is a rich manor and you will be close to your son there. I also make you the champion of my son Henry Fitz Empress!"

I smiled, "That I will accept."

"Sir Raymond, I give to you the manor of Arromanche in Normandy. The baron there was a traitor and he is under sentence of death in Caen."

"Thank you, my lady."

"Sir Miles, I give you St. Briavals Castle and the manors thereof. I fear that my cousin has taken your right to be constable of Gloucester. This should make up for that."

"Thank you, my lady, but I serve you and that is enough."

"Nonetheless you shall have a reward and now we must plan our next move."

I had already thought this through. "That is simple enough. We must make the west your land. There are royal garrisons at Worcester, Winchcombe, Cerne and Hereford. We strike now with the forces you would have sent to aid us and we make this as safe a stronghold as any."

"And then?"

"It will be winter then, my Empress, and the land will be too hard and cold for fighting. This is not Normandy nor Anjou. This is England and here the winter bites." She nodded. "Besides, we need to win back the support of your brother. Without his knights, we have not enough men to face Stephen in open battle. Next year we must do that. This year we secure your base and when we have built up your forces and mended relations with your brother, we take back the rest of the country."

Sir Miles clapped me on the back. "And with you to lead us, Earl, we shall!"

We left earlier than I had planned for the weather began to change. Wintry showers of sleet and rain drove in from the west. If they had been from the north then they would have had snow in them. We gathered our forces and headed for Hereford. Sir Miles brought forth Geoffrey Talbot who had captured the castle in the early days of the civil war. Stephen had retaken it but Sir Miles and Geoffrey knew the defences well. Sir Pain also had useful knowledge. When we reached Hereford, which was but twenty odd miles from Gloucester, we surrounded it.

I held a council of war. "This will need siege engines. I will take my men and those of Sir Raymond and we will take Worcester. It is close enough for us to reach there quickly."

Sir Miles agreed, "Aye, lord, and we will prosecute the siege with more vigour than Stephen did at Wallingford."

As we headed northeast towards Worcester, I sent Ralph and my archers ahead. I had spoken with those knights who came from the area and knew that there was no castle there but an island, Bevere, two miles upstream. It was a place the locals used as a refuge in times of peril. Ralph and my archers were sent to capture it. The other information we had was that they had fortified a manor house. When they saw our approach, they would bar themselves within. I planned a sudden strike with my knights and men at arms. We would use the speed of our horses to overpower them before they had time to react and organise their defence.

We had travelled fifty miles by the time we reached Worcester. The river was high; that was due to the rains. It passed perilously close to the road. The cathedral, which was still being built, rose high above the river and we used that as a landmark for our approach. We galloped over the bridge which led to the city so quickly that the sentries who stood their watch were slain by Dick and my household knights before they could utter a cry. However, the noise of the hooves on the bridge acted as a warning for the rest. I heard a cry as my standard was seen. "It is the Wolf of the North! The Warlord comes! Flee!"

Fear is a deadly foe and it filled the hearts of those in Worcester. Most did not run to their sanctuary of the manor house but fled north taking whatever they could carry. We reached the fortified dwelling and could go no further for the press of refugees fleeing north filled the road. I left Sir Raymond and the rest of the knights and men at arms who accompanied him to pursue the citizens. Arrows were loosed at my men from the manor house and Cedric fell clutching his leg.

"Withdraw out of bow range."

As we wheeled around, Oswald had his horse slain by two arrows. We took shelter behind a row of houses. Dismounting, I handed my reins to Richard. "Gilles, give Richard the standard. You shall come with me."

We returned to the main street. Sir Raymond and his men had emptied it. The bodies of those they had slain lay scattered along its length. I shouted, "Whoever is in the manor house, surrender and I will treat you fairly!"

I was answered by an arrow which thudded into the building next to me and a defiant shout, "You are the Earl of Cleveland and a traitor. We would sooner surrender to the devil."

"Then be it on your own head."

I looked at the manor house. It was sturdily built. There was a ditch running around it and we would have to cross a small bridge to reach the door. The door itself had four stairs before it so that a ram could not be used. I knew that my archers would be holding Bevere Island but I regretted sending them hence. I needed them. I spied two dead bowmen in the road. "Gilles, fetch those two bows and those quivers."

He ran the gauntlet of the crossbows and arrows from the manor house but he was quick and he was lithe and they were expecting an attack, not a youth running away.

"Dick, Harold." My two knights joined me as Gilles returned. "You two will have to become archers once more."

"Aye, lord." They both looked with distaste at the war bows. "These are poor weapons, lord, and the arrows..."

"They are all that we have. Do your best. I am going to lead a tortoise to break down the door." As they went to identify their targets, I waved over Sir John, Sir Tristan and Edgar. "I want four axe men. We will make a shelter of shields and advance to the door. Dick and Harold will clear the archers and crossbowmen."

"Aye, lord. "

I held my shield over my head. Sir Tristan stood next to me and did the same. Edgar and John stood with Gurth and Wilfred. They would break the door down. The rest of my men at arms formed up behind us.

"Ready, Dick."

"Aye, lord. Go!"

I heard the two bows twang as the arrows were sent speeding towards the roof of the manor house. I heard a cry and, as we crossed the road, saw the body of a crossbowman lying awkwardly in the middle. Arrows and bolts thudded into our shields. One managed to penetrate through to the other side but, as Dick and Harold became used to the new bows, they silenced more of the defenders. We reached the steps.

"One hacks the other defends." Edgar held his shield over Sir John as he smashed his war hammer at the door. After ten blows, Edgar took over and used his axe. I could see that the door had lines gouged in it. The metal studs would slow down the destruction but we would break it down eventually.

Gurth and Wilfred took over. It was Wilfred and his mighty hammer who finally broke down the door.

"Stand aside!"

The four men would be tired. Sir Tristan and I leapt through the shattered door. A spear was thrust at me. I deflected it with my shield and rammed my sword through the knight's thigh. The blood spurted high. I had struck an artery. I pulled his body aside and stepped into the hallway and the stairs. More men were massing and racing towards us. This was no time for finesse and fine stroke work. Tristan and I hacked and slashed about us with scything sweeps. There were so many men trying to get at us that blows managed to get through our defences. A sword rasped along my helmet and a spear caught my mail. Alf had made both well and they held. When Sir John and Edgar reached us, we had managed to empty the stairs of defenders but I knew that more would be on the first floor waiting for us.

We advanced slowly up the stairs with our shields held above us. It was fortunate that we did so for stones were dropped from above. One was so large that it cracked my shield and numbed my arm. Whoever had dropped it had to have been a mighty warrior. As we neared the top of the stairs, I saw a leg. I stabbed at it and my sword sliced through the calf. As the man dropped, I brought my sword up and ripped through his throat.

I had had enough of this and I roared as I punched upwards with my damaged shield. I brought my shield down and swept my sword before me. It clanged against another and I saw the huge knight who had dropped the stone. He was a head taller than I was and had a chest like Alf, my blacksmith. He made the mistake of trying to swing from over his head but he was too tall and his sword caught on the ceiling. I stabbed upwards and my sword found a gap in his mail. I saw the tip emerge from this left shoulder. He shouted and brought his sword's pommel down to strike me on the side of the head. I brought my shield up and it softened the blow but I was still knocked sideways and my shield broke in twain. The two halves fell to the floor. As I stumbled to the side, I grabbed my dagger with my left hand. Still falling, I slashed with my dagger and it ripped across his knee. He still had the strength to bring his sword down and I was barely able to block the blow with my sword. I raised my dagger and stabbed him through the foot. He stumbled backwards and I managed to get to my feet.

He was a bloody mess but he was a strong warrior. He came forward using his sword to swing sideways at my middle. This time I spun around and his blow hit the air. I continued my swing and brought the edge of my blade across his back. His mail held but it was a powerful blow and he started to lose his balance. Alan son of Alan was coming up the stairs and, as he saw the giant, he rammed his spear upwards. The weight of the falling knight drove the spear through his neck. Finally, he tumbled to the ground, dead.

The knight was the last of the serious opposition. We worked our way through the rooms and up to the roof. The last to die were the two remaining crossbowmen. Sir John hurled one to the road below us. We stood on the battlements at the top of the house and we cheered. It took us until dawn to finally clear the town of all those who opposed us. Ralph and my archers returned driving animals before them. The townsfolk had fled to the island and their men were slaughtered by my archers. The animals would feed our army and deprive the enemy of supplies. After burning the manor house, we headed back to Hereford and the siege.

We arrived in the middle of the next afternoon. We had many animals to drive back. The siege was being prosecuted with great vigour. Geoffrey Talbot knew something of siege warfare and they had dug up the graves of St. Guthlac's church to make a ramp. It was gruesome but effective. The catapults hurled broken pieces of gravestones towards the walls. The men working the war machines must have had no sense of smell for they were surrounded by festering bodies.

Sir Miles greeted me warmly, "Well done, my lord! The capture of Worcester and the fresh meat has put heart into our men."

"Good. When will you be ready to assault?"

"The day after tomorrow. The east wall is weakened already."

"Good. I have time to ride to Gloucester and report to the Empress."

I took just my squires with me for it was not a long journey. We reached Gloucester just after dark. As we arrived, I saw a great number of tents had been erected and there were many more armed men than there had been. I left my squires with the horses and was hurrying to the hall when Margaret accosted me. "My lord, the Empress' brother, the Earl, is here."

"Good."

She lowered her voice, "Be careful, my lord. Be careful I beg of you."

I trusted both Margaret and her judgement. I nodded, "Thank you, Margaret, you serve your mistress well."

She smiled, "As do you, my lord. None better."

I recognised the Earl's livery. His men guarded the doors to the Great Hall. The two looked at each other as I approached, "My lord, the Earl is within."

"And I have great news so stand aside and let me enter."

"We have orders to admit no one."

I stepped close to him and said, quietly, "While you and your fellows have been hunting and pleasuring yourselves in Bristol, my men and I have been fighting the forces of Stephen. We have killed many. Unless you wish to join them, move!"

He looked at his fellow and then nodded and moved aside.

"A wise move."

I opened the door. The Earl had his back to me and he shouted, "I said I wanted no interruptions!"

He turned and saw me. His mouth dropped open. I smiled and spread my arms. "Not even a comrade and warrior who brings good news."

The Empress smiled, I think it was with relief, and said, "A timely entrance, my lord. My brother was just telling me how we will never defeat Stephen without his aid. We do not have the skills to do so. Is that not right, brother?"

I saw that he was angry. What I could not discern was the cause of that anger. Was it my presence or the fact that the Empress had mocked him? I sat down next to the Empress and poured myself a goblet of wine. "I have just come,

Empress, to tell you that we have captured Worcester and driven off the garrison. We have captured large numbers of supplies. We can feed the army for the winter. Hereford will fall tomorrow."

"Excellent, and I was trying to tell my brother how you relieved the siege of Wallingford and drove Stephen from Trowbridge." She smiled at her brother and I saw that he did not know how to respond.

I decided to build a bridge of sorts, "And, my lord, if you join with us then we can finish off Stephen by next summer."

"If I command!"

"It matters not to me but the men with whom I have fought, Fitz Count, Fitz Walter and Fitzjohn are all happy with the way we have fought together."

He sneered, "Your own little faction, eh? Not content with those mercenaries you lead, you now subvert those who should be loyal to me."

"Firstly, my lord, I thought that we all served the Empress and her son or am I wrong, and secondly, I take exception to your denigration of my men."

He rounded on me, "And what will you do about it? Challenge me?"

I said, quietly, "If I did then we both know the result, don't we?"

"Are you threatening me, pup!"

I laughed, "It seems I am always compared to an animal; it used to be a wolf and now it is a pup."

"Aelfraed is right, brother, we need you at our side but it is I who command, not the Earl of Cleveland and not you. If that is not acceptable then leave now. I will send for my husband and bring over more of our men from Anjou."

That worried the Earl, "We have enough here already. Very well, sister, you command but you do not lead on the battlefield, do you?"

That moment showed me what a great woman the Empress was. She looked her brother in the eye and said, "If that is what it takes to bring harmony to my army, then yes I will. I know that I will be safe on the battlefield for there are knights who will protect me."

He shook his head in resignation. "Very well then, I will return here after winter and we will combine our forces." He went to his sister and kissed her on the cheek.

He was about to stride past me but I put my hand out. "And I would be friends Earl Robert. We cannot have this division between us."

He hesitated and then nodded and clasped my arm, "You have courage and you did well to drive Stephen east but you have ideas above your station." His eyes flickered towards his sister and then he was gone.

The doors remained open. Margaret entered. "Close the door, Margaret, and guard them."

"Aye, my lady."

I took Matilda's hand, "What was that about?"

"I think that your success has irritated him. He sees himself as Alexander the Great but every deed which is spoken of by my people is to do with you: the Battle of the Standards, the capture of Lincoln, the defeat of the Earl of Derby. The list goes on. He is desperate for the same sort of fame."

"Yet I do not seek fame."

"It follows you, Aelfraed."

"What I meant was the comment about ideas above my station. He looked at you."

She flushed, "He suspects a liaison between us."

Margaret burst out, "Not a word has passed my lips, my lady!"

"I know. I think it is because Henry looks more like your son, my lord. He has little in common with his brothers. My husband does not see it but the Earl... well, he has sharp eyes and a suspicious nature."

"Then when Hereford is taken I shall winter in Stockton. There must be no hint of scandal or we will lose support for your cause. I will leave now and return to the siege."

"But you have just arrived."

"Your honour is more important than my discomfort. I will leave. I must give no cause for gossip."

I stood and the Empress impulsively stood as well and, throwing her arms around me, kissed me passionately.

Margaret discreetly looked the other way, "Life is so unfair, Aelfraed."

"I know. Fate plays tricks with us. We can do nothing about it and must bear our burden." I held her tightly and then, reluctantly, pulled away, "And now I must leave."

"I would that you would stay. Always."

"As would I but that cannot be."

I found Richard and Gilles in the guard room tucking into a hot stew and warmed ale. I smiled, "When you have finished that then we return to the siege."

"But we have just got here, my lord!"

"I know Richard and now we leave!" I smiled, "Finish your food first, though. I will meet you at the stables." I headed towards the stables. They were guarded. Horses had been stolen before now and in the present circumstances, horses were worth more than gold. I recognised the guard.

"I am going to saddle Rolf, Alan."

He cocked his head to one side, "Leaving, my lord? It seems you have just arrived."

"I was a mere messenger this day and now I return to my men. Hereford is about to fall and I would like to be there to see it."

"I will help you to saddle your horse, lord."

"Thank you for the offer but I can manage. Besides, my squires are still eating." I found Rolf eating grain. These were the Empress' stables and her horses had the best. If I took things easy on the way back to Hereford, Rolf would not suffer too much. I spoke to him as I saddled him. It was the way a father spoke to a baby. It was not the words that mattered but the tone of voice. I had just finished and was leading Rolf out when Gilles and Richard arrived. Gilles handed me a fresh loaf. "Margaret said you had not eaten, lord. She said to make sure you ate this. I have a skin of wine too."

"Thank you, Gilles, Margaret is thoughtful." I put my shield over my back and donned my cloak.

"She is, lord." He looked at the sentry and then began to saddle his horse. We were half a mile from the stables and I had finished the deliciously warm wheaten bread when he said, "Lord, I did not want to say anything in the stables but Margaret said to take care and to watch for knives in the night."

"Alan is a good man. I trust him." However, as I washed down the bread with wine from the skin, I wondered at her words. There were others who might wish me harm. I reined in Rolf and handed the skin back to Gilles. "Margaret does not worry over gossip. She fears for us. Eyes and ears open. The road is straight but it is night. If you suspect anything then tell me."

"Aye, lord."

Gilles said, "Before you came, some of the Earl's men stormed through the guard room. They looked angry. Could they be the ones Margaret means?"

"They could be. Where did they go?"

"Out, lord. Perhaps to the stables. I know not."

"From now on we use no words. Just signals."

They both nodded. I slid my sword in and out of my scabbard and then pulled my cloak tightly about me. The night was cold and there would be a frost soon. I wondered as we rode the old Roman Road if I should have taken the quieter, though longer, Tewkesbury road. If someone wished me harm, they would not follow but lay an ambush. It was too late to worry about that now. Like my squires, I listened. There was little to see save blackness. It was our ears and noses which would alert us.

We were ten miles from Hereford and I had begun to wonder if Margaret had been wrong and my suspicions unfounded when we heard, in the distance, the sound of hooves. They were behind us and they were riding hard. We had walked our horses to save them. In normal circumstances, I would have slowed to speak with fellow travellers but I feared whoever this was meant us harm. I drew my sword and said, quietly, "Gilles, lead. Richard, in the middle."

We passed a track that crossed the road and I smelled the wood smoke of the hut which lay there. In more peaceful times I might have considered asking for help but who knew, in these parlous times, who was a friend and who was a foe. We passed on.

We did not speak but Gilles spurred his horse and we began to trot down the road. Rolf was a mighty horse with a big heart but the mounts of Gilles and Richard were not. We had to take it steadily. The sound of the hooves behind us grew closer. It was fortunate that we were not going fast for Gilles' nose and ears picked something out. He reined in and Richard almost ran into the back of his horse. "Lord," he whispered. "There are men ahead."

I trusted Gilles. I looked for another way out and there was none. There was, however, a second deserted woodman's hut just off the road. I rode Rolf towards it and we dismounted behind it. The hooves continued to thunder up the road. There were four riders. In the dark, I did not recognise them but I saw their mail. Richard looked at me but I pressed my finger to my lips. The hooves receded as they moved toward Hereford and then they stopped. The silence intensified the suspense. I guessed the four riders had stopped because they had met up with the ones Gilles had detected.

It was faint but I heard the sound of voices and then I heard hooves as horses came back down the road towards us. They halted close to the hut and looked around them.

"We cannot have passed them. They must have taken the Tewkesbury road."

"No, Ralph, they are on this road. We passed that pile of fresh horse shit two miles past. They have hidden somewhere."

They drew closer. I did not move. If we stayed still then they might not see us.

"There is that track we passed and that hut. They may have taken shelter there. If not, we will return to the place we last knew they passed and search."

They began to trot back down the road. There were four men there and I knew not how many lay ahead but if we waited then those four would find us. I did not risk speech. Gilles knew me well enough to copy my actions and not panic. I now regretted bringing Richard. He was new and I did not know how he would handle the situation. I mounted and started to move along the verge at the side of the road. Our progress would be slow but we would be silent. We now knew that, ahead of us, were men waiting in ambush. I did not know the numbers. Their smell gave them away. I had no doubt that my squires and I smelled too but these men smelled differently.

I slowed Rolf down and peered ahead. The men were there. I spied two horses. They waited not in the woods but on the road. They were forty paces from us. I had to resist the urge to risk the two horses and gallop past them. I was rewarded when a third led his horse from the woods. He spoke. "Any sign of them?"

"Nothing. Sir William blames us! We left as soon as we were ordered and we rode as hard as we could."

"I still think this is a mistake. Just because the Earl is annoyed with the Empress' lackey is no reason to kill him."

"This is our best chance. He has two boys with him. Would you wish to try to kill him when he is surrounded by the outlaws he uses?"

"I would not take on the Wolf of the North. It is a good job we are being paid well."

Now that I knew their numbers I could plan. We had to eliminate these three first and then try to outrun the other four. I dismounted and handed my reins to Richard. I pointed to Gilles to follow me. He nodded, handed his reins to Richard too, and stepped carefully into the woods. I took out my dagger. I would need two weapons. We moved towards the men who continued to grumble and moan. They held their horse's reins. One sat astride his horse. I would have to stop him but the other two were easier targets. The one on the horse was in the middle of the road and the other two were on our side. I pointed to the man on the right and Gilles nodded. I knew I was asking a great deal but Gilles had done this before.

We took steps to close with them. I could see them clearly now. My eyes had adjusted to the darkness. They were men of the retinue of Sir William de Villiers. He was one of the Earl's men. I thought I had recognised his voice. I

glanced at Gilles. We were close enough now to strike. I
nodded. Running forward, I thrust my sword into the throat
of the nearest man at arms. His horse reared as he fell. The
one sitting astride his horse had to use two hands to control
his own horse which also became skittish at the smell of
blood. I brought my sword over and hacked into the thigh of
the man. He fell from his horse, screaming.

"Lord!"

I turned and saw that the third had managed to cut Gilles'
arm and he was about to finish him off. I dived towards him
with the dagger in my left hand. I managed to hit him under
his raised arm and we fell in a tumble on the ground. He was
dead but the shout would have alerted the other four. Gilles
was bleeding. After sheathing my sword and my dagger, I
took a piece of cloth from the dead man and tied it around
his upper arm. Richard had brought the horses and I helped
Gilles to mount. I clambered on Rolf's back and heard, in the
distance, the sound of horses.

"Ride." I grabbed the reins of one of the dead men's
horses and followed my two squires up the road. "Richard,
watch out for Gilles, he is wounded."

"Aye, lord."

"Do not stop even if I drop back. I will be safe!"

"Aye, lord."

We had ten miles to go. Our horses had had a short rest
but we were outnumbered. Gilles could not fight and Richard
would be outmatched. Sir William was a knight and I had no
doubt that the other three were killers all. All we could do
was to run for as long as we could and then turn and make a
last stand. Wulfstan had always told me that a true warrior
never gave up until his enemy was prising his sword from
his dead fingers. Where there was life there was hope. I had
to believe that my fate was not to die on the road from
Gloucester to Hereford.

I knew that I had some little time. They would halt at
their comrades. I scanned both sides of the road for anything
which would help me. Half a mile up the road, by a Roman
mile marker, I saw a track crossing the road. I stopped. There
was a holly tree and I cut a branch. I went to the left side of

the road and tied the reins of the captured horse around the cantle. I could hear the approach of the hooves. I jammed the holly under the saddle of the horse and clapped its rump. The pain and the prickles were enough to make it start. It leapt across the road and its hooves clattered on the cobbles. A heartbeat later the four riders galloped up in time to hear the riderless horse as it raced, in panic and pain, away up the track to the north.

"There, lord! They are heading off the road."

"John, you wait here in case they double back. You two, come with me."

I watched as three of them raced down the trail. The man at arms they left behind watched the trail to the north. I waited until the other three had ridden into the woods. I had my sword out and I burst out of the undergrowth swinging my sword as I went. The man was so surprised that he did not shout. My sword smashed into the side of his helmet and he fell, stunned, to the side of the road. I grabbed the reins of his horse and hurried up the road after my squires. The odds were now a little more even. I was another mile down the road, having seen another mile marker, when I heard the shout from the road behind. It was followed by the sound of hooves. There was no sign of my squires and I took that to be a good omen. It meant they might reach my men.

The sound of the hooves drew closer. They were gaining. I let go of the reins of the second horse when I came to a clearing. As soon as the reins touched the ground, it stopped and began to graze. I spurred Rolf. When the three saw the horse, they would slow. They would expect a trick like the other one. Following someone at night was difficult. I had a reputation as a trickster. I would play upon that. Inevitably, however, they began to gain. As I passed the marker showing just three miles to Hereford, I glanced over my shoulder and saw them hurrying after me. It was a man at arms leading; he had a helmet but no mail. The knight was behind him.

I drew my sword and leaned forward, "Come on, Rolf. Just a little further!"

I did not risk turning again. I kept myself low to help Rolf travel faster. I could hear the rider behind and he was gaining. I could hear his horse snorting and then I felt a huge blow as he hit my back. Had I not had my shield there it would have done for me. The blow hurt but did no harm. Turning, I swung my sword horizontally. He was raising his sword for a second strike. My sword smashed into his hand, making him drop his sword and then it continued across his front, just above his cantle. It bit into his reins and the palm of his hand. The sword was sharp and cut through to the bone. His horse stopped and he fell from its back.

The two mailed men had taken their chance and now rode at me. They started to overtake me. One was to my left and one was to my right. Rolf had given his all and could go no further. I slowed down and prepared to sell my life dearly. I had two men to fight. I wheeled around Rolf's head and the manoeuvre took the man at arms by surprise. He thundered past me. I went directly for the knight. I had met Sir William de Villiers before. He was not known as a great leader but I knew him to be ambitious. Perhaps he thought to end my life and gain favour with the Earl. I brought my sword around and he blocked it with his own.

I heard the hooves of the man at arms behind me. I needed to defeat the knight and hope that would discourage his man at arms. Rolf was too weary to be used as a weapon and so I drew my dagger. As Sir William swung at me, I blocked his blow with my dagger and thrust at him. Hooves thundered behind me and as my sword struck Sir William's mail, his man at arms swung his sword at my back. It was a powerful blow. Rolf's legs gave way and I found myself tumbling to the ground.

I tucked my head and rolled with my arms held before me. I knew that I had to hang on to the sword and dagger. It would be bad enough to be afoot against two horsemen without being defenceless too.

Sir William saw his chance and he galloped at me. Rolf staggered to his feet as the knight neared me. It made Sir William's horse veer to the side. As the killer knight tried to control his horse, I swung my sword at Sir William's leg. I found flesh and the edge of my sword ripped into bone. I barely had time to spin around and deflect the man at arms' sword as it swung at me. I made a cross of my dagger and my sword.

Sir William managed to control his horse and he whipped the head around to run me down. This time there was no Rolf to help me. I gambled that the horse, despite the knight's urging, would not trample me. I could also hear the man at arms as he turned to charge my back again. This time he would strike, not at my back, but my head and I would die. Sir William's horse veered at the last moment. I saw a gap above the cantle and, even as I was knocked over, I stabbed forward with my sword. It was torn from my body and I turned, with just a dagger to face the man at arms.

The rider had a look of joy on his face as he leaned forward to take off my head. He was but three paces from me and if I dropped to the ground I would be trodden on and killed by his horse. I would die as I had fought, on my feet. Even as the sword was raised, I saw his face contort in pain and he threw his arms in the air. His body tumbled from his horse and I saw Richard with his bloody sword in his hand.

"Gilles said you needed help, my lord!"

I laughed, "And he was right. I turned and saw that Sir William's horse had stopped. My sword was still stuck in his middle. He was dead but I think it was my blow to the knee which had caused it. I had severed an artery.

Hooves clattered down the road and I saw Dick and Sir Harold with half a dozen of my men. "Gilles found us, my lord! What happened?"

I walked over to pat Richard on the back. "My new squire became a warrior today and saved his lord and master. Come. When this siege is over, we will quit the west and head home. I grow tired of this treacherous war."

Epilogue

Stockton Christmas 1139

We stayed in Hereford just long enough for the siege to be ended. I wrote two letters: one to the Empress and one to the Earl. I told them of Sir William's treachery and attempt on my life. I cared not if I offended the Earl. If it had not been for my squires then I might be dead on the Gloucester Road. We went home richer for Hereford was filled with all kinds of treasures. Our journey had, perforce, been slower than normal. We travelled in winter through the lands of the Earl of Chester. He was still Stephen's man.

My castle looked solid and welcoming as I rode through its gates. My mason and my men had not been idle and it was improved. I also saw that Henry of Brotton and his family had made it safely to my castle. For some reason that gave me more hope than anything. He would know soon enough that his former lord was a traitor but the family had found sanctuary and that made me happy. Gilles' wound healed and Rolf recovered from his exertions. The year ended well.

As I sat in my west tower, I pondered on the year. We could have had victory but the defection of the Earl of Chester and the arrogance of the Earl of Gloucester had stopped that. Sir Miles and Sir Brian had shown me that I was not alone. I was not the only knight who fought for the Empress but I also realised that this war was far from over. The Anarchy had just begun and the enemy was still at the gates.

The End

Glossary

Allaghia- a subdivision of a Bandon-about 400 hundred men (Byzantium)

Akolouthos - The commander of the Varangian Guard (Byzantium)

Al-Andalus- Spain

Angevin- the people of Anjou, mainly the ruling family

Bandon- Byzantine regiment of cavalry -normally 1500 men (Byzantium)

Battle- a formation in war (a modern battalion)

Booth Castle – Bewcastle north of Hadrian's Wall

Butts- targets for archers

Cadge- the frame upon which hunting birds are carried (by a codger- hence the phrase old codger being the old man who carries the frame)

Cadwaladr ap Gruffudd- Son of Gruffudd ap Cynan

Captain- a leader of archers

Chausses - mail leggings. (They were separate- imagine lady's stockings!)

Conroi- A group of knights fighting together. The smallest unit of the period

Demesne- estate

Destrier- warhorse

Doxy- prostitute

Fess- a horizontal line in heraldry

Galloglass- Irish mercenaries

Gambeson- a padded tunic worn underneath mail. When worn by an archer they came to the waist. It was more of a quilted jacket but I have used the term freely

Gonfanon- A standard used in Medieval times (Also known as a Gonfalon in Italy)

Gruffudd ap Cynan- King of Gwynedd until 1137

Hartness- the manor which became Hartlepool

Hautwesel- Haltwhistle

Kataphractos (pl. oi)- Armoured Byzantine horseman (Byzantium)

Kometes/Komes- General (Count) (Byzantium)

Kentarchos- Second in command of an Allaghia (Byzantium)

Kontos (pl. oi) - Lance (Byzantium)

Lusitania- Portugal

Mansio- staging houses along Roman Roads

Maredudd ap Bleddyn- King of Powys

Martinmas- 11th November

Mêlée- a medieval fight between knights

Moravians- the men of Moray

Mormaer- A Scottish lord and leader

Mummer- an actor from a medieval tableau

Musselmen- Muslims

Nithing- A man without honour (Saxon)

Nomismata- a gold coin equivalent to an aureus

Outremer- the kingdoms of the Holy Land

Owain ap Gruffudd- Son of Gruffudd ap Cynan and King of Gwynedd from 1137

Palfrey- a riding horse

Poitevin- the language of Aquitaine

Pyx- a box containing a holy relic (Shakespeare's Pax from Henry V)

Refuge- a safe area for squires and captives (tournaments)

Sauve qui peut – Every man for himself (French)

Sergeant-a leader of a company of men at arms

Serdica- Sofia (Byzantium)

Serengford- Shellingford Oxfordshire

Surcoat- a tunic worn over mail or armour

Sumpter- packhorse

Tagmata- Byzantine cavalry (Byzantium)

Turmachai -Commander of a Bandon of cavalry (Byzantium)

Ventail – a piece of mail that covered the neck and the lower face.

Wulfestun- Wolviston (Durham)

Maps and Illustrations

Stockton Castle c 1136

Historical note

The book is set during one of the most turbulent and complicated times in British history. Henry I of England and Normandy's eldest son, William died. The king named his daughter, Empress Matilda as his heir. However, her husband, the Emperor of the Holy Roman Empire died and she remarried. Her new husband was Geoffrey of Anjou and she had children by him. (The future Henry II of England and Normandy- The Lion in Winter!)

There was never an Earl of Cleveland although the area known as Cleveland did exist and was south of the river. At this time the only northern earls were those of Northumberland. The incumbent was Gospatric who rebelled against England when King Henry died.

The Scots were taking advantage of a power vacuum on their borders. They did, according to chroniclers of the time behave particularly badly.

"an execrable army, more atrocious than the pagans, neither fearing God nor regarding man, spread desolation over the whole province and slaughtered everywhere people of either sex, of every age and rank, destroying, pillaging and burning towns, churches and houses"

Robert of Hexham

)

Books used in the research:

- The Varangian Guard- 988-1453 Raffael D'Amato
- Saxon Viking and Norman- Terence Wise
- The Walls of Constantinople AD 324-1453- Stephen Turnbull
- Byzantine Armies- 886-1118- Ian Heath
- The Age of Charlemagne-David Nicolle
- The Normans- David Nicolle
- Norman Knight AD 950-1204- Christopher Gravett

- The Norman Conquest of the North- William A Kappelle
- The Knight in History- Francis Gies
- The Norman Achievement- Richard F Cassady
- Knights- Constance Brittain Bouchard
- Knight Templar 1120-1312 -Helen Nicholson

Griff Hosker
March 2016

Other books by Griff Hosker

If you enjoyed reading this book, then why not read another one by the author?

Ancient History

The Sword of Cartimandua Series
(Germania and Britannia 50 A.D. – 128 A.D.)
Ulpius Felix- Roman Warrior (prequel)
The Sword of Cartimandua
The Horse Warriors
Invasion Caledonia
Roman Retreat
Revolt of the Red Witch
Druid's Gold
Trajan's Hunters
The Last Frontier
Hero of Rome
Roman Hawk
Roman Treachery
Roman Wall
Roman Courage

The Wolf Warrior series
(Britain in the late 6th Century)
Saxon Dawn
Saxon Revenge
Saxon England
Saxon Blood
Saxon Slayer
Saxon Slaughter
Saxon Bane
Saxon Fall: Rise of the Warlord
Saxon Throne

Saxon Sword

Medieval History

The Dragon Heart Series
Viking Slave *
Viking Warrior *
Viking Jarl *
Viking Kingdom *
Viking Wolf *
Viking War
Viking Sword
Viking Wrath
Viking Raid
Viking Legend
Viking Vengeance
Viking Dragon
Viking Treasure
Viking Enemy
Viking Witch
Viking Blood
Viking Weregeld
Viking Storm
Viking Warband
Viking Shadow
Viking Legacy
Viking Clan
Viking Bravery

The Norman Genesis Series
Hrolf the Viking *
Horseman *
The Battle for a Home *
Revenge of the Franks *
The Land of the Northmen
Ragnvald Hrolfsson

Brothers in Blood
Lord of Rouen
Drekar in the Seine
Duke of Normandy
The Duke and the King

Danelaw
(England and Denmark in the 11th Century)
Dragon Sword *
Oathsword *
Bloodsword *
Danish Sword
The Sword of Cnut

New World Series
Blood on the Blade *
Across the Seas *
The Savage Wilderness *
The Bear and the Wolf *
Erik The Navigator *
Erik's Clan *
The Last Viking

The Vengeance Trail *

The Conquest Series
(Normandy and England 1050-1100)
Hastings
Conquest

The Aelfraed Series
(Britain and Byzantium 1050 A.D. - 1085 A.D.)
Housecarl *
Outlaw *
Varangian *

The Reconquista Chronicles
Castilian Knight *
El Campeador *
The Lord of Valencia *

**The Anarchy Series England
1120-1180**
English Knight *
Knight of the Empress *
Northern Knight *
Baron of the North *
Earl *
King Henry's Champion *
The King is Dead *
Warlord of the North
Enemy at the Gate
The Fallen Crown
Warlord's War
Kingmaker
Henry II
Crusader
The Welsh Marches
Irish War
Poisonous Plots
The Princes' Revolt
Earl Marshal
The Perfect Knight

**Border Knight
1182-1300**
Sword for Hire *
Return of the Knight *
Baron's War *
Magna Carta *
Welsh Wars *
Henry III *

The Bloody Border *
Baron's Crusade
Sentinel of the North
War in the West
Debt of Honour
The Blood of the Warlord
The Fettered King
de Montfort's Crown
Ripples of Rebellion

Sir John Hawkwood Series
France and Italy 1339- 1387
Crécy: The Age of the Archer *
Man At Arms *
The White Company *
Leader of Men *
Tuscan Warlord *
Condottiere

Lord Edward's Archer
Lord Edward's Archer *
King in Waiting *
An Archer's Crusade *
Targets of Treachery *
The Great Cause *
Wallace's War *
The Hunt

Struggle for a Crown
1360- 1485
Blood on the Crown *
To Murder a King *
The Throne *
King Henry IV *
The Road to Agincourt *
St Crispin's Day *

Enemy at the Gate

The Battle for France *
The Last Knight *
Queen's Knight *
The Knight's Tale

Tales from the Sword I
(Short stories from the Medieval period)

Tudor Warrior series
England and Scotland in the late 15th and early 16th
century
Tudor Warrior *
Tudor Spy *
Flodden*

Conquistador
England and America in the 16th Century
Conquistador *
The English Adventurer *

English Mercenary
The 30 Years War and the English Civil War
Horse and Pistol

Modern History

The Napoleonic Horseman Series
Chasseur à Cheval
Napoleon's Guard
British Light Dragoon
Soldier Spy
1808: The Road to Coruña
Talavera
The Lines of Torres Vedras
Bloody Badajoz
The Road to France

Waterloo

The Lucky Jack American Civil War series
Rebel Raiders
Confederate Rangers
The Road to Gettysburg

Soldier of the Queen series
Soldier of the Queen*
Redcoat's Rifle*
Omdurman

The British Ace Series
1914
1915 Fokker Scourge
1916 Angels over the Somme
1917 Eagles Fall
1918 We will remember them
From Arctic Snow to Desert Sand
Wings over Persia

Combined Operations series
1940-1945
Commando *
Raider *
Behind Enemy Lines
Dieppe
Toehold in Europe
Sword Beach
Breakout
The Battle for Antwerp
King Tiger
Beyond the Rhine
Korea
Korean Winter

Tales from the Sword II
(Short stories from the Modern period)

Books marked thus *, are also available in the audio
format.
For more information on all of the books then please
visit the author's website at www.griffhosker.com
where there is a link to contact him or visit his
Facebook page: GriffHosker at Sword Books or follow
him on Twitter: @HoskerGriff or Sword
(@swordbooksltd)
If you wish to be on the mailing list then contact the
author through his website.

Made in the USA
Monee, IL
26 November 2024

71338040R00140